moors after dark. Marion Grayle had heard that story from babyhood. Old Emm, who lived down in the Thatch Cottage, repeated it with relish, and tales of crime had a queer fascination for Marion.

Twenty years ago, a solitary rider had been attacked by an escaped convict from Princetown and brutally done to death. It was said that his headless corpse, seated upright on a spirit-horse, galloped wildly over the moors, seeking vengeance.

Clop . . . clop . . . clop. Marion stood motionless, her eyes straining to penetrate the misty darkness ahead of her, her heart racing. Then a shape loomed up before her. She gave a little scream that changed to a note of relief as she saw, not a gory, decapitated body, but a very virile, red-faced man on a grey mare.

'Oh, it's you, Jet!' she said.

'Why, Marion—you out in this rotten weather?' said the man, pulling up his mare, and dismounting. 'You ought to be home.'

'That's my affair,' said Marion, tossing her head. 'I'm not afraid of storms, anyhow.'

'Nor of anything nor anybody,' said Jet Saddleman a trifle gloomily, surveying the girl's slim, supple body and the face which was famous throughout Devonshire for its rare beauty.

He wished that Marion were a bit more shy and dependent; the sort of maid who could cling to a man for protection; rouse his

2

tenderness. But Marion was not that kind. She roused mad passion, hot admiration, deep interest—never tenderness. She was wild, independent; a true creature of the wind and rain and moors . . . a law unto herself.

Jet Saddleman had known her since she was a child. He owned Double-Styles Farm, the fields of which skirted the garden of Marion's home. She lived at the 'Travellers' Rest', Tom Grayle's inn and the only public-house and hostel for miles around; it was three miles across the moors from Moorcoombe Village.

Marion had no mother. Mrs. Grayle had died at her birth, and Marion had had her own way with her father, who adored her for her beauty and strength and fearlessness, even while he dreaded that some harm might come to her one day; for she had a strange, deep mind, and a fierce temper when roused.

She could be adorable when she wished to, however, and Jet Saddleman was one of the many Moorcoombe men who had tried to woo and win her, in vain.

'Can I take you back to the "Travellers' Rest" on my horse, Marion?' he asked. 'You're carrying a great basket—and—'

'No, thanks,' she broke in. 'I prefer to walk.'

'Why are you so proud and stand-offish with me?' he said. 'You know I'm crazy about you, Marion, and I'm not badly off as a farmer goes these days. There's many girls roundabout would like to be mistress of Double-Styles

Farm '

'Marry 'em, then,' said Marion, with her most provocative smile.

Jet clenched his fists. Passion was rising in him, turning his sun-browned face a dusky scarlet. He was a huge man of some thirty years, handsome in a rugged way. But Marion did not care for him. She was a publican's daughter, a child o' the moors. But she had dainty, fastidious ways. If she married, it would be to a gentleman—a lover of refinement and brains. She was not going to throw herself away on a hulking farmer. A few months ago, just before her twenty-second birthday, she had amused herself by flirting with Jet. But she did not find him amusing any more. He had grown too serious, too insistent.

'Goodnight, Jet,' she said, sweetly. 'See you at church on Sunday, maybe.'

'When are you going to church with me, Marion?' he asked hoarsely, seizing one of her hands . . . a slender, soft hand, yet strong as steel, and tanned to gold by the summer's sun.

'Never, you great mutt!' she laughed at him.

His body shook. He stared at her with bitter, furious eyes, through the mist and rain. She was beautiful; a maddening, lovely creature; an enchantress, with flame-gold hair which was bobbed and curled crisply over her small head; a smooth, milky skin, a small red mouth with a short upper lip; and wonderful eyes, darkly brown, sparkling under thick dark lashes and

4

straight, narrow brows.

'You'll come to no good, Marion,' he shot at her. 'You tempt men and play 'em up—you've played with me—but I swear I'll get you yet.'

'Pooh!' she said. But her pulses stirred uneasily as she looked up at him; there was such bitterness, such thwarted passion in the man's blue eyes. Jet Saddleman was not a callow youth . . . he was a full-blooded man, as lawless and savage in his way as she was in hers. Could he do her any harm? Then she laughed and moved away from him. 'Goodnight,' she repeated. 'Great boob! I'm not likely to marry you—I've other ideas.'

He ran after her, caught her roughly in his arms, and before she could resist, had pressed a hot, fierce kiss on her mouth. Then he released her, jumped on to his mare and galloped off, vanishing in the thick fog which continued to curl up from the valley.

Marion stood staring after him, her brows knit with anger, her breast heaving. Clop . . . clop . . . clop—the horse's hoofs grew more muffled and finally died away. The girl drew a hand across her lips and spat on to the turf.

'I'll pay him back for that,' she said between her teeth. 'The beast!'

She felt that if Jet had stood before her now, and she had a revolver in her hand, she would have shot him for daring to desecrate her lips.

She hurried on home. The fog was not so

5

thick here as below. Her father's inn came in sight; an old Tudor house with gabled roof, diamond-paned windows and timbered walls. A charming place in the summer. But in the autumn and winter very lonely and depressing. The sign, jutting out from the roof, flapped dismally in the wind. *The Travellers' Rest.'* There were no lights to be seen save in the bar-parlour. There were no visitors at the inn at the present time.

As Marion walked toward the door, carrying her basket of parcels, she was stopped again; this time by an old woman in an ancient black bonnet and shawl, who came tapping along on an ebony stick. The old woman was not pleasant to look at; wrinkled, red-nosed, with one eye blind and one open, which had a queer, malevolent expression.

'Oh, good evening, Emm,' said Marion, pleasantly. She hated old Emm from the Thatch Cottage, because she knew that Emm hated her. Emm was a weird, Celtic creature, believed to have second sight. Marion was pleasant because she was afraid of her—the only person in Moorcoombe she did fear. She was superstitious, and dreaded the uncanny powers the old woman was supposed to possess.

'A wild night, my lass,' croaked old Emm, peering with her one eye at the girl's lovely, rain-wet face. ' 'Tis time you were safe in the inn. The Travellers' Rest . . . ha! ha! ha! 'Tis

6

the last long rest for many a one that sleeps in there. Ha! ha! ha!'

Marion shivered. The old woman's cracked laughter disturbed her. Her significant words were sinister enough to disturb any girl. *The last long rest* . . . hateful old woman! She was forever making those remarks about Grayle's inn . . . and not without reason, which Marion well knew. The pretty, Elizabethan inn had a sinister reputation with the natives of Moorcoombe.

Many a traveller during the past hundred years had stayed there, gone out and *never come back.* A mile away there was a dark, gloomy spot avoided by folk around Moorcoombe, a stagnant pond known as 'The Suicide's Pool.' Inmates of the 'Travellers' Rest' had sometimes been found in that pool, drowned; dragged forth with pale, agonised faces and staring eyes.

Marion, when a child, had seen one of the suicides, and never forgotten it. It had been a Londoner—one of her father's visitors, staying on Dartmoor for the fishing season. A clear case of suicide. Another proof that the evil place was haunted . . .

Old Emm clutched at Marion's arm:

'There's dark, treacherous thoughts behind your pretty face, my maid,' she croaked. 'Dark thoughts . . . leading to the dark death . . . and tonight . . . who knows but tonight there'll be a handsome stranger knocking at your gates . . .

7

one to tear the heart out 'o the body o' you, and squeeze the life-blood from it with the passion o' love you'll bear him ...'

'Oh, be quiet, you raven!' interrupted Marion with a gasp, half of fear, half of anger. 'You're crazy, you old witch!'

She ran into the inn and banged the door in Emm's face. Long afterwards she heard the croaking, discordant laughter mingling with the sobbing of the storm. As she took off her soaked mackintosh, put on dry shoes and brushed her red-gold hair into flaming glory about her head she remembered Emm's words:

'A handsome stranger ... at the gates ... one to tear the heart out of her body ...'

Was that a prophecy? So many of Emm's prophecies came true. Marion looked at her reflection in her looking-glass, holding a small oil-lamp close to it. Her beautiful, radiant face smiled back at her. A face for a lover to worship ... to kiss ... not for Jet Saddleman, anyhow ...

'Come soon, come soon, my lover,' Marion crooned to herself. 'If I love, I shall love to the death ... nothing shall come between me and the man of my choice ...'

Her father's voice interrupted her reverie, shouting from the kitchen below:

'Marion— Marion, come down. You're wanted. Charlie Hodges says there's been a motor accident just down the road, and there's

8

a young man injured . . . come and help get him in.'

A queer, excited look flashed into the girl's eyes. A stranger . . . Emm's prophecy . . . had he come already? Would he be handsome? Would he be her lover? She snatched up a shawl, and rushed downstairs, her heart beating madly as though she were suddenly intoxicated with life.

CHAPTER TWO

In the fog-bound road about two hundred yards away from the 'Travellers' Rest,' there had been a nasty accident. When Marion joined her father and Charlie Hodges, the barman, she found a two-seater car in the ditch, turned on its side, and a girl kneeling beside the prone figure of a man.

'Thank heaven you've come!' said this girl, in a hysterical voice. 'I can't stop the bleeding . . . he must have been cut by broken glass . . . and his arm is twisted . . . broken . . . I'm sure . . .'

'What happened, miss?' asked Tom Grayle, flashing a torch-light on the scene.

'We were . . . driving over the moors . . . and got lost in the fog . . . then ran into this ditch,' she sobbed.

Marion ignored the girl, and stared eagerly

down at the injured man. He was young and looked as though he would be tall and slim. His leather motoring-coat was splashed with mud and blood. His neck was bleeding, but his face and head seemed untouched. Marion gasped a little as she looked down at him. The stranger was the most handsome man she had ever seen. It was a pure Greek head, pillowed on the lap of the girl who had been his companion; a fine head with thick dark hair, now dishevelled and spattered with mud. The face was pale, as though carven out of ivory, with straight features; a boyish, chiselled mouth, a square dented chin. Marion felt a strong desire to push the other girl away; to take that dark attractive head on her own lap and watch for his eyes to open. What colour would they be?

She moved nearer.

'I'm Marion Grayle,' she said. She had a rich, caressing voice; more cultured than one would expect to hear from a publican's daughter on the wilds of Dartmoor. 'Let me help you, Miss—'

'Marshall,' filled in the girl. 'And—and this is—Mr. Courtland.'

She sounded frightened, and she was crying now. Marion looked at her a trifle contemptuously. Miss Marshall was smartly dressed in a fur coat and tailored skirt, but in the light of Tom Grayle's torch, she looked a pale, insignificant little thing. Marion spoke to

10

Miss Marshall with great sweetness, however:

'You poor little soul . . . what a frightful shock for you . . . come along in and have a drink and warm up, and my father and Charlie'll carry the gentleman in.'

Half-an-hour later the handsome victim of the accident had been put to bed in one of the best rooms of the inn. A fire had been lit, and a doctor sent for. While this medical man was attending Mr. Courtland, Marion took Miss Marshall into her own bedroom where she could wash and recover from her fright.

Marion stood by the dressing-table, watching the other girl brush her hair. Without the big fur coat, in a dainty georgette jumper, with Eton collar and silk tie, Miss Marshall looked quite pretty. She was exceedingly fair—with a silky, shingled head—and had sweet eyes of gentian blue, and an innocent, rather wistful mouth. Her expression was at once gentle and appealing. She was not more than nineteen or twenty. She was of that clinging, dependent type that invariably attracts strong men. Marion thought her weak and silly. But as a matter of fact, Hope Marshall was a charming little thing, with a heart of gold and an unusually white mind. Life had not been very kind to her, nor had she had much chance to find happiness. She was unnerved and shaken by the accident on the lonely moors, and glad to confide in Marion Grayle, who seemed to her a veritable tower of strength.

11

'It's the most dreadful business,' she said, as she laid down the brush and sat down on a chair to drink the hot coffee Marion had brought upstairs for her. 'I ought not to be with Dion . . . and now it'll be found out for sure.'

Marion's eyes narrowed.

'Dion?' she murmured. 'You mean—?'

'Mr. Courtland . . . the gentleman I was with.'

'Ah,' said Marion, with a secretive smile. She liked the name, Dion. She was burning with impatience to go to the man in the room opposite; to sit by him, nurse him, watch and wait for Emm's prophecy to justify itself. But first she wanted Hope Marshall's confidence, and she got it by keeping silent and subtly giving Hope the impression that she was to be relied upon.

Hope poured out her story—was more talkative than usual, possibly because she was in a nervous condition and frightened . . . and Marion seemed sympathetic and kind.

Hope belonged to a good family in Torquay, but her mother was mid-Victorian—distressingly strict and down on the 'moderns.' Hope had no liberty; was given clothes and luxuries but no chance to spread her wings as she yearned to do. A few months ago, at a dance she had met Dion Courtland, only son and heir of Sir George and Lady Courtland, who lived in London and had recently been in

12

Africa after big-game. He was 'terribly attractive,' Hope shyly confided in Marion. But he had a reputation for being a flirt. Mrs. Marshall disapproved of him, although really he was only an impulsive charming boy of twenty-five. He had fallen in love with Hope . . . she was crazily in love with him, but the Marshalls would not hear of an engagement . . . at least until Hope came of age.

'Dion ran down from town in his car this morning,' Hope finished, her pretty, pale face puckered and wet with tears. 'He persuaded me to go out on the moors and lunch at Princetown I told Mummy a lie about it . . . and this is my punishment . . .'

Marion gave her a few encouraging words, but inwardly despised her. The little fool! Why care what her people said, if she loved Dion Courtland. How could Dion want to marry a baby like this . . . a mere child who could not know the wild, tempestuous passion of love as Marion visualised it.

Hope blurted out more. Dion wanted her to become engaged, despite her parents; she yearned to agree; she adored him; he gave her the tender love her starved little heart desired; but she was under her mother's thumb; life-long habit, the obedience of years, had made her refuse Dion . . .

'Now what shall I do? How shall I get home?' she finished. 'If I stay here, where Dion is, mother will never get over it.'

13

Marion thought a moment. Then she said:
'You can get back. The fog is lifting. We've got an old Ford we use for marketing. Charlie can drive. I'll make him take you back to Torquay at once. You'll have to confess about your drive, but you can say you were nearly killed, and your mother will be so glad to get you back, she won't rate you much.'

Hope gave a nervous laugh.

'Thank you most awfully,' she said. 'If you could arrange that, I'd be so relieved.'

Marion's heart leaped. Splendid! She wanted Hope Marshall out of the 'Travellers' Rest' . . . for many reasons.

'I'll see Charlie about it now,' she said.

'Just let's come and see how Mr. Courtland is,' said Hope timidly, laying a hand on Marion's arm. 'And I shall never forget your great kindness, Miss Grayle.'

Marion wanted to shake her, but she kissed the pale face Hope offered, and accompanied her to Dion's room. There they found him more comfortable, his arm in a splint, his cuts bandaged; lying back on his pillows, watching the firelight flicker in the big, old-fashioned grate.

As the two girls entered, he looked at them . . . his gaze met Marion's. For the first time she saw his eyes open . . . they were brilliant, hazel-green eyes with thick black lashes; arresting eyes that made Marion's heart shake. She bowed to him demurely.

14

'I hope you're better,' she said. 'I'm just going to arrange for Miss Marshall to be driven home. She is so worried about her people.'

'By jove, yes . . . my poor little Hope,' said Dion, a trifle weakly. He was in pain, and still suffering from shock and loss of blood. But he held out his uninjured hand to Hope, who ran to him and knelt by the bed, weeping. 'I'm terribly sorry for getting you into this mess, sweetheart.'

'That'll be all right. I . . . I shall manage mother,' she said, trying to be brave.

'If only you'd take the plunge,' he said. 'Brave 'em all, and marry me, Hope . . .'

'Oh, I daren't,' she said, her face flushing painfully. 'But I'll write tomorrow . . . every day . . . try and come to see you, Dion darling.'

'Do,' he said. 'Promise you'll try and fix up an engagement.'

'I promise,' she said.

She bent her fair head, and kissed him. Dion was an ardent lover, and very much in love at the moment with this gentle, charming child whose life had been so dull and tiresome. But even while his lips touched hers, his eyes were drawn, in a curious, magnetic fashion, to the other girl in the room. She was standing at the foot of the bed, looking straight at him. He thought he had never seen a more beautiful woman than the innkeeper's daughter . . . Marion, with her exquisite brown eyes and straight brows, and curling scarlet lips; Marion in a grey frock with a frilly apron and Puritan collar and cuffs; her red-gold hair curling about her head.

Half-an-hour later, Hope had gone back to Torquay with Charlie Hodges, and Marion prepared to act night-nurse to Dion Courtland. She was glad that he was left entirely to her care now, and that she had knowledge of nursing. She had been taught a lot by an aunt who was at Guy's Hospital, and who came to the inn for her holidays.

It was peaceful and cosy in the big bedroom with its timbered walls and ceiling, pretty casement and fine old oaken furniture. Dion alternately drowsed and talked to his charming nurse.

Her beauty had a flaming fascination about it which intrigued him. She was an excellent nurse, too: did not 'fuss' him. She was cool and subtle and quiet.

Once when she drew the clothes about him, her slender, sun-tanned fingers touched his chin, and he was amazed by the thrill of that touch.

He did not mean to be disloyal to Hope. He loved Hope; admired her sweet, gentle nature. But very different thoughts rioted in Marion's brain. Before that long night's vigil ended, she was hotly, passionately in love with Dion Courtland. This was the lover whom Emm had spoken of . . . who could 'tear the heart out of

16

her body' . . . and with supreme egotism, in her mind she had already wiped Hope Marshall off the sheet—in her imagination had possessed Dion and was wholly his.

Dion remained in bed for a week. Marion nursed him tirelessly and devotedly. Every morning he wrote to Hope . . . passionate letters, imploring her to break with her people and marry him. And every day a letter came from Hope, bidding him to be patient and wait until she could make up her mind.

But those letters never reached their destination. Dion gave his to Marion to post. She slipped them all into a drawer in her room, and kept them under lock and key. And each note that bore the Torquay postmark was destroyed before it reached Dion.

He began to fret a little. One day he confided in Marion, who was sitting by his bed, sewing—a charming picture of domesticity.

'I can't understand about Miss Marshall—why she never writes. And she must have got my wire yesterday. You sent it, didn't you, Miss Grayle?'

'Yes,' lied Marion, frankly meeting his gaze.

'Oh, well,' he said moodily. 'Perhaps she's fed up with me.'

'To be honest, I'm afraid she must be,' said Marion. 'But please, please don't let it worry you. I do so want you to get well.'

'You've been an angel of goodness to me,' he said, giving her his hand. 'You must be tired out.'

She let him hold her hand. Her heart leapt at the clasp of his fingers. And for the first time, passion stirred in the man. Her beauty, her strange, subtle charm had been working on him all this week, rousing those primitive emotions which can be very real and strong . . . stronger temporarily than the more genuine and tender affection which he bore Hope.

'I must get up tomorrow, somehow,' he said. 'I can't encroach on your goodness. I must try and get back to town.'

Marion dropped her needlework. 'No, no,' she said, under her breath. 'You can't go. Let me nurse you, till you're quite strong. I love doing it—honestly I do.'

He was afraid of his feelings in that moment. He dropped her hand and leaned back on the pillows, breathing rapidly.

'God, what a rotter I am,' he thought. 'I can't be so disloyal to poor little Hope. But why doesn't she write?'

Another few days passed. Every one of Hope's letters were intercepted and locked away by Marion. And now Dion ceased to write. He was annoyed and resentful of what he called 'Hope's weakness.'

'If she cared, she would at least write me a line,' he blurted out to Marion one afternoon—the first afternoon he was down in the smoking-room, where Marion had placed him before a roaring fire, and covered his

18

knees with a plaid rug. 'I suppose she hasn't forgiven me for running into the ditch that night and getting her into a row.'

'H'm,' said Marion. 'She can't care much. If I loved a man . . .'

'Well?' said Dion, suddenly forgetting Hope, and interesting himself with Marion. 'How would *you* love?'

'With all my heart and soul and body,' she said, in a low, thrilling voice. 'Nothing, nobody should keep me from my lover.'

'He will be a lucky fellow,' said Dion.

He could not tear his gaze from her. She was entrancing this afternoon. She wore a severe frock of black velvet which clung to her lissom figure, and accentuated the milky whiteness of her arms and throat. She was sitting on a stool at his feet, mending a pair of his socks. The sunlight slanted through the casements, and fell upon her, turning her hair a molten gold. There were violet shadows under her eyes.

'You look dead tired,' he said. 'You've worked too hard nursing me and helping in the inn.'

'No,' she said, smiling at him. 'I'm not tired.'

'But you look as though you've had no sleep.'

'Perhaps that is true.'

'Why—Marion?'

His use of her Christian name sent the blood rioting through her veins. She looked at

19

him, shivering. He was still pale and weak, but extraordinarily handsome; his dark hair smoothly brushed, his arresting eyes drawing the very heart out of her as Emm had predicted. Her head drooped.

'I—I can't tell you,' she whispered.

'Is it something to do with me, Marion?'

'Don't ask,' she said.

'I'd better go tomorrow,' he said, hoarsely.

'No, no—don't,' she gasped, turning to him. 'Dion—don't go—I couldn't bear it.'

For an instant he drowned in the great black pools of her splendid eyes. Then he caught her close to him with his uninjured arm, and with a graceful movement she swung herself into his embrace and locked her arms about his throat.

His lips sought and found her mouth.

That kiss was long and terrible in its intensity. To Marion it was the most amazing and marvellous thing; the kiss she had waited for, hungered for, schemed for . . . the kiss for which she had sinned and would sin and sin again.

Deep and long, Dion drank in the sweetness of her mouth. Then he drew back, spent and trembling.

'Marion!' he said. 'You witch . . . you enchantress!'

'I love you—I love you,' she said. 'It is *you* I would love to the very death, Dion.'

He believed her. And he held her close, kissing her flame-gold head and milky throat.

20

After this . . . this mad rapture, this intoxication, his love-affair with Hope seemed a stupid, insipid thing. Never again could he find delight in Hope's cool; innocent little kisses.

'I love you,' he said, hoarsely. 'You've shown me what love can be. Once or twice in my life I've thought I cared for a woman. In Africa there was someone . . . and then Hope . . .'

'Ah—Hope,' said Marion, her arms still about his neck, her eyes sparkling at him. 'But you don't love her now, do you?'

'I shall always be fond of her,' he admitted. 'But she's treated me shabbily—absolutely deserted me. If she'd cared, or been ill, or written . . . but her silence has been rottenly unkind.'

Marion hid her face in his breast. She was feeling guilty—remembering all Hope's pathetic, appealing letters, up in her drawer. But she soon forgot Hope. She took Dion's head between her hands and kissed him passionately between the brows.

'Mine—my Lover,' she said, exultantly.

'Yes, yours, Marion,' he said. 'You are going to marry me.'

Her heart leaped.

'If you want me, Lover.'

'I want you,' he said, thickly. 'When I leave Moorcoombe, you will come with me; we will get married by special licence . . . then I shall take you to France and introduce you to my

21

people.'

'Will they mind?'

'I don't care if they do. I have money of my own. But they will have to admit you will make the loveliest Lady Courtland for generations.'

'Lady Courtland?' she repeated dreamily.

'Yes. I inherit that title when the pater dies.'

'I don't care much about the money. Only for you,' she said. 'For you I would . . . die.'

He held her close, but shivered a little.

'You mustn't love me quite so much, you marvellous girl. I'm not worth that.'

She laughed and kissed him on the mouth. And once again Dion Courtland was lost . . . lost to all reason, all calm, all honour . . . as he took his fill of kisses from her beautiful lips.

Suddenly she opened her eyes, and her face lost its lovely, passionate colour. For over Dion's shoulder, through the casements, she saw the face of Jet Saddleman. He beckoned to her. Uneasily she obeyed his silent summons. She drew away from her lover's arms.

'You are not strong yet—you must rest, my beloved,' she said. 'I will come back to you in a moment.'

He leaned back on his cushions and closed his eyes. He did feel tired . . . exhausted with the emotions this strange, beautiful creature roused in him. His head was whirling. Only one fact was clear to him. He loved Marion Grayle, and he was going to marry her . . . at once. No more waiting, no hanging about; no fussing such as Hope had done. Unkind Hope! She could not have cared, otherwise she would have written . . .

But once Marion had left him, he began to feel guilty about Hope. Such a short while ago he had vowed eternal love and fealty to her. If she had not neglected him, deserted him, he would still be her lover . . .

Outside the Travellers' Rest, Marion met Jet Saddleman. She had put on a woolly coat, but her curls were bare to the breeze that blew freshly over the moors.

'What d'you want? What do you mean by spying on me?' she asked.

He eyed her angrily.

'I wasn't spying. I didn't know you were spooning. I just glanced in to see if you were there. Now I know the truth. You're fooling around with this Londoner. But I won't have it.'

'How dare you criticise me?' she asked in a furious undertone. 'I don't belong to you, Jet Saddleman, and never did.'

'But you will one day, Marion.'

'No. I am going to marry Mr. Courtland.'

'Pooh!' he sneered at her. 'Not on your life. He'll not marry an innkeeper's daughter. What about the young lady from Torquay?'

'He's done with her.'

'You aren't so clever as I thought, Marion. I reckon the truth is that while his young lady is away, he's amusing himself with you, but once she comes back, you'll get the go-by.'

Marion shivered with rage. Her eyes sparkled wickedly at him. But she did not lose her temper. She crossed her arms and gazed at him with a slow, scornful smile.

'Well, you're just wrong—as you'll see,' she said. 'I'm going to be married to Mr. Courtland next week by special licence.'

He seized her by the shoulders.

'You're going to be married to me, Marion Grayle.'

She shook herself free and marched past him. He laughed—a mocking laugh that maddened her. How dared he say Dion was amusing himself . . . that if Hope turned up, she, Marion, would be shelved. It was not true.

It was true that Dion would not marry her if he found out the disgraceful way in which she had intercepted his letters. But he would never find that out. He was going to marry her before he left Dartmoor. He had said so.

As she walked along, she met the postman. At once her expression became wary. She greeted him with that sunny, charming smile which gave one the impression of utmost candour.

'Afternoon, Hepworth. Anything for little me?'

'Naw, missie,' said the postman, genially. 'Only one fur Mister Grayle, and that gentleman staying at the Inn.'

'Oh,' said Marion. 'Right-oh, Hepworth—I'll take them in.'

He gave her the letters without hesitation. Marion pocketed her father's; a bill; and looked at Dion's. The Torquay postmark . . . Hope again.

Up in her bedroom, Marion opened and read Hope's note without scruple. It was a piteous note, stained and blotted with tears. The poor little thing was broken-hearted because he had not written. Her mother was bullying her into an engagement with an elderly man with money and a title. She ended thus:

'I don't think I can bear it much longer, darling Dion. There must be some reason why you haven't written. Perhaps you are too ill. I can't stand it. I am coming to see you as soon as I can . . .'

Marion ground her small white teeth.

Hope must not come; must not see Dion. It would drive her mad if the girl turned up and spoiled things now . . . now that Dion had begun to love her . . . meant to make her his wife. More than anything on earth she desired to marry Dion Courtland.

She heard her father calling. Hastily she pocketed Hope's pathetic epistle, and ran downstairs. Dion was tired and wanted to be helped back to his bedroom. His arm was

25

throbbing tonight.

Marion tended him with the greatest concern.

'We must get that arm well soon, darling,' she said, once he was back in bed. She was shaking up his pillows—making him more comfortable.

He pulled her face down to his, and kissed her with passion.

'You wonderful thing!' he whispered. 'What would I do without you? Yes—I must get fit. I want to marry you—make you my very own, Marion. Tonight I am going to write to Hope, and tell her that you and I are engaged.'

Marion's eyes glowed. But she said:

'Poor little Hope—in a way I pity her, Dion.'

'I don't,' he said roughly. 'She can't care a jot for me. She hasn't even troubled to send a postcard.'

A little later that same evening, a grey Autumn twilight, Marion put on a thick coat and a pair of brogues, and set forth for a walk. She was splendidly healthy and liked open-air exercise. She had been sitting with her lover most of the day, and felt the need for fresh air now.

As she walked over the moors, her fierce young heart exulted within her at the memory of Dion's arms and lips.

'I love him—I love him!' she sang within her. 'Nothing shall take him from me . . . certainly not that fool of a girl from Torquay.'

She drew near that grim, solitary spot known as the Haunted Glen. Here lay the Suicide's Pool; dark, quiet, sinister; protected by a clump of bushes and a few stark poplars stripped of their leaves by the October wind.

Marion stood on the fringe of the pool, staring into it. Her own face grinned up at her, dusky, distorted. She usually avoided this haunted spot. But today it fascinated her. The 'Dark Death' held no terrors for her. She was burning and thrilling with the intensity of her feelings for Dion.

The sound of quick, light footsteps rustling the dry leaves, startled her. She looked up and saw, to her amazement and dismay, the small figure of Hope Marshall; Hope in the short musquash coat that Marion remembered; and a little brown felt hat with a diamond-arrow through the brim. As Hope saw Marion, she rushed up to her with a glad cry.

'Oh, Miss Grayle . . . thank goodness you're here. I've lost my way—walking from Moorcoombe Station.'

'Oh!' said Marion, stepping back a pace.

'I just had to come,' continued Hope, her blue eyes distressed and tired. 'Mother's led me an awful life, and I couldn't stand it. I wanted Dion. In fact . . . I've run away . . . taken the plunge at last . . . and I know when I see Dion he'll take care of me.'

Marion did not speak. She stared at the girl in a stupefied way. But she noticed that Hope carried a suitcase; began to realize what this meant. Hope had come to Dion . . . and when Dion saw her, he would find out about the letters, and turn against her, Marion . . . he would recognize his responsibility to Hope, and marry her.

Hope did not notice the almost fiendish look of anger in Marion's eyes.

'How is Dion? And why do you think he hasn't written to me?' she was saying in her confiding way. 'You were so kind to me, Miss Grayle . . . perhaps you can help me again . . . tell me why he hasn't written . . .'

Marion's face grew crimson, then deathly pale.

'I can't help you,' she said. 'Go back to Torquay, you little fool!'

The change of tone; the sudden alteration in Marion from a sweet, girlish friend to a furious, shaking woman, horrified Hope.

'Miss Grayle!' she said, aghast.

Marion felt her forehead damp. She fumbled with shaking fingers for her handkerchief. As she pulled it from her coat pocket, a letter fell to the ground. Hope's gaze followed it, and she recognized her own handwriting. Her face grew amazed and stern. She picked up the letter and held it out to Marion.

'Why have you got this?' she said. 'It is the note I wrote to Mr. Courtland, yesterday.'

Marion did not answer. She was in one of

28

her blind, white-hot rages; the sort of rage that robs a being of sanity. She only knew that this yellow-haired chit of a girl was going to come between her and Dion; that if Dion saw her tonight, she, Marion, would never again feel the wild thrill of his arms and his lips—never become his wife.

'I do believe you are a wicked, dishonest woman!' Hope was saying in a shocked voice. 'You opened my letter and read it. Perhaps you have read all my letters. Perhaps that is why Dion hasn't written to me . . . or have you opened and destroyed his to me? I—'

She paused, abruptly. She saw such hatred, such primitive, jealous fury in Marion's face, that it petrified her. Then Marion rushed at her with clenched fists.

'You shan't take him—you shan't come between us!' she said between set teeth. 'My God—I'll *kill* you first!'

Hope was on the edge of Suicide's Pool. And she stepped sharply back as Marion attacked her. She lost her balance, and fell backwards into the water, with a shrill cry.

The pool, treacherous, quiet, even sinister, seemed to be waiting for her. The dark waters closed over that fair little head. There was a horrid, gurgling sound as they sucked their victim under.

The red mist cleared from Marion's brain. She stared with fascinated eyes at the widening circles about the spot wherein Hope had fallen. A fair head appeared . . . a white face agonised, convulsed.

'Help!' she choked. 'Help . . . I can't swim . . .'

Marion stood rigid, merciless. Hope was drowning before her very eyes. And if she drowned, she, Marion, would gain her heart's desire . . . Dion would never see Hope again . . . never know the fatal truth.

Hope Marshall rose and sank for the third time.

Now the Suicide's Pool was quiet and smooth, as though satisfied—its hunger appeased.

Peace settled over the haunted glen. But Marion went on staring down at the dark waters wherein Hope had perished. And she knew as she stood there, that the crime of murder was upon her soul.

CHAPTER THREE

The sun went down.

In the haunted glen dark shadows slanted through the stark poplars and cast fantastic shadows over the Suicide's Pool. The wind dropped and it was deathly quiet over the moors. Great grey clouds came billowing up from the North, and it seemed to the guilty girl who stood there staring down into the gloomy water, that nature, herself, held her breath for very horror of the crime which had been done.

Hope was dead . . . had perished miserably in that stagnant pool. Marion had a vivid imagination, and suddenly she pictured her victim lying at the bottom . . . her golden hair floating like seaweed piteously about her pallid, agonised face . . . the eyes still staring accusingly up at her murderess.

From the distance came the low rumble of thunder. One or two great drops of rain began to fall, pattering on Marion's face and figure, and making little punctures in the pool. Again came the growl of thunder. A storm was approaching. A vivid flash of lightning lit up the haunted glen, and made Marion's heart leap with fear. To her feverish, distorted imagination, the Almighty Himself was showing the face of His anger. The thunders of the heavens; the lightning; the storm accused and condemned her. Perhaps she would be struck . . . Divine justice . . . struck down on the very spot where her crime had been committed.

The lethargy of horror which had consumed her after Hope had sunk for the last time, was replaced by a frightful sensation of terror. She put her hands up to her ears as though to shut out the sound of the storm which seemed charged with Hope's last, despairing cry for mercy. She gave a shrill scream, turned and fled from that dark and sinister spot.

31

She ran blindly, without pausing once, her eyes dilated, her face white, her breath coming in gasps. The storm was growing fiercer. She felt almost that it followed her . . . that it was a Thing . . . chasing, snarling after her . . . trying to get at her. She began to sob as she ran . . . a pain stabbed her side . . . the thunder crashed over Dartmoor, and the lightning flashed vividly across the sky.

Then as Marion came within sight of the Travellers' Rest, she slowed down. Common-sense came to her aid and thrust back the hysteria that was rising in her. She wanted to scream and scream . . . to run to Dion, be folded in his arms, feel his kisses on her mouth . . . compensation for the frightful crime she had just committed in order to retain his love. But she reminded herself of the necessity to appear before Dion, and the world, as though nothing had happened; nothing had frightened her. She was a murderess . . . she was haunted by a secret which she could never forget. But she had let Hope Marshall drown in order that Dion should not be taken from her. Now it was essential, vital, that she should keep him for whom she had stained her immortal soul.

She walked steadily toward the Inn, taking an iron grip of herself. She was not a weakling. She was a strong-minded girl at all times, and in this hour of crisis and horror, she conquered the weaker self that threatened to betray her. She must remember that nobody at

Moorcoombe knew that Hope had come to see Dion. Dion had not received her letter. Nobody, therefore, would guess that she had met anybody on her walk, or even that she had been to the Suicide's Pool.

She walked into the Inn, and began to take off her drenched coat and the little felt hat which was sodden with rain. As she mounted the stairs to her bedroom, she ran into her father who was coming downstairs. He was a stout, rosy-faced man of tremendous height and breadth, with white curly head and a series of little chins which made him look like a ridiculous, over-grown baby. A simple-minded, God-fearing man was Tom Grayle; unlike this strange, fierce, passionate daughter he had begotten, and whom he idolised. He smiled at her and patted her shoulder as he met her.

'Hullo, Marion-girl! You're a sight—wet through. Got caught in the storm?'

'Yes, Dad,' she said carelessly. She smiled at him with her innocent, childlike smile. She had begun to act, as she knew she must act for the rest of her days. She snuggled her head against her father's arm with more affection than she generally showed him. 'How's my Dad?' she added.

His face glowed with pride and pleasure. He liked his beautiful daughter to be demonstrative. He gave her a kiss on the top of her head, and she ran lightly on up to her own room.

Some queer, fastidious feeling made her change every piece of her clothing, have a hot bath, and dress in fresh things again before she approached her lover. She did not want ever to see that dress or coat or hat again. In them she had stood by the Suicide's Pool . . . acknowledging herself a guilty creature . . . a *murderess.* She would destroy those clothes . . . or give them to the poor.

When she had put on a pretty, flowered ninon frock with a square neck and short, baby sleeves; a blue velvet narrow band about the hips, she looked at herself in the mirror. The lamplight threw up the lovely lights in her hair. She had rubbed her face with a rough towel, after her brisk bath, and brought a soft, carnation pink to her cheeks. She looked cool, sweet, fair as a flower in her dainty gown . . . ready for a lover's caresses. Who, looking at her now, could associate her with that livid, savage, passionate creature who had sent Hope Marshall to her death, an hour ago?

A few minutes later, Marion was in Dion's bedroom. She took him a light supper of buttered eggs, toast and Ovaltine. He sat up eagerly as she set the tray beside him, and held out his uninjured arm.

'You're back, then, darling?' he said.

'Yes . . . got caught in the storm, Dion. I found myself at Hunter's Hill' (she mentioned a place in the opposite direction to the haunted glen) 'and had to run all the way

34

home.'

'You look as fresh, as glowing as a rose,' he said in a low voice. 'Marion, Marion, is it true that you love me . . . that before you went out, you promised me to be my wife?'

She fell on her knees by the bed. His arm encircled her, pressed her red-gold head to his breast. She began to breathe swiftly; looked up at him with great dark eyes magnified by sudden tears . . . tears of passion and longing rather than remorse. She had no remorse in this instant, with her lover's arms about her, his face close to hers. She had sinned for this . . . broken the Commandments for it; she gloried in it now. A sort of savage pleasure swept over her. Hope Marshall could never now separate her from Dion. She put up her arms and wound them around his throat.

'Dion, Dion indeed I do love you—adore you!' she said. 'Hold me close, hold me close, sweetheart . . . tell me you will never stop loving me . . . oh, tell me you will always want me, Dion!'

'Always,' he said recklessly, the blood hotly pulsing through his veins. 'Always, you Enchantress . . . you lovely woman . . .'

He kissed the white arms around his throat, from dimpled elbow to slender wrist, then he put his hand behind her head and his lips closed over her mouth. Marion closed her eyes during that long kiss. In the rosy, lamp-lit room with its charming rafters, blue-and-white check curtains, drawn across the long, narrow casements, all was quiet and peaceful. The storm was abating. It had been swift and fierce. There was no sound now, save the occasional rumble of thunder from far away.

Marion and Dion clung to each other. The man was under a spell, completely enslaved by this girl who had bewitched him since first he had become intimately acquainted with her. Thoughts of Hope were far from his enamoured mind at this moment. But Marion could not help thinking of her.

Only for an instant did she surrender wholly to the rapture of her lover's caresses. Then she drew away and he felt her shudder in his encircling arm.

'What is it, Beautiful?' he asked.

'Oh—nothing,' she said. 'I'm a little cold . . . after my hot bath.'

'You mustn't get a chill,' he said tenderly. 'Run down to the fire, Marion. And after supper we must talk of our marriage.'

'Yes, yes,' she said feverishly. 'Let us talk of that.'

They discussed their marriage that night. Old Tom Grayle was let into the secret. He was delighted. He liked and respected Dion Courtland. He was what Grayle termed a 'proper young gent,' and he was not surprised that Dion should prefer his lovely daughter to the fair-haired young lady who had broken down in the car with him that foggy night. He gave his consent to a speedy wedding. He did not want to part with Marion, but he felt proud to think she was going to be Lady Courtland, one day . . . that she would have plenty of money. It was a much better marriage than one with a chap like Jet Saddleman would have been.

It was finally fixed between them that Dion and Marion should be married at Moorcoombe Church by special licence next week. Dion's arm would be better then. They would go on to London where they would stay a night before going on to Monte Carlo, to Dion's people.

Monte Carlo! Marion's eyes sparkled at the thought. She had always dreamed of that place as a fairyland; the Playground of the Rich. And she would be going there now as Mrs. Dion Courtland. The thought enraptured her.

But the evening did not end as happily for Marion as it began. After all the arrangements had been discussed, and Mr. Grayle had retired, discreetly leaving the lovers to say goodnight, Dion insisted upon talking about Hope.

He had written to her, telling her of his engagement.

'She can't blame me, can she?' he asked Marion, rather anxiously. 'She deserted me, first—never even bothered to send a card, or answer any of my wires or letters.'

'Quite so,' said Marion.

She was sitting by his bedside, and he was playing with her hands. He was happy, but a little troubled in his mind, about Hope. He could not quite forget her sweet, gentle face and clinging ways.

'You don't think I've treated her shabbily, do you, Marion?' he persisted.

'No, no, of course not, darling,' she answered.

'I hope when she gets my letter, she'll be as relieved as I am to end it all,' added Dion.

Marion drew her fingers away from him. The talk about Hope made her feel nervy and almost irritable. She wished Dion would stop it. Guilt knocked at her heart and she was forced to listen to the inner voice that accused her . . . to think of the girl who lay at the bottom of the Suicide's Pool. Hope would never receive Dion's letter . . . Hope was not in Torquay with her mother tonight. She was drowned . . . dead . . . an inanimate Thing sleeping the last, long sleep in those dark and icy waters, this stormy night.

Dion felt Marion shiver.

'You're cold again, dearest,' he said. 'You look tired, too. Go to bed, my lovely one . . . don't sit up any longer.'

At any other time she would have found it hard to drag herself from his side. But since he persisted in turning the conversation to Hope, she felt glad to depart. She kissed him passionately before she went . . . left him

38

shaken and thrilled by the wonder of her caresses.

She sought her own room; undressed, slipped into bed and tried to sleep. But for the first time in her life she knew what it was to suffer from insomnia . . . to be nervy . . . to feel her heart jerk at the bulging of the curtains in the wind, or the creak of a footstep outside her door. She lay wide awake in the darkness, staring up at the ceiling. She was haunted by the picture of the girl she had murdered . . . lying in the Suicide's Pool . . . only a mile from the Travellers' Rest. Her teeth began to chatter . . . her whole body grew ice-cold and shuddered violently. She felt remorse . . . terrible remorse creep over her. She seemed to hear Hope's voice, moaning: 'Save me . . . Help . . . I can't swim . . .'

When would Hope's loss be discovered? What would be done? Would the body ever be found?

Marion huddled under the bedclothes, turned her face to the pillow and stifled the cry that forced itself to her lips. The sweat poured from her forehead. She groaned aloud:

'Dion . . . Dion . . . it was for you . . . Dion . . . I worship you . . . I want you . . . I must never be found out . . .'

She did not find oblivion in sleep until the grey light of dawn dispersed the haunting shadows of that night.

CHAPTER FOUR

Then, early in the morning, came the first discovery of Hope Marshall's disappearance.

A telegram arrived at the Travellers' Rest for Miss Hope Marshall. Old Grayle took it in, and before Marion could prevent him, carried it straight to Dion, who was not yet out of bed.

Dion regarded it perplexedly.

'I can't understand it. She isn't coming here, so far as we know. What do you think about it, Marion?'

Marion, who was almost as pale as the handkerchief she twisted in her nervous fingers, shrugged her shoulders.

'Haven't the least idea, Dion,' she said.

Two hours later came another wire. This time Dion elected to open it.

'I'd better see what it's all about,' he said.

The wire proved to be from Mrs. Marshall, Torquay:

'Exceedingly annoyed you left home without telling us to go to Mr. Courtland. Come home at once.'

'Mother.'

Dion's face was a study in astonishment as he read this wire aloud. He looked at Marion, who looked straight back at him, deliberately.

40

'I can't understand this at all. Hope must have run away to come to me. But why, when she didn't write or bother to answer my letters?'

'It's a mystery,' said Marion, keeping a firm hold on herself.

'We'd better wait till later on in the day, and see what happens,' said Dion.

At lunch-time, Mrs. Marshall herself arrived at the Travellers' Rest to rescue her daughter from the clutches of a 'young rotter,' as she called Dion Courtland. Marion was forced to interview her, with Dion, who was now dressed and down in the smoking-room. Mrs. Marshall was a plump, grey-haired woman with blue eyes rather like Hope's, but a prim, tight little mouth and disapproving expression, suggesting that she was continually shocked by the wicked world. She was fond of her only daughter, but narrow-minded.

'Where is Hope?' she demanded of Dion. 'What have you done with her?'

'I have not seen. Hope since the night of the accident to my car, Mrs. Marshall,' said Dion, coldly. He had never liked Hope's mother.

'That's rubbish,' she said. 'Hope left Torquay to come to Moorcoombe, yesterday. I found a note from her when I came back from a bridge party, and wired at once.'

'Left yesterday afternoon to come here? Are you sure?' asked Dion, frowning.

'Positive. I have made inquiries, and Hope's

41

personal maid, Williams, has now confessed that she drove with my daughter to the station, took a ticket for Moorcoombe, and left her in the train.'

'But how extraordinary!' exclaimed Dion. 'She ought to have reached here yesterday evening.'

'Quite so,' said Mrs. Marshall. 'Where is she?'

Dion turned to Marion, who had been standing by very silently. Her slender fingers, behind her back, had torn her handkerchief to shreds. When interrogated, however, she met her lover's glance with a sweet, innocent smile.

'It is strange, isn't it, Dion,' she murmured.

Mrs. Marshall put up lorgnettes to regard Marion.

'Who is this?' she inquired.

'My fiancée—Miss Grayle,' said Dion, with slight sarcasm.

'Fiancée!' echoed Hope's mother.

'Yes. So you will see, Mrs. Marshall, that I have not lured your daughter here,' said Dion, in a short tone.

Mrs. Marshall went red, then white.

'Well, I don't pretend to understand the situation at all,' at length she said. 'But if this is true—if you have transferred your—er—affections from Hope to this—er—Miss Grayle—where is Hope?'

'I don't know,' said Dion.

'It's extraordinary,' murmured Marion.

But she wanted to shriek . . . to say to the prim-mouthed, arrogant woman: 'I know where she is . . . at the bottom of the pool . . . drowned . . . murdered . . . by *me!*'

She swallowed and shook her head as though to ward off the madness that rose in her.

'I must keep quiet . . . behave sanely,' she told herself. 'If I am not careful, I shall give myself away and lose Dion for ever . . . and be hanged . . . hanged by the neck until I am *dead . . .*'

The interview with Mrs. Marshall was long and distressing. Hope had come to Moorcoombe yesterday and had mysteriously disappeared. Mrs. Marshall drove away from the inn in a state of panic, to make full inquiries at Moorcoombe Station. When she returned, she was in a greater state of panic than ever. She was no longer haughty or prim. She was pathetically human . . . a mother, fearing for her child.

'The station-master saw Hope get out of the Torquay express at five o'clock, and described her . . . her clothes . . . accurately. There can be no mistake,' she told Dion and Marion.

'Then what has become of her?' said Dion.

'The station-master said she refused a cab, and said she wanted the fresh air—decided to walk to the Travellers' Rest over the moors. He told her the way. But it is obvious that she must have lost her way and come to some harm. Oh, dear . . . oh, dear . . . what shall we do?'

Dion lit a cigarette and smoked in silence, his brow knit. He was honestly upset and alarmed on Hope's account. If the poor thing had suddenly taken it into her head to come to him . . . what could have happened to her?

Marion felt the need to act a part at once. She pulled herself together, walked to Mrs. Marshall's side, and put an arm about her.

'Oh, poor, poor Mrs. Marshall!' she said. 'How frightfully worrying for you. And Miss Marshall was such a sweet, gentle young lady. But don't cry . . . we will find her . . . if she has got lost on the moors, we will find her.'

Mrs. Marshall, completely shaken and unnerved, clung to Marion for support and wept in her ams . . . wept in the arms of her daughter's murderess! Marion was a charming girl, she thought . . . so sympathetic . . .

It was Marion who insisted upon Hope's mother remaining at the Inn, while an extensive search was made for the missing girl . . . Marion who waited on her, comforted her while the anxious hours dragged by.

Dion watched Marion with passionate love and admiration in his eyes.

'You're being absolutely topping,' he said, when she was alone with him for a moment. 'As sweet to Mrs. M. as you can be . . . and just as anxious about Hope as we are.'

The 'we' sent a flame of jealousy across

44

Marion.

She put her arms about his neck.

'You don't regret loving me . . . now you've heard Hope was coming to you?' she said, panting.

'No, no, of course not,' he said, kissing her on the lips. 'I love you, Marion—only you. But I was fond of little Hope. I naturally don't want any harm to come to her.'

'Naturally not,' Marion agreed.

But a queer, haunting terror possessed her from that hour onward that Hope would be discovered in the Pool, and that Dion would guess the truth and shrink from her in horror.

That same afternoon the men of the village who, in conjunction with the police, had searched Dartmoor for Miss Marshall, without success, decided to drag the Suicide's Pool. Mrs. Marshall screamed and fainted when they suggested this. Her daughter could not be drowned . . . nothing so horrible could have happened . . . when she recovered her senses, she clung to Marion and protested against the idea. But Marion, who was ice-cold with nerves, patted her shoulder and comforted her.

'Of course nothing will be found there . . . Miss Marshall must have hidden herself deliberately in some hotel or cottage . . . but they always drag the Suicide's Pool when people are missing on the moors . . . as a matter of course.'

When Dion heard that the men were going to drag the Suicide's Pool, he whitened and felt physically sick.

'Marion,' he said. 'Good God . . . they can't think that! . . .'

She caressed him and murmured words of courage and hope.

'Don't feel badly about it, Dion. They must make every possible search for her.'

He hid his face in his hands.

'My God . . . the poor little thing can't have . . . come to harm like that . . . I don't believe it!'

Jealousy tore at Marion again. But she stroked his head, clung to him with passion.

'It's all right, Dion . . . it's all right . . . and you've always got me.'

'Yes, always got you,' he repeated. And he tried to shut out the thought of Hope, by surrendering to the thrill of Marion's arms and lips.

When the search-party set out for the haunted glen, Marion felt irresistibly drawn to the same spot, with them. She felt she must go . . . nerve herself to go . . . face the ultimate horror of seeing the wet, limp body taken from the water. She *must* be there. A guilty person could not have joined the party and watched the pool being dragged. It would further establish her innocence, her ignorance of the affair, if she went . . .

Old Emm, hobbling on her ebony stick, met

the grim little party as it walked toward the haunted glen. Marion tried to avoid her, but Emm thrust out a claw-like hand and gripped her arm.

'I see the fires of passion and madness of fear in your eyes, Marion Grayle!' she croaked. 'You've found the lover to tear the heart out o' your body . . . but I see more than that. I see the Dark Death . . . the Dark Death . . .'

Marion's face became drained of colour. Livid, furious, she pulled away from the old creature.

'What rot you talk, Emm!' she muttered.

'Ha! ha! ha!' cackled Emm. 'I see more in your eyes, my lass, than I will tell . . .'

The perspiration stood in little beads on Marion's forehead. She hurried away from the old woman and went on with the search-party. She talked lightly and cheerfully with the various Moorcoombe men whom she knew. No one could have guessed the terror, the sick fear that knocked at her guilty heart as they neared the haunted glen.

When at last she stood again by the Suicide's Pool, and her vivid imagination brought back the memory of Hope Marshall's death, she was forced to lean against a tree for support.

Suddenly she became aware that Jet Saddleman was one of the party, and that he was watching her . . . watching her with queer, malevolent blue eyes. She met his gaze, but it frightened her and she looked away again. What was Jet thinking? Why had she come? When would they find Hope's body . . . ?

They began to drag the pool.

Marion's fascinated eyes watched the movements of the men as they let down their nets.

But in a few minutes' time the men ceased work.

'We're wasting our time,' said the Moorcoombe constable. 'There's no body here.'

No body there. Marion stared at the man as though transfixed. No body in the pool . . . and they said they had touched the bottom. It was not a bottomless pond . . . and *she knew that Hope Marshall was there.*

Her first feeling of relief was replaced by one of terror and perplexity. This was some devilish magic . . . Hope's body had been removed from the Suicide's Pool. But by what . . . by whom? If not by the dark, supernatural powers . . . then by what human?

She had to bite her lower lip till it bled to keep herself from screaming at the men:

'You fools . . . she is there . . . she *is* there!'

'Come on home, Miss,' said the policeman kindly. 'You look all white, and no wonder. It bain't a place fur womenfolk . . . nor ought you'm to have come.'

But she stayed there, leaning against the tree, as though rooted to the spot. The party

48

began to walk back toward the Travellers' Rest, discussing the mysterious disappearence of the young lady from Torquay.

Jet Saddleman walked up to her. The others had gone. Only Marion and Jet remained in that sinister spot.

Jet touched her on the arm.

'You haven't said how-do-you-do to me yet, my Pretty,' he said.

She stared as though stung. The colour rushed back to her ashen face.

'Let me be, Jet. And I'm not your "Pretty".'

'Oh, yes, you are,' he said quietly. 'And very soon you'll be my wife and mistress of Double-Styles Farm.'

'You great boob!' she laughed at him wildly. 'It's no good stuffing yourself up with that idea. Happens that I'm engaged to Mr. Courtland. I've told you already that I'm being married to him by special licence next week.'

Saddleman folded his arms over his chest, and looked down at her. It was another bright, autumnal afternoon, and the sun was just setting. The red rays fell upon Marion's bare head, turning it to fire.

'You will never be married to Mr. Courtland, Marion,' he said. 'You are going to marry me.'

'Don't keep on!' she said furiously. 'I won't listen to you. And don't try and bar my way, or I'll call out to Hepworth and the others.'

'Oh, no you won't,' he said, with a soft

significant laugh that chilled her. 'You don't dare.'

She began to tremble at the knees.

'What do you mean, Jet Saddleman?'

He looked down at her with an expression of terrible passion and horror, mixed. He suddenly flung his arms around her, holding her in an embrace that made her faint and ill.

'I know,' he said under his breath. '*I know* about Hope Marshall, you little fool!'

She would have fallen to the ground if he had not been holding her. Her eyes looked up at him piteously from a livid face.

'You don't . . . what are you saying? What— do you know?' she stammered.

'That you murdered her, Marion Grayle,' said Jet with his lips close to her ear. 'And I saw you do it . . . here by the Suicide's Pool, yesterday. I know . . . and you're going to marry me, *or swing for it.* Now you can choose, my Pretty Dear!'

CHAPTER FIVE

Just for a moment, Marion leaned against Jet's shoulder, her eyes shut, her breath coming in quick gasps. Just for an instant she knew the meaning of extreme fear—the fear that she had been found out. She thought she would faint dead away in his arms. But like lightning

50

flashed across her intelligence the knowledge that if she gave herself away through bodily weakness like this; that if she allowed Jet to get the upper hand; all would be lost.

'Come, Marion,' she heard him say in his hoarse voice which had just the suspicion of a Devonshire drawl. 'Come, my dear, and tell me what made you do it.'

She recovered herself. She pushed him away from her with the strength of a young tigress, and faced him with blazing eyes and scarlet cheeks.

'How dare you, Jet Saddleman!' she cried. 'You're mad—mad as a hatter. What are you trying to insinuate, you great brute?'

He folded his arms on his chest, his vivid blue eyes narrowing to slits.

'You can't get out of it like that, Marion,' he said. 'You got to own up.'

'Own up what?' She stamped her foot with well-assumed impatience and anger. 'What are you driving at, you great mutt?'

'You'll call me a "mutt" once too often, Marion,' he said quietly. 'I'm not the mutt you think me. Come, my Pretty, you're very handsome with that colour and that sparkle in your big black eyes, but it's best for you to stop acting, and own to the terrible thing you've done.'

Marion shuddered. For an instant her eyes sped to the Suicide's Pool which had just been dragged in vain. Her mind turned to Hope

Marshall's body . . . what in heaven's name had become of it? Had Jet Saddleman truly seen the crime committed . . . had he, personally, disposed of the drowned, murdered girl? Her teeth began to chatter. She was fast losing courage again. But she tried to laugh . . . a wild laugh, her head flung back, her hands on her hips, defiantly.

'You're crazy!' she panted. 'I've done no terrible thing. I shall tell Mr. Courtland how you're persecuting me, and trying to frighten me.'

Jet echoed the laugh, but his was a sinister sound. He came up to the girl and swung her back into the circle of his arm again.

'You'd be well advised, my Pretty, not to tell Mr. Dion Courtland anything of the sort; otherwise I shall have a much more interesting tale to tell him, concerning the disappearance of the young lass from Torquay.'

His persistent insinuations and the sinister attitude he maintained proved too much for Marion's nerves, which were already strung to breaking point. She began to moan and struggle in his embrace.

'Let me go—let me go, Jet . . . don't be cruel to me . . . don't go on suggesting such horrible things!'

'Own up, then,' he said harshly.

'There's nothing to own,' she gasped, her face as white as milk.

'Then I'll tell *you*,' he said, his own patience

52

exhausted, his nerves as raw as hers. 'That night when you met Miss Marshall by this pool, I was coming by for a walk, and when I saw you two girls, I stood behind a tree yonder . . .' he pointed to a clump of poplars fringing the dark and gloomy water . . . 'I stayed there—and I saw you push in the young lady and leave her to drown. It was murder, Marion . . . murder, my girl, and you know it!'

Hysteria gripped her. She began to sob helplessly . . . great shuddering sobs that tore her throat and convulsed her body. Jet continued:

'After you'd run away in that blinding storm, I came forward and thought over what you'd done. I decided to cover your guilt . . . to make things safer for you. I knew when the young lady was missed they'd end by dragging the pool. They always do. I waited till it was dark. Then I fetched a grappling iron and a net, and I fished up the body and the suitcase . . .' (Marion, listening to him in frenzy of terror, felt him shiver now although he spoke callously) . . . 'Then I carried them to Linton Wood—half a mile yonder—and I buried them there.'

Marion looked up at him in a dazed way.

'You—buried them?'

'Yes—body and suitcase . . . with a spade. A fine undertaker I made and a fine sexton.' Jet gave a grim laugh. 'Murder's a dirty thing, but once 'tis done, 'tis done, and to me a dead body's no more than a Thing to be hidden out o' sight, quick and sharp.'

'Oh—my—God!' gasped the girl, covering her eyes with her hands.

'I buried Miss Marshall deep,' said Jet, more sombrely. 'I was sorry for the poor little thing, but there it was, and you done the crime, and it's you I love and wanted to cover.'

Marion felt no gratitude—only an unreasoning hatred and chagrin because he had spied on her and knew her for the crime-stained creature she was. And he had made himself partner in her crime—accessory after the fact.

'You fool—you fool!' she flung at him. 'Why didn't you leave things alone—why did you interfere?'

'Ah! You own up, now, eh?'

'What use to deny it if you saw it and have b-buried her?' she said, shivering as though with ague. But her teeth were clenched with fury, and she felt she could have killed this great brute of a man . . . willingly choked the life out of him if she had had the strength in her delicate hands.

'She lies six foot down in Linton Wood,' said Jet. 'And there she'll lie in peace. Nobody'll find her. I strewed dry leaves and twigs about where I'd dug, so that it looks like the rest o' the woods. Unless they get the blood-hounds out to search Linton Woods, Miss Marshall will never be heard of more.'

The blood-hounds! Marion's eyes dilated. It was natural now for her to turn to Jet in the extremity of her fear.

'They won't do that, will they, Jet? Say they won't!'

'They won't,' he soothed, pleased, triumphant that he had this girl in his power now . . . that she would learn to grovel, to plead to him. 'In any case, 'tis no proof you've done it if they do find her.'

She bit her lips till the blood came.

'Come, pull yourself together, Marion,' he said. 'I've taken on part o' your guilt, and now it's up to you an' me to keep quiet about it and act as though we're innocent.'

'Yes,' she muttered. 'I know that.'

'I know why you did the murder,' he said. 'For Dion Courtland.'

'Yes,' she admitted through her teeth.

'But you won't ever marry him, my girl. You must give him up at once—and marry me.'

'No,' she gasped. 'No—never!'

'If you don't, Marion, I shall say what 1 know.'

'You daren't. You'd be hung with me.'

'I'll be hung rather than see you wedded to Dion Courtland!' he said fiercely, drawing her close to him. 'I tell you, I'm mad for you, Marion. I'm not a man of half-measures. It's all or nothing. It's you, or gaol and the gallows. I don't mind. If you're convicted, I'll be convicted along with you. But if you choose to marry me, I'll keep a still tongue.'

Marion felt distracted. Marriage with Jet had always seemed abhorrent to her fastidious taste. He was too coarse, uneducated; too rough for her. And now . . . now that he shared her guilty secret, it made him a hundred times more repellent. Imagine being married to a man, sitting opposite him at the table, living with him day after day, knowing that he *knew* . . . the ghost of that unfortunate girl forever between them, haunting them, accusing them!

'Ah, no, no, no,' she moaned. 'You can't be so cruel—you can't make me give up the lover for whom I've sinned.'

'I can and I will,' said Jet, savagely.

Despair gripped her. She knew that Jet was adamant; half mad with love for her. But when she thought of Dion, of forfeiting his kisses, his caresses, it was more than she could bear. For Dion she had murdered Hope Marshall. It was not likely she would give him up after that! But she saw the need to capitulate, to gain time. She made a giant effort to control her emotions which were running riot, playing havoc with her. She drew a hand across her hot eyes, and pushed the curly masses of hair back from her damp forehead.

'Jet,' she said. 'You must give me time.'

'Time—what for?'

'To send Dion Courtland away.'

'Ah—then you will do it?'

'Yes,' she said, knowing that she lied. 'I will

56

do it in good time. But I've only just become engaged to him, and it would look queer if I gave him up suddenly and married you. I don't want to arouse suspicion.'

Jet Saddleman was a passionate, unprincipled man. At the same time he was possessed of a dull wit. A clever woman with education and brains like Marion Grayle could do what she wanted with him—very soon blind his eyes to reason and truth. Marion had changed her mood. She was no longer angry, terrified, exhibiting her blind fury. She had become soft, kittenish, yielding. She even put her arms around his neck.

'After all, you're a bit of a dear, Jet,' she murmured. 'I oughtn't to quarrel with you, seeing that you have proved your love by wanting to cover me, to shield me.'

He hugged her, foolishly infatuated and delighted.

'You mean that, you lil dear?'

'Why, yes,' she said softly, stroking his head. 'I'm not so crazy about Dion that I wouldn't prefer you, in the end. But you'll be a dear and give me time, so as to stop anybody being suspicious, eh?'

'Yes, all right,' he agreed. 'I'll not be unreasonable. But swear you'll give him up and marry me, Marion.'

'I swear it,' she said, looking straight up into his eyes.

But in that very moment she could willingly

have plunged a knife into his heart. She loathed and feared him. She went on stroking his head, partially surrendering, making a dozen promises, throwing dust into his eyes. He would have pressed a dozen hot kisses on her lips, but she pretended to be shy, giggled like an innocent village maiden, turned her head so that his kisses fell on her hair. She felt she would have been sick if he had touched her lips . . . those lips that belonged to Dion. In her queer way, Marion was fiercely reticent. She loved Dion utterly . . . for him she had committed a crime; she belonged to him and him alone. But she had completely deceived and enslaved Jet Saddleman before they parted in the haunted glen that evening.

She thanked him for what he had done; for disposing of Hope Marshall's body so successfully. She promised to meet him on the morrow at Double-Styles Farm and to tell him in what manner she intended to get rid of Dion.

He went his way, exulting. But she went back to the Travellers' Rest with a heavy heart and a brain still seething with anger and fear. It was a catastrophic thing for her that anybody—particularly Jet Saddleman—should have seen what had taken place that fatal night at the Suicide's Pool. She was in his hands, for the moment. But she must think of a way to outwit him . . . match her brains against his. Nothing would induce her to marry him, to give up all her hopes of becoming Dion Courtland's wife.

She found her lover sitting with the wretched Mrs. Marshall in the parlour, trying to console her. Mrs. Marshall was weeping bitterly.

Dion looked at Marion as she entered. She appeared weary and white, as though she had been through a severe mental and physical strain. He quickly walked up to her and took her hands. Mrs. Marshall left them, sobbing, poor woman, as she walked away.

'My darling—are you all right? Where have you been? You didn't go with that horrible search-party, surely?'

'Yes,' she said, in a gloomy voice. 'I had to go. But I'm sorry I did, now. It was—frightful!'

'You oughtn't to have been there,' he said in a shocked voice. 'It was no place for a woman.'

She clung to his right hand feverishly.

'I had to go,' she repeated. 'I'm so sorry for poor Mrs. Marshall—so anxious Miss Hope should be found.'

'It is like you to be so tender-hearted, my Beautiful,' said Dion, putting his uninjured arm around her. 'But try not to worry too much. It will make you ill. I know it is all most distressing. I feel rotten tonight . . .' and he sighed and shut his eyes wearily. He had been through a very painful hour with Hope's mother, and all the time he was haunted by the memory of the girl who had been so sweet, so simple, so clinging; she had loved him once, and once he had thought to marry her. Had he treated her shabbily? She had set out to come to him; what had happened to her? Surely she had not done away with herself? She was not that sort . . .

He felt a hot kiss on his hand . . . thrilled to the touch of Marion's lips. He opened his eyes and looked down at her with an expression that made her pulses leap in response.

'Ah, Marion, my own,' he murmured.

'Dion, my Dion,' she said under her breath.

He forgot Hope . . . only remembered his wild infatuation for this girl and his forthcoming marriage to her. And she tried to forget, too . . . but it was horribly difficult now that Jet Saddleman had complicated matters so.

She looked at Dion's handsome face, and her fierce heart rebelled against Jet.

'I shall never give Dion up—never—never—never—' she inwardly vowed.

And meanwhile, to Dion and Mrs. Marshall and all the others, the mystery of Hope Marshall's disappearance remained unsolved.

CHAPTER SIX

That following morning, Hope's mother returned to Torquay. Worn, anxious, pathetically humble, for the once proud woman that she was, she took her leave of Dion and Marion.

Marion, after a sleepless night, ought to have looked haggard. But she had a fine constitution, magnificent vitality, and she appeared quite fresh and sparkling on this bright, autumnal morning. With her arm through Dion's, she bade Mrs. Marshall farewell and wished her luck.

'I *do* so hope you'll hear news of Miss Hope quite soon,' she said. 'Somehow I think you will get a note from some quite different part of England, saying she is safe and well.'

'I pray you are right; and a thousand thanks for your kindness and sympathy, my dear girl,' said Mrs. Marshall. 'It is plain that my poor Hope is not in this vicinity. The search-party can find no trace of her, and they think the Moorcoombe station-master must have made a mistake when he said he saw her get out of the Torquay express.'

'It does seem as though it's a mistake,' said Dion, nodding. 'If she had come here, we should have found her by now. I think Marion is right—that you will find that Hope has gone away to some other part of England.'

'Yet her maid is sure she took a ticket for Moorcoombe,' sighed Mrs. Marshall. 'It is all most mysterious. However, the matter is in the hands of the police, and very soon, if I don't find her, I shall get Scotland Yard on to it.'

61

Marion dared not move a muscle. But she felt a shiver down her spine at the mention of that dreaded name. Then Hope's deluded mother leaned forward to kiss her daughter's murderess.

'You've been a dear,' she said. 'Good-bye.'

Marion had the grace to avoid kissing the woman whose only child she had sent to a terrible death. She turned a cheek to that kiss. After Mrs. Marshall had gone, she walked back into the inn with Dion. He looked healthier, brighter today, and his arm was greatly improved. But his brows met in a worrying frown.

'It's all most unnerving,' he confessed to Marion. 'Somehow I feel responsible about Hope . . . and yet . . .'

'Rubbish!' interrupted Marion. 'You can't feel in the least responsible. It was nothing to do with you if she did leave home, darling. She didn't write to you or answer any of your letters.'

'That is so,' he sighed.

Jealousy burned Marion.

'Don't let the thought of that girl spoil our love,' she urged, nestling her head against his arm.

Dion felt uneasy. But Marion's beauty and passion never failed to stir him. He pressed her close . . . their lips met in a lingering kiss. And while Marion thrilled under that embrace, her sharp brain was working . . .

wondering what to do about Jet . . . how to manage him . . . silence him . . . without surrendering her lover.

Hope's mother had returned to Torquay. But the Moorcoombe police would go on investigating . . . and if they failed and if Mrs. Marshall did not hear from Hope, detectives from Scotland Yard would be put on the track. Marion grew cold at the thought. She must silence Jet, and get away with Dion before that much more thorough and cunning investigation began.

Things were somewhat precipitated by a sudden wire from Dion's mother at Monte Carlo, which reached him that morning just as he was talking to Marion of their marriage and future. It was to the effect that his father had had a stroke and was dying. He asked that his son should, if well enough himself, go to him before he died.

This wire was a mixed blessing for Marion. It gave her time . . . yet it took her lover away from her . . . and somehow she never felt happy or secure save in the passionate circle of his arms. She tried to cheer and comfort him when he received this news.

'Oh, my poor darling—what a tragedy for you—I know how you love your father—my poor boy! I'm so sorry!'

She was her sweetest self, tenderly kissing and caressing him, and he abandoned himself to her in his grief.

'I'm terribly fond of the pater—it's rotten—
he went South as fit as a fiddle . . . of course he
is the big, ruddy type . . . liable to apoplexy . . .
the poor mater will be in a fearful stew . . . yes,
I must go at once.'

'But are you strong enough?' she asked,
anxiously.

'Quite. My arm is healing and I feel much
better altogether. I must go to the pater,
Marion.'

'Of course,' she murmured.

'I must catch the next train up to town, and
then cross over. I hope I'll be in time.'

She was silent. She was dreading the
thought of letting him go from her . . . of losing
sight of him for an hour. At the same time she
remembered what his father's death would
mean to him—and to her. He would inherit
the baronetcy. When he came back he would
be Sir Dion Courtland. She, as his wife, would
be Lady Courtland. The whole idea was
ravishing to Marion.

Then Dion said:

'Come with me, Marion beloved . . . come
with me . . . as my future wife . . . let me show
my father the loveliest woman in the world . . .
then marry you over there.'

She trembled with love and longing. His
impulsive invitation tempted her almost
beyond endurance. To get away from
Moorcoombe; to get away from the shadow-
haunted place wherein Hope had met her

death; from Jet's persecution! God! it would be wonderful . . . and to go to Monte Carlo with Dion as his fiancée . . . ah, that would be sweeter than a dream. But she dared not go. If Jet heard . . . he would follow and carry out his threat. She could not, dared not risk it . . . risk Jet telling Dion the horrible truth.

'No, I won't come, Dion,' she said. 'I would rather wait—marry you when you come back. Your father is dying—your poor mother will want you, her son, to herself. I will not intrude on her grief.'

Dion covered her face with kisses.

'My Lovely One,' he said. 'That is typical of you—always understanding, generous, unselfish. Very well, then, we will wait until you see me again. But that will be very soon, my Marion—in a few days . . . and then we will not wait any longer—we will marry and go away.'

After Dion had gone to London that afternoon, a terrible depression gripped Marion. Without her lover, the charming Tudor inn which had been her home from her birth, seemed a gloomy, lonely place—a veritable tomb. She missed Dion intolerably. She realised, in truth, how much she adored him . . . how deeply she could and would sin for his sake . . . for her own . . . in winning him forever.

She had promised to go to Double-Styles Farm to tea. Well—she must keep that

65

promise. But what was she going to say to Jet Saddleman? How could she silence him?

She *must* achieve something, definitely, before Dion returned . . . Sir Dion . . . to claim her for his wife.

Dion left Moorcoombe directly after lunch. Between two o'clock and four, Marion sat in her bedroom, staring out at the purple and gold of the moors, brooding, scheming. And while she sat there, dark thoughts came to her . . . dark, terrible thoughts such as she had hoped to avoid and quell after Hope's death. But like mocking demons, those thoughts insisted on crowding back into her brain, stirring her to madness.

She must get rid of Jet Saddleman just as she had got rid of Hope Marshall . . . if she wanted to secure Dion Courtland's love for ever. She dared not let him tell the truth; tell the authorities what he had witnessed by the Pool; send her to the gallows along with himself. She believed he would do so, rather than see her give herself to Dion. He was as mad to win her as she was to win Dion. She knew he would stop at nothing to gain his own ends. But she would outwit him yet.

There was nothing for her to do but to silence him—for good. She felt sick horror at herself for even allowing such an idea to come into her head. But she had already crossed the Rubicon once for Dion . . . and the second time would be a little easier. The first time the terrible thing had happened in the heat of the moment. This time she was forced into contemplating cold-bloodedly, another, a fresh crime.

At half-past four, Marion was at Double-Styles Farm, which stood on the brow of a hill, overlooking the village of Moorcoombe. It was a rather gloomy, grey stone house without creeper or much of a flower garden. Jet had no time for floral decoration. He was bent only on money-making, and was satisfied with his acres of brown, ploughed land; his cattle, his sheep, his fowls. The farmhouse, run by an elderly housekeeper, a widow named Sarah Pollock, who had been with him for twenty years, needed a mistress like Marion—somebody young and pretty to cheer it up. It had been Jet's ambition ever since he had known Tom Grayle's daughter, to take her as his bride back to his lonesome and depressing farm.

Today, knowing that she was coming, he had sent Sarah into the village. He wanted to be alone with Marion . . . to talk things over with her. He greeted her eagerly, his huge, mahogany-coloured hands closing over her slender ones.

'My Pretty,' he said, breathing hard and fast. 'So you've come—at last.'

She wanted to snatch her fingers away, but with perfect self-control, she refrained and smiled at him with soft brown eyes that made his heart-beats race.

'Yes, I've come, Jet,' she said. 'And Mr. Courtland has gone away—back to London.'

'You mean you've sent him off?'

'Yes,' she lied. 'I've done what you asked.'

Jet was beside himself with delight. He seemed to forget completely that this beautiful girl before him was a criminal; he thought of her only as the Marion he had loved and courted since she left school . . . exquisite, bewitching, wholly desirable.

He led her into the house.

'Sarah's made a special iced cake for you, my Pretty. I didn't say who was coming, but I mentioned a young lady that might soon be Mrs. Saddleman.'

'Better not tell Sarah it's me,' said Marion, sarcastically. 'She hates the sight of me.'

'She'll get kicked out if she says one word against you,' said the infatuated farmer. Now, my pretty dear, tell me when you're going to church with me?'

'I feel stifled here,' said Marion, shivering a little as she looked round the gloomy, old-fashioned dining-room into which she had been led. 'Take me out for a walk, Jet. It's early yet for tea. I like to see the sunset from Hunter's Hill. Let's walk there.'

'Anything my dear likes,' he said, his blue eyes beaming with satisfaction and good humour. 'Be you warm enough?'

'Quite,' she said, buttoning her tweed coat about her throat, and pulling her little felt hat well over her hair.

Ten minutes later they were out on the moors, walking toward Hunter's Hill. The sun was setting; like a great fiery ball sinking slowly in the West. A lurid, blood-red glow hung over Dartmoor. Against this scarlet sky the stark trees stood like black sentinels. It was a wild, picturesque sight, and Marion felt a queer, fierce pleasure in it this afternoon. She walked with her arm tucked through Jet's, the picture of soft, contented girlhood. She might have been a humble Devonshire maid, walking out with her lover; innocent, with no thought of evil in her mind.

Half way up Hunter's Hill lay a disused quarry, known as Hunter's Hill Quarry. Here Marion paused, telling the man that she wanted to look down at the old pit. It was dark and dreary down there, full of great boulders that had rolled down, loosely, and grey slate. Once the quarry had been worked for slate.

'Don't go too near the edge, my Pretty,' said Jet, drawing her back a little. 'I can't abide looking down, myself, from any height.'

'Great baby!' she laughed at him, her dark eyes sparkling in the sunset. 'Fancy having such nerves.'

Then she changed . . . stiffened . . . stared down into the depths of the quarry.

'Good heavens!' she ejaculated.

'What is it, Marion?' he asked, startled.

'There's somebody down there, Jet . . . at

69

least it looks like a human body.'

Jet blenched.

'Gracious heavens . . . where, Marion?'

'Look!' she gasped, pulling at his arm.

The man, ignorant of the fiendish thoughts that lay behind those lovely eyes which shone so sweetly at him today, slouched in front of her and peered down into the quarry. In an instant she had pushed him from behind with all her strength. He did not expect the push, and he pitched over, with a hoarse scream.

Marion heard his body fall on to the stones below with a sickening crash. Then there was silence. Her heart-beats shook her body. She bent over and strained down to see him. She could just glimpse his great body twisted, motionless; his white face upturned to the sunset sky. And she took it for granted that he was dead . . . that no man could survive a fall on to sharp boulders and stones from that height. Mingled horror and relief seized her. Jet was silenced—forever . . . and now Dion was hers.

There was nobody to see but the birds and the trees, and a little later the stars, which see everything but tell no secrets.

Then suddenly, some queer intuition made her swing right round, her hands pressed to a heart that began to gallop and jerk. She had made a mistake. *She was not alone* on Hunter's Hill. A little way down was a shadowy figure . . . so shadowy that she could not see by its

70

shape whether it was man, woman or child; the light was too indistinct. But it was a human being, moving . . . and moving away from the Quarry. The question was, had that human being *seen* . . . seen her send Jet Saddleman to his death, over the quarry cliffs?

Marion began to shudder violently. She felt the same sick fear and horror of herself that she had felt when she had murdered Hope Marshall. But it was more than horror—it was a terrible fright that seized and shook her. Who was this person walking down Hunter's Hill? Had he, or she, *seen* . . . ?

Marion dared not pursue that figure. She turned and began to walk quickly away from the Quarry, taking a short-cut over the moorland, instead of going direct to the Travellers' Rest down Hunter's Hill.

The twilight had fallen. Purple shadows hung over Dartmoor. A thin white autumnal mist curled up from the low valleys. They seemed to Marion like pallid ghosts, wreathing, swaying toward her, and she wondered if Hope was amongst them . . . not only Hope, but Jet . . . her two victims, hand in hand . . . writhing toward her . . . leering, pointing . . .

Marion reached the thatched cottage wherein old Emm resided. She began to run past that dreaded cottage. She did not want to face the old witch-woman of Moorcoombe just now. But the door opened as she passed, and

71

Emm hobbled out on her stick. She beckoned to the girl, and Marion was forced to stop.

'What do you want, Emm? I'm in a hurry,' she said.

'Little doubt . . . little doubt,' said the old woman, with a cackling laugh. She drew close to the girl, and peered up at her with one, malevolent eye. 'Hurrying from t'quarry where . . .'

'Be quiet!' interrupted Marion, thickly. 'You're mad, you old fool.'

'Mad, am I? Ay, maybe, but I'll get even wi' you for all your arrogance and rudeness one day, my girl,' said Emm, in a sinister voice. 'I know more than you think. I see everything in my crystal. I was looking over you, Marion Grayle, and the Dark Death . . . Ha! ha! ha! My time will come, and I'm biding it . . . you wait and see!'

That night Marion calmly sat down to supper with her father, in the cosy, lamp-lit dining-room of the Travellers' Rest.

'Where've you been all day, dearie?' he asked her.

'I lay on my bed for a bit after Dion caught his train,' she said, with her sweet smile. 'Then I took a walk on the moors . . . then came home again.'

'Seen anything o' Mrs. Angus . . .?' he began, then paused. A sharp rat-tat on the front door broke the silence of the night. 'Who's that?' he added, rising to his feet.

Marion sprang to hers. Again the knocking broke the silence and played havoc with her nerves. Who was it? For a moment her heart quailed in her, lest it was the hand of the Law, knocking accusing her . . .

Then her father opened the door. To her unbounded relief, it was Charlie Hodges. The colour flamed back into her cheeks. But at his first words, it receded again.

'Have you heard what's happened?' he asked, excitedly.

'No—what?' asked Tom Grayle.

'Jet Saddleman's been found in Hunter's Hill Quarry,' said Charlie.

'Good God!' It was Marion who made the exclamation, and her hands gripped the back of her chair. 'What—dead?'

'No,' he said. 'Unconscious and badly hurt, and 'tis believed foul play.'

Marion felt sick and faint. Not dead . . . great heavens, what a mistake! She should have made sure . . .

'He's precious near dead,' added Charlie Hodges. 'The search-party, looking for Miss Marshall, found him . . . took him back home an hour ago. The doc. says he's been hurt by falling on his spine, and he's alive but completely paralysed.'

Something jerked at Marion's guilty heart.

'Paralysed!' she repeated.

'Yes, he can neither move nor speak,' said the barman. 'And the doc. says he may live like that for years. But he can't make no sign, so he won't never be able to say whether he fell into the quarry, or whether he was pushed in.'

CHAPTER SEVEN

'Saints alive!' ejaculated old Grayle, his rosy face paling with horror. 'What a catastrophe, to be sure. Marion girl, you'll be grieved to hear o' this—he was once a sweetheart o' yours, eh?'

Both the men looked at Marion. She was still gripping the back of her chair, her knuckles gleaming like ivory. Her face was a set mask. She wondered whether they would see the guilt written behind that mask; whether they could hear the thud, thud, thud, of her frightened heart which seemed to shake her whole body. But they looked at her with kindly eyes; her father's expression was now one of compassion for her.

'Poor Marion—'tis upsetting for you,' he added.

Then she recovered her equilibrium.

'Steady, steady, you fool!' she said to herself. 'Play up to this—play up—or you'll give yourself away . . .'

And at the same time, Charlie Hodges' words reiterated through her brain . . . *'He can't make no sign . . . so he won't never be able*

74

to say whether he fell into the quarry . . . or was pushed in . . .'

'What could make you suggest Jet was *pushed* in, Charlie . . . ?' she gasped.

The barman's rather heavy, stupid face turned to her blankly. He scratched his thick shock of tow-coloured hair.

'Dunno, I'm sure, Miss Marion, save that the folks around here think there might 'a' been foul play. 'Twas strange he should have got to t'bottom o' the quarry by himself.'

'Not at all strange,' contradicted Marion, now quite calmly. 'It's been a misty night—these autumn evenings are very treacherous on the moors when there's a fog—and he might easily have fallen in.'

'That's what happened, no doubt,' agreed her father, filling his pipe, thoughtfully. 'Poor old Jet—what an end to a great strong, hulking chap like him—paralysed in all his limbs! Double-Styles Farm'll go to rack and ruin now.'

Marion swallowed hard. Her throat felt very dry.

'Have a glass o' beer, Charlie,' she said. 'You look hot and bothered.'

'T' news o' Jet Saddleman's come as a bit o' a shock,' said the barman. 'I liked old Jet. He often come into the Inn here for a pint o' bitter wi' me. And if it *was* foul play . . .'

'Oh, don't—you give me the creeps, Charlie!' interrupted the girl, with a shudder.

'Don't let's put the worst construction on it. I'm sure there are no horrid murderers knocking about dear old Moorcoombe.'

She handed him a glass of foaming ale as she spoke, giving him a sweet, friendly look from her great brown eyes. Charlie Hodges had always liked and admired Tom Grayle's lovely daughter. Tonight he was her slave . . . because of that smile and the friendly drink. It would never have entered his dull brain in a thousand years that the sweetness, the friendliness, hid terrible, ghastly thoughts . . . that Marion Grayle was responsible for Jet Saddleman's frightful 'accident.'

He began to talk volubly about the 'accident,' and Tom listened, sucking at his pipe, putting in a word or two. Marion calmly picked up a pair of her father's socks and began to darn . . . a fair, attractive picture of innocent young womanhood, sitting there at the table with a rosy lamp-light throwing up the glorious tints of her red-gold hair, and suffusing her cheeks with colour . . . cheeks that were actually ghastly pale. Yet she had admirable self-control, and the slender fingers plying the long darning-needle now, were quite steady. She listened to Charlie's gossip, the slightest suspicion of a sarcastic smile on her lips. He thought he knew a lot; was repeating important information! But how little he really knew, and what a lot she could have told him had she wanted to!

Charlie said that Patterson, the Moorcoombe constable, and his little search-party, had taken it into their heads to look into Hunter's Hill Quarry in case poor Miss Marshall of Torquay had come to grief there. They had found, to their horror and astonishment, the twisted, injured body of Saddleman . . . not Miss Marshall as might have been expected. Jet was covered with bruises and cuts from his fall, and was now lying at home like an inanimate log.

'Better he had been killed by t'fall,' added Charlie, 'instead of having to live for years, like that!'

'I agree,' said Tom. 'That's a cruel fate for a lively chap like Jet.'

'It's too terrible,' put in Marion. 'Poor, *poor* Jet!'

'He was very sweet on you, Miss Marion,' sighed Charlie.

'Oh, I know!' she said, with a flush. 'But I never wanted to marry poor Jet. I'm engaged to Mr. Courtland, anyhow.'

'We must go and visit the poor chap tomorrow,' said Mr. Grayle.

'Why, of course—we'll do anything we can for him,' said Marion.

Charlie, looking at her over the rim of his mug, thought how sweet she was; how fortunate the poor paralysed farmer to have her pity and friendship.

But she was inwardly shuddering at the

thought of looking upon Jet Saddleman again. Why, why had her luck been out? Why hadn't that fall into the quarry killed him outright? Now she would always be tormented with the fear that he might recover his speech and give her away . . . accuse her not only of trying to murder him, but of murdering Hope Marshall.

She tried not to remember that she was responsible for Jet's frightful fall, and to concentrate on what the two men were saying. They were talking of Hope now. If only they would speak of something else!

'Queer happenings in Moorcoombe of late,' Charlie was saying with gloom. 'First the mysterious disappearance o' the young lady from Torquay . . . now poor Jet's accident.'

'Yes, it is queer,' said Tom, puffing at his pipe. 'Moorcoombe's bewitched.'

Marion laid down a sock she had finished, and stood up; folding her other mending and putting it neatly into a basket.

'I really can't see what right anybody had to suggest Jet was pushed into the quarry,' she said coolly. 'Who should have such a grudge against poor Jet as to want to kill him?'

'That's it,' said Charlie.

'And as far as Miss Marshall is concerned, I don't believe she disappeared round these parts,' added Marion. 'Much more likely she's in some other part of England.'

'Don't you worry your pretty head about it, anyhow, darling,' said her father, holding out his hand to her. 'You've had plenty of worry already. You run up to bed, my girl.'

She kissed and hugged him. She was genuinely fond of her father, and she made a charming picture, with her beautiful head against his white one. What horror would have filled that proud father's heart could he have known the dark and guilty secrets in his daughter's mind!

Just as she walked toward the door, Charlie said something that made her catch her breath with sudden terror:

'Mrs. Pollock's told the police that she spent the afternoon at the village, and that when she left her master he had said a young lady was going to have tea with him. I bet that young lady knows something about this accident.'

Marion stood stock-still. Her brain worked swiftly. She had forgotten that Jet had told Sarah Pollock that his 'young lady' was coming to tea. And her father knew she had been absent all yesterday afternoon from four o'clock onwards. She decided to make a bold stand.

'You're wrong there, Charlie,' she said calmly. 'It happens that *I* was invited to tea by Jet yesterday.'

'You!' he said lamely.

'Yes,' she said. 'And when I got to Double-Styles Farm, it was all shut up and I couldn't make anyone hear, so I walked home again. I thought at the time it was strange, as Jet had asked me to tea. But I didn't think twice about it, really, afterwards. Now, of course, I can understand what happened. He must have met with his accident at the quarry, and that was why he didn't turn up at the farm to meet me.'

'That's it,' said her father. ' 'Tis very queer. You must tell Patterson that, Marion. Good night, my girl.'

She walked out of the room, smiling. But once she was in her own little bedroom, she gave way. The rection came after the strain of this evening's conversation with the two men. She locked her door, then flung herself on her bed, biting her lips till they bled to keep herself from screaming aloud. She buried her face deep in the pillow, moaning, sobbing, like a furious, tortured creature.

What a mess she had got herself into! What a net was closing about her . . . a network of intrigue, lies, deception . . . and soon she would be so tangled, so involved that she would find difficulty in extricating herself. She must be very, very careful what she said, what she did. But she had *had* to state that she had gone to Double-Styles Farm. It was better to be frank and open like that. It would prevent suspicion being directed against her. Nobody had seen her depart for Hunter's Hill with Jet. She was positive of that. All the farm-labourers had gone home to their own cottages. On the other hand, who had been walking down the hill, after she had pushed Jet in? Would that person soon come forward and state that he, or she, had seen Marion Grayle on the edge of the quarry with Jet?

Why had she done it? Why had she sent Hope Marshall to her death in the Suicide's Pool? Hope lay buried in Linton Wood, and Jet Saddleman knew it . . . and Jet was still alive . . . even though his was death in life . . . and while he lived she would be in constant danger.

Why had she done it? One crime invariably led to another. Old Emm had seen the shadow of the gallows over her in the crystal . . .

Marion's vivid imagination played havoc with her. She screamed . . . moaned . . . stifling the sounds in her pillow. Half that night she lay awake, fully dressed, clenching and unclenching her slender hands . . . her beautiful face ravaged and distorted with the fear and remorse that consumed her.

But gradually she regained composure. She remembered *why* she had done these things . . . for what she had sinned. She sat upon the edge of her bed, the little oil-lamp flickering beside her, and examined a photograph which Dion had given her—a big one of himself taken at Oxford in his college days, and very like him. She stared down at the handsome face which smiled back at her . . . looked with feverish love and longing at every feature . . . the arresting eyes . . . the chiselled lips and dented chin . . . the fine head with its thick, dark hair

. . . the graceful, virile body. And she began to cover his photograph with passionate kisses, sobbing his name . . . calling up every remembrance of him as her lover . . . his kisses, his caresses, his passion for her.

'Dion! . . . Dion! . . . Dion! it was all for you . . . for *you*! Dion, I can't really regret anything that I've done . . . I love you so . . . I couldn't let you go . . . Dion, it would kill me to lose you now!'

It was half-past two in the morning before Marion recovered her nerve sufficiently to put that photograph down, to undress and get into bed and behave in a normal fashion. And when she did sleep, it was an uneasy sleep, haunted by two faces . . . the despairing, girlish face of Hope with the dark waters of the pool closing above her head . . . the sinister, accusing face of Jet whom she had made the victim of a fate more terrible than death.

CHAPTER EIGHT

All that following day, Moorcoombe was ringing with the news of Jet Saddleman's 'accident.' Marion hung about the inn in a state of acute nerves, listening to every word that was said in her hearing, and making her plans accordingly. She used rouge for the first time in her life, and with the skilfully-applied pink in her cheeks, appeared well and almost radiant. She simulated just that touch of sadness on behalf of 'poor Jet,' to make people think her sympathetic and compassionate; indeed, she sent Charlie Hodges in the old Ford to the nearest shop wherein he could buy a few grapes for Jet.

'I'll walk to the farm with Dad and see the poor chap tomorrow,' she told a certain Mrs. Jessop who was married to a farmer whose fields adjoined the Saddleman farm. 'What do you think of it all, Hilda?'

Hilda Jessop, a nice, plump Devonshire girl—already a young matron with two babies; and who was one of Marion's many admirers—had come over with her husband for a 'bit of gossip' in the Travellers' Rest. A good many Moorcoombe folk had gathered round the bar there to discuss Jet's strange tragedy.

'I think it's rather queer, Marion,' she said. 'So do Bob and others up our way. We spoke to Arthur Patterson this morning, and he's going to the Torquay police about it. He don't like all these goings-on, what with that young lady's disppearance and all.'

Marion clutched a coral necklace which she wore. Her eyes looked beyond Hilda Jessop's placid face to the distant moors which were grey and forbidding this morning—the last day of October. So Patterson had the 'wind up' and was going to the Torquay police? And Mrs.

Marshall was going to Scotland Yard? Worse and worse. Marion wished passionately that Dion would come home . . . come and marry her and take her away from all this before she was found out. Moorcoombe had a sinister atmosphere now. She was afraid to go out alone today . . . afraid to pass old Emm's cottage lest others should hear the terrible, witch-like creature hint at her guilt . . . point at her with the skinny finger of condemnation.

'You'm got a lovely colour today, my dear,' remarked Hilda, guilessly, smiling at her companion. 'When's that fine sweetheart o' yours coming back to Moorcoombe?'

'Soon,' said Marion. And she inwardly laughed at the thought of that 'lovely colour,' and how it had been put on this morning.

Before lunch she was forced to interview Patterson, the constable. He was a big, bearded fellow who had known Marion since she was a dainty, intriguing little baby with a mass of red-gold curls, and great laughing eyes. He had called her 'Bubbles' then, and still called her 'Miss Bubbles.' The ridiculous name comforted Marion's guilty heart this morning when he addressed her:

'Tell me about this visit o' yours to Jet's farm, Miss Bubbles,' he asked her, writing down what she had to say on his pad.

Marion secretly despised the policeman, who was dull-witted and totally unable to deal with mysterious cases of crime. But today she

84

blessed his cloddish brain and gave him her loveliest smiles. She told him of her visit to the farm; of how she found it closed up; gone away again.

'Poor, *poor* old Jet must have been lying at the bottom of the quarry all the time!' she said, with a handkerchief to her lips. 'Oh, Patterson, isn't it awful? But do you *really* think he was pushed in?'

'Gawd knows, Miss Bubbles, but truly I don't,' said the good man, pulling his beard. 'Thank'ee for what you've told me. Now us had better push along to Torquay, and give the case into better hands than mine.'

At this juncture Charlie arrived at the inn, back from Moorcoombe. He brought an orange envelope for Marion.

'Telegram for you, Miss Marion.'

She took it, her pulses racing, her cheeks on fire. A wire . . . from Dion . . . of course.

She scanned it rapidly.

'Father died in my arms so thankful in time coming home with mother at once expect me Moorcoombe Thursday all my love Dion.'

'Thank God for that,' she murmured to herself. 'He is coming back sooner than I expected.'

Today was Sunday. Four more days, and Dion would be with her. Then she would agree to an immediate marriage and leave Dartmoor with him as his wife . . . Lady Courtland . . . yes, she must not forget that . . . his father was dead, and he was Sir Dion Courtland, now!

She completely obliterated the memory of Jet and Hope for the moment. She revelled in a rioting imagination . . . pictured herself going away with Dion . . . titled, rich, adored . . . and—still greater rapture—thought of the moment when she would feel Dion's kiss on her lips . . . know herself wholly his own, his bride . . . could shake the sinister dust of Dartmoor off her feet.

She literally danced into the Inn, and caught Hilda Jessop round the waist.

'Dion's coming home on Thursday, and I shall be Lady Courtland, Hilda . . . what do you think of that!' she cried.

Mrs. Jessop looked at the girl, admiring her beautiful shining eyes and rosy face.

'How lovely, Marion!' she said.

The two girls spent a delicious half-hour discussing Marion's future wedding . . . the clothes she would wear . . . the wonders of the world which marriage to Dion would open to her. Nobody on earth would have dreamed that Marion Grayle was a guilty, crime-stained creature as she sat there, gossiping innocently and radiantly with her friend.

But after lunch, Marion was forced to face stern reality. She had agreed to go with her father to visit Jet Saddleman. She nerved herself for the ordeal, trying to think of Dion and her forthcoming wedding; to regard this visit to Jet as a necessity to be got over quickly and quietly, then forgotten.

She took Jet a basket of grapes and some jellies made by her own fair hands.

Sarah Pollock opened the front door of the farm to the Grayles. She was a thin, angular woman with iron-grey hair and sharp eyes behind black-rimmed glasses. She adored Jet, whom she had taken care of for years. Of other women she was jealous, and she had always been particularly jealous of Marion, and of Mr. Saddleman's passion for the Moorcoombe beauty. She greeted Mr. Grayle warmly enough, but for Marion had only a sour nod.

'Come in,' she said. 'Poor Mr. Saddleman can't talk nor move, but no doubt he'll be pleased to see you both.'

' 'Tis a sad business, Mrs. Pollock,' said Old Grayle, removing his cap as he entered the wide hall of the farmhouse.

'More than sad. 'Tis very strange,' said Sarah Pollock, her thin lips compressed. 'Mr. Saddleman knew every inch of the moor, and I reckon he were not the one to fall over into a quarry.'

Marion clenched her hands. She hated Sarah Pollock. Were those cold grey eyes behind the glasses looking at *her* with suspicion or doubt? No—it was her fancy. And yet . . .

'Come, Mrs. Pollock,' she said sweetly. 'Don't you be one of these folks talking of foul play. Who could want to harm poor Mr. Saddleman?'

'I reckon he were pushed over the edge,' said Mrs. Pollock, with her habitual frankness. 'He had an enemy somewhere, and the Almighty God will bring that person to justice—you'll see.'

Marion passed a tongue over her lips, which had grown suddenly dry. Sarah Pollock was her enemy . . . she realised that and she was curiously loth to face that grim-faced housekeeper who worshipped her master. She bent over her basket and said:

'Well, well, let's see poor Mr. Saddleman.'

She entered Jet's bedroom with loathing and a revulsion of feeling very difficult to control. She felt that all the time Sarah Pollock was watching her . . . Sarah was a dangerous enemy . . . jealous because Jet had loved her and meant to marry her; yet resentful, perhaps, because she had not married him; had made him wretched by engaging herself to the London gentleman. Sarah knew that she had called at Double-Styles Farm yesterday. Did Sarah believe that she had accompanied Jet out for that walk on the moors? Was it . . . *could* it have been Sarah, herself, who had walked down Hunter's Hill?

Marion's knees shook beneath her as she

entered Jet's bedroom, but she managed to approach the bed with the sweetest smile on her face. Ugh! how ugly it was, this huge bedroom with its dark rafters and old-fashioned furniture. The heavy blue damask curtains were faded; the carpet was a hideous pattern of blue and yellow; the wall-paper hidden by family photographs, groups, and some religious texts. The Saddlemans were all devoted Wesleyans.

Jet, himself, was terrible, repulsive to behold. He lay like a log, in a huge four-poster bed, the blue curtains spread out round him. His brown hands, piteously useless now, were folded in front of him. His face, mahogany-burned, his hair dark against the white linen pillow-cases. A white bandage was neatly bound round his forehead. His face was scratched and bruised, his lower lip swollen as though he had hit it against a stone or boulder when he fell. He was absolutely still, and out of the brown mask of that terrible face burned two vivid blue eyes . . . dreadful, agonised eyes, as though he were in some physical or mental pain which he could not express. Marion had to gather all her strength and courage to draw near the bed and face those dreadful eyes. From the moment she had entered the room, the eyes had fastened on her, and now they never left her . . . they watched her every movement. They seemed the only living things in his deadened body.

Marion realised the frightfulness of his case. It was worse than death to Jet Saddleman, who had loved fresh air, exercise; worked with his hands on his farm; ploughed the earth, sowed the seeds, reaped and harvested . . . to be totally disabled—paralysed! Better for him had he broken his spine and died.

Marion reached the bedside. Jet's terrible blue eyes stared at her. She met their gaze, trying not to shudder and flinch. She knew what he was thinking . . . she read the accusation and scorn in their depths . . . she knew how he must despise and hate her for the treachery, for the thing she had done to him.

'Poor Jet!' she said. 'I am sorry about this terrible accident. And Dad is sorry—he is coming up in a moment—we thought it better not to worry you, both at once. I have brought you some grapes and jellies, Jet. Later I will bring some books, and read to you.'

He went on staring at her. It was an almost murderous stare, and Marion began to feel sick. She shivered and spoke again:

'Poor Jet—it is terrible for you.'

She knew that Mrs. Pollock was behind, watching her. If only her knees did not feel so wobbly! She could not bear to remain in this room. Those frightful eyes were penetrating to her guilty soul. She rose hurriedly.

'I'll—come again—soon, Jet,' she stammered.

She had to pass Sarah Pollock to leave the

room. She gave Sarah an entreating look.

'It is too terrible!' she whispered.

The housekeeper looked at her almost balefully.

'It must have been more terrible for him, or her, that done the dreadful thing,' she said. 'I wouldn't like to have that criminal's conscience, tonight.'

Marion's thick lashes hid the expression in her eyes. Hot colour stung her cheeks. She passed on and ran down the stairs, shuddering, eager to get away from Double-Styles Farm, from Mrs. Pollock, who hated her; and from Jet Saddleman's dreadful, staring accusing eyes.

What did Sarah Pollock know? Why did she look at her in that penetrating way . . . make that remark about 'him or *her*' who did the evil thing?

Assuredly in this moment, Marion's conscience pricked and tortured her. She clung desperately to the belief that nobody knew . . . that she was only nervy and worried . . . that she would win through if she played her part with courage and defiance to the very end. And she thought with passion of her lover . . . clasped his wire to her bosom . . . longed for his return and for the departure with him, which would make her utterly safe.

Four days later, Dion Courtland returned to the Travellers' Rest.

Marion was expecting him. She had

received a wire announcing his arrival at 6.30 that evening at Moorcoombe Station, and had sent the Ford to meet him. But she had stayed behind. She wanted to enjoy this meeting in private, not to look upon her lover in full view of the Moorcoombe gossips who might be hanging around the station. She had thirsted, burned for this hour . . . she had dressed herself in the black velvet frock he liked; brushed her beautiful hair into gleaming curls about her small head. Her large dark eyes were shining with passion and eagerness; her face flushed like a rose-carnation. She had never looked more entrancing; and when Dion jumped out of the car and saw her standing in the doorway of the Inn, with the lamp-light behind her, welcoming him from the dusk of the November evening, he felt his pulses thrill. He knew then how he had wanted her while he was in France . . . how much he loved her.

'Marion!' he said huskily.

'Dion!' she said, and held out both her hands to him. He took them, and she drew him into the sitting-room, which was deserted, and shut the door. The next moment he had flung off his coat and hat, and had her in his arms in a tight, fierce embrace, his lips on her mouth, assuaging all her longing; every kiss a terribly sweet recompense for what she had suffered since he had left. She wound her arms about his throat and clung to him madly. For a moment or two they swayed locked in that passionate embrace. Then Dion lifted his head and looked down at her.

'Marion, Marion, my darling,' he said, 'it is sheer delight to have you in my arms again.'

She did not, could not speak. She felt extraordinarily young and helpless just then . . . as though she wanted to break down and cry; beg him to forgive her her sins; to protect her and love her for ever. She knew just how much she cared in this moment of reunion . . . and she wished there were no shadows of guilt between them . . . that she need never have stained her soul with such crimes, in order to win him. Yet she felt it was worth any sin to feel his arms about her and his kisses on her mouth—like this!

She opened her eyes . . . soft, dazed, brilliant with unshed tears. She noticed that he was haggard and tired, made him sit down by the fire; crouched at his feet; leaned her lovely head on his knees; asked him a dozen questions about himself, and all that he had been doing.

He kept an arm about her, leaning over now and then to kiss her hair. He was genuinely upset by the death of his father, and embarrassed by his new dignity.

'I hate being called "Sir Dion" . . . but there it is . . . and I've always told you you would make the loveliest Lady Courtland our family will have known.'

She kissed the hand that rested about her

shoulder.

'Dion, Dion, never leave me again—I love you so!' she said. 'Darling, I missed you intolerably.'

'And I you. My dearest, don't shiver so . . . are you cold . . . or is, it just your emotions . . . you are such a wild little creature, sometimes you make me afraid . . .'

'Afraid of what?' she caught her breath.

'Oh, I don't really know,' he said, laughing. 'Anyhow, when are you going to marry me?'

'At once,' she said.

'You mean that?'

'Yes. I am ready now . . . when you will.'

'Then it must be the day after tomorrow,' he said firmly. 'I will go into Torquay tomorrow and get the special licence and your wedding-ring.'

She gave a great sigh of relief. She dared not speak; could not unburden her guilty soul, tell him what it meant to her . . . what it would mean to be taken away from Dartmoor as his wife.

'I'm beginning to dislike this part of the world,' he said, with a little frown. 'Such nasty things are happening. First poor Hope . . . who has never been found . . . then Jet Saddleman.'

'You know about Jet?' Marion bit her lip.

'Yes, Charlie told me . . . rotten affair. I wonder if some dangerous criminal is at large about these parts?'

Marion swallowed hard.

94

'I—don't know. But don't talk of horrors. Let me look at your poor arm—' she tried to speak lightly and to smile up at him—'why, it's practically well—and you held me so tightly just now—it's splendid, Dion!'

'Oh, yes, that's all right now,' he said. 'I got some first-rate massage all for nothing in Monte Carlo . . .' he laughed. 'Matter of fact, the mater had a girl staying with her—she's brought her home with her, too . . . a topping young woman who used to do massage and V.A.D. nursing during the War. Just about my age . . . daughter of an old pal of the mater's, and recently orphaned. I'm glad about it, because the mater's lonely now Dad's gone, and this girl, Patricia Westby, will probably live with mother for a bit.'

Marion's expression altered. All the rapture seemed to die within her. Another girl on Dion's horizon . . . this Patricia Westby. Loving him as madly as she did, Marion could not bear to hear Dion speak of another girl with affection or friendship.

'Don't look like that, you darling duffer!' said Dion, bending to kiss her. 'I won't have you being jealous. Pat is a dear . . . a very capable, charming young woman . . . but not you, my Loveliness!'

She flung herself back into his arms, speechless, adoring, forgetting Pat Westby. After a moment, she said in a thick little voice:

'Swear you'll never love anybody . . .

anybody but me . . . I couldn't lose you now . . . I couldn't, Dion!'

He caressed and comforted and promised her everything she asked. He did love her, passionately. But he felt just a twinge of uneasiness tonight. He wished she were not quite so tempestuous, so possessive. He had spent these last few days in the company of two such different women to Marion Grayle. Lady Courtland, dignified, gentle, old-fashioned . . . Patricia Westby, good-looking, healthy, a great golfer and motorist—a typical 'British sportswoman,' and at the same time, charming, sympathetic, magnetic, with some of the reserve and innocence that poor little Hope had possessed. Dion had felt drawn to Pat in a platonic way. He could not help wishing that Marion would cultivate some restraint. What was it she lacked? Breeding, perhaps . . . dignity . . . yes . . . and yes, she made him a little afraid, sometimes, of he knew not what.

Still, he was a man and bewitched by her beauty and obviously genuine passion for himself. He was just about to kiss her again when the door opened and Tom Grayle entered, followed by Patterson, the Moorcoombe constable. Tom's ruddy face was pale, and Patterson looked grave, almost scared.

Marion stood up, clinging on to her lover's arm. She glanced from her father to Patterson.

'Something's wrong—what is it?' she said.

'There's been a shocking discovery,' said Patterson, taking off his helmet. 'I hesitate to tell you, Miss Bubbles . . .'

'But she'll have to know,' said Grayle, 'and so will Mr.—I mean Sir Dion. It's just as well he's come back, as he was a personal friend of the poor young lady's.'

Marion's nerves went to pieces. Before she asked, she knew what had happened. But she said, hoarsely:

'Oh, God . . . what is it?'

'The body of Miss Hope Marshall, along with her suitcase, was found in Linton Wood by the Torquay police, today,' said Patterson, gravely. 'And it is a case o' murder, of course . . .'

CHAPTER NINE

The silence that followed this announcement was frozen . . . frozen with horror. Dion was the first to pull himself together. He was ghastly pale. He had faced horrors at the Front during the War without flinching. But this horror, at home, in peace-time, and of so intimate and terrible a nature, threatened to shatter his nerves. He spoke quietly, however:

'Patterson—are you sure?'

'Quite sure, sir. The body of the poor young

lady has been taken to a woodman's cottage that b'ain't been used for some years, and left there. They made it into a kind o' mortuary.'

Dion sank heavily into a chair. His forehead was wet.

'Hope—poor little Hope—*murdered!*' he said in an incredulous voice. 'Good God! Good God! How frightful!'

Marion swayed on her feet. Her eyes held a look not only of horror, but of fear—stark naked fear. Neither Patterson nor old Grayle read the fear in those beautiful eyes, however. Tom Grayle made a swift movement toward his daughter.

'This isn't talk for women,' he said gruffly. 'You aren't going to faint, are you, Marion girl?'

Marion tried to speak but could not. Her teeth chattered in her head. She leaned against her father's arm and a little moan broke from her.

'Oh, God . . . oh, God!'

'Poor Miss Bubbles, it's properly upset her, and no wonder,' murmured Patterson, with a kindly glance at the girl.

Dion rose to his feet again. He went up to Marion, and took her away from her father, with a protective little gesture.

'My dearest—it's horrible for you—for us all—but pull yourself together—we mustn't give way—any of us. This is frightful for Mrs. Marshall—poor woman! I can't imagine it yet, can you?'

She clung to him, shuddering and gasping.

'No, no, I can't—oh, who could have done such a thing, and why—why?'

' 'Tis very strange,' said Patterson, pulling a pipe from his pocket. 'The doctor says she didn't die from a blow of any sort—but from drowning.'

'Drowning!' repeated Dion, his brows knit.

Marion's beautiful brown eyes stared wildly at the constable.

'Drowning!' she repeated in a piteous voice.

'Yes, that's what he said, Miss Bubbles. The poor young lady was drowned first and buried afterwards.'

Dion drew Marion closer to his side as though seeking to protect her from the horror of these ghastly details. But he had a too-vivid imagination himself, and he was picturing Hope, sweet, gentle little Hope, with her fair hair and gentle blue eyes . . . Hope, drowned, brutally murdered . . . Hope's body dragged out of the sod in Linton Wood . . .

'How—long had—she been there?' he asked.

'About ten days,' said Patterson.

'It was ten days ago that she was seen by the station-master at Moorcoombe,' said Dion. 'So it was true—she did come.'

'Looks like it, Mr.—I mean Sir Dion,' said the constable, with respect. 'Looks like she was murdered on her way, don't it?'

'She was so young, so gentle,' said Dion. 'God! The murderer of a child like that must be inhuman—beyond redemption. I pray God he is brought to justice, speedily. I know I shall never rest until he has been found out. Whoever it is must be mad—only a mad creature could have taken the life of a girl as innocent and harmless as Hope Marshall.'

He broke off. He felt a dead weight against him. Then he gave a cry of distress. For Marion had fainted dead away.

He imagined she was overcome by the horror of what she heard. How could he dream that her nerves had momentarily given way under the strain . . . that his solemn, terrible words had completely unnerved her . . . that *she* was the 'mad creature' . . . she, the brutal murderess of Hope Marshall . . . that it was she whom he prayed might be brought to justice speedily! He picked her up in his arms and laid her on the couch. Old Grayle rushed for brandy. Patterson tactfully withdrew from the room, muttering something about 'poor Miss Bubbles.' Dion knelt by the couch and looked down at her.

'Marion!' he said. 'Marion—darling—wake up!'

Her eyes opened. She looked up at his face. Then she remembered . . . and a long shudder passed through her body. She flung her arms around his neck.

'Dion—Dion!' she gasped.

She burst into passionate weeping. Nothing he could do or say consoled her. She was hysterical, and he put it down to natural distress. It was horrible for a girl like Marion to know that poor little Hope had been murdered. She sobbed heartbrokenly in his arms. He begged her to be calm, not to think of the horrors.

'You're unstrung, and no wonder, dearest, but try not to cry,' he said.

She went on crying. Gradually her weeping exasperated Dion. His own nerves were none too good. He had loved Hope once, and he was haunted by the thought that she had been found in Linton Wood . . . drowned . . . brutally murdered. He wanted to comfort and support Marion, but he felt no single thrill of passion this evening, after what he had heard. He wished Marion would be more controlled, more helpful to him.

She stopped crying for a moment and saw his face, stern, anxious, a little irritated. Her heart gave a sick jerk. Fool—fool that she was to give way like this. She was giving herself away—over-doing it. She had not known Hope Marshall long. Dion would be surprised soon if she continued to sob in such an hysterical fashion. She *must* control herself. She was annoying him. After all she had gone through, she could not bear to drive Dion away from her.

She buried her face on the sofa cushions.

Dion smoked fiercely at a cigarette.

'Do you mind if I go outside for a breath of fresh air, Marion?' he said, after a pause.

She lifted her head. She was not beautiful now. Her face was ravaged by her violent weeping. But her great dark eyes stared at him wildly.

'Yes—of course—do go,' she stammered. 'But kiss me—kiss me first, Dion.'

He came up to her, leaned down and kissed her on the brow. She dragged his head down to hers, insisted on a more passionate caress.

'Don't stop loving me—don't stop loving me, Dion!' she said in a hoarse voice.

He was curiously shocked by her demeanour.

'My dear, of course I won't. But I am very upset by this terrible news. I have known Hope for years, and I was very fond of her. I can't bear to think about it . . . what effect it will have on her unfortunate mother.'

Marion bit her lower lip till it bled. With an effort she restrained her desire to cling to him; scream at him to stop thinking of Hope, and turn his thoughts to her. Hope was dead . . . yet even now she was jealous of the dead . . . she begrudged every kind, compassionate thought Dion gave the unfortunate girl. But she realised that she would estrange herself from him if she acted in this unforgiveable way. Besides, she would rouse suspicion. She let her arms fall away from him.

'Forgive me, Dion—of course, I understand it is terrible for you. I am shattered by the news, myself. Poor, poor Hope!'

Dion's eyes softened. He patted her head.

'I'll be back in a moment, darling. Buck up, won't you? We shall all need to be calm over this. It's a shocking business. And we can't let our love for each other be entirely selfish— can't even think of our marriage—with Hope's body lying there in that cottage—'

He broke off, shuddered and turned away. Marion gripped the couch with both hands and watched him walk from the room. Her father came running in with brandy, and she allowed him to give her a stiff dose. The fiery liquid ran through, stimulated her, gave her the strength she so sorely needed. A pulse in her temples beat, beat, maddening her. This was a dire catastrophe, this discovery of Hope's body. Already it had taken away a particle of Dion's love . . . he had said that he could not think of their marriage just now . . . and she was frozen with the fear that he would let this 'murder' separate him from her altogether. How could she bear it? Supposing he refused to marry her now, after she had gone through so much . . .

Marion's wild and frightened thoughts chased each other like black demons through her tormented brain. But gradually she grew composed. She dried her tears, powdered her nose, smoothed her tumbled curls, never again must she be so ungoverned, so hysterical. Now that the first shock had passed, she was more herself . . . strong, practical, resourceful, cunning . . .

She heard voices outside the front-door, drew near the window, and strained her ears to listen. Dion was talking to a little group of men outside the inn. She heard most of what they said; stood crouching against the window, her teeth clenched.

Patterson was answering Dion's questions. Hope had been found through the aid of bloodhounds. They had worried that spot where Jet had buried the body, until the Torquay search-party had examined more closely, and finally dug down until they had seen a human foot in a suede walking-shoe . . . then to their horror they had discovered the body of Miss Marshall; partially decomposed, but recognisable. The doctor was certain that death was due to drowning . . . there were no marks of violence . . . all the clothing was rough-dried, as though it had been under water for some time and dried in that earthy grave in the wood . . . tomorrow morning there was to be an inquest at the cottage . . . Mrs. Marshall had been wired for . . . the only identification so far had been through the description given to the police. But it left no doubt . . . it was poor Miss Marshall all right . . . etc, etc.

Marion felt physically sick as she listened.

But the more she heard of the ghastly details, the more cool and composed she grew. She knew so much more than they did . . . and she need not be frightened . . . how could they ever discover that she, Marion Grayle, had sent Hope to her death in the Suicide's Pool? Jet could not speak. What would Jet think when he knew that the body had been found . . . since it was he who had buried that body in Linton Wood? But probably he would not hear. Sarah Pollock would guard him from the distressing news.

Marion started and turned from the window. Her lover had come back into the room. And this time she met him without a trace of her former agitation. Relieved to find her so much more composed, he sat down and began to talk to her sadly and quietly of the 'shocking murder,' without once realising that every word he spoke shook her guilty heart.

CHAPTER TEN

The inquest was over.

Mrs. Marshall, having identified that piteous, drowned body as that of her daughter, Hope Gladys Marshall, returned to Torquay a broken-hearted woman. It was said, in Moorcoombe, that she went through the inquest very well, her tragic face hidden behind a thick veil; but that her hair had turned snow-white after the identification of Hope's body. She saw Dion for a few moments at the Travellers' Rest. Marion was with him. She embraced them both.

'I believe in God's justice,' she said, looking pathetically aged and shocked. 'My Hope never did harm to anyone on earth, and she was little more than a child. God will bring the murderer to justice. I shall pray every day and night that he will be found and made to suffer as my poor darling child must have suffered.'

'I shall pray that, too, Mrs. Marshall,' said Dion, much moved.

The poor mother kissed Marion. Marion received that kiss in silence, in horror at herself. After Mrs. Marshall had gone, Marion went out for a walk with her lover.

'Poor Mrs. Marshall,' said Dion, with a heavy sigh.

'Yes, I pity her from the bottom of my heart,' said Marion.

'It's such an extraordinary business,' said Dion. 'The verdict was brought in "Death from drowning, murder by person or persons unknown" . . . but there seems no clue of any sort.'

Marion's heart exulted at this.

'What will they do now, then?' she asked.

'Carry on investigations quietly,' he said. 'Scotland Yard will be on the business, now.'

He felt her shiver against his arm. For the

first time since yesterday he turned his whole thoughts to her. After all, he loved her, his beautiful, wonderful Marion . . . she was going to be his wife. He must not allow his horror and grief at Hope's unspeakable death to obsess him. Poor Marion . . . she looked so pale and ill today.

'Let's talk of ourselves for a bit,' he said, generously.

Her face brightened.

'Oh, yes, Dion—I want to!' she exclaimed.

'I don't see the use of postponing our wedding,' he went on. 'I feel in many ways that I am to blame for Hope's death, and yet . . .'

'Oh, you can't—you mustn't feel that!' she broke in. 'It was nothing to do with you.'

'Yet she was murdered on her way to see me,' he said gloomily. All last night he had been picturing Hope, running away from home, wanting him . . . and while she had been coming, he had been giving his kisses, his caresses to Marion . . . he had been disloyal . . .

'She ignored all your letters . . . deserted you first.' Marion argued. 'You can't blame yourself for this.'

'Anyhow, we won't go all over it again, dear,' said Dion, with a sharp sigh. 'About our wedding . . . I'll go into Torquay tomorrow morning and get a special licence. Fix it for the end of this week, Marion, and then I'll take you away from Moorcoombe, and these horrors.'

She wanted to say 'Thank God.' She was bursting with relief . . . with joy at the thought of being taken away; at being made Lady Courtland. But she nestled her head against his arm, and said:

'Are you sure you wouldn't rather wait until the mystery is cleared up, Dion darling?'

He hesitated. In his heart of hearts he would rather have waited until the investigations by Scotland Yard had proceeded further. He did not consider it quite the thing to marry Marion, on top of this frightful murder. It was hardly decent . . . with the girl he had once intended to marry only just cold in her grave. Piteous little Hope! Yet, he had a duty to Marion. She was all on edge, anxious to get away from Moorcoombe. His duty was to the living rather than to the dead.

'That's all right, dear,' he said abruptly. 'I think it best for us to be married at once and get away.'

She was speechless with relief. Now all would be well for her, she was sure. Dion began to talk about Jet Saddleman:

'That's another mystery, Marion. Seems to me there's an escaped lunatic about Dartmoor . . . a sort of criminal maniac . . . first Hope's murder . . . then the attempted murder of Jet.'

'Who said it was murder?' said Marion, quickly. 'Everybody thinks that an accident.'

'I doubt it,' said Dion grimly. 'Saddleman doesn't appear to be the chap to fall over a quarry, knowing the moors so well. There was foul play there, no doubt. But I daresay he will recover his speech one day and throw some light on the matter.'

Marion said no more, but her hand grew ice-cold in her lover's warm fingers.

She dreaded passing old Emm's cottage on the way home. But Fate was against her. The witch-like creature hobbled out from the cottage and greeted them at her gate. Her one, sinister eye fastened on Marion with a mocking expression.

'Good day to you, Marion Grayle,' she croaked. 'And to you, Sir Dion.'

'Good evening, Emm,' said Dion, courteously.

Emm's withered face softened.

'Good luck to you, and I see prosperity and luck in the crystal for you, sir,' she said. 'There's blood and tears to cross your path, but happiness in the end.'

'That's good,' he said, with a light laugh. 'And will you come to our wedding, Emm?'

The old woman's face grew sinister again.

'I see a wedding . . . but the Dark Death for Marion Grayle . . . and I see . . .'

'Oh, take me away from her, Dion—I hate her—she's a wicked, vicious old woman!' interrupted Marion, growing livid.

He stared at her, astonished.

'Why should you be afraid of her? And what's all the nonsense about "Dark Death"?'

he laughed. 'Let's listen to what she has to say.'

'No, no!' cried Marion.

'Ha! ha!' said Emm, with a cackling laugh. 'Ha! Ha! 'Tis a guilty maid hanging on to you, Sir Dion, sir . . . and my time will come . . . as she'll see.'

Marion literally dragged her lover away from the cottage. Dion glanced at her with a worried look in his eyes.

'You surely aren't afraid of that old fool, Marion?' he said. 'And what reason could she have for calling you guilty?'

With a superhuman effort Marion smiled.

'Guilty of throwing stones at her window when I was a kiddie,' she said lightly.

'Oh, I see,' laughed Dion, and thought no more about it.

CHAPTER ELEVEN

Two days later, a special licence had been procured and a platinum wedding-ring lay in Dion's pocket. His marriage with Marion Grayle was arranged to take place at Moorcoombe Church on the third day.

The funeral of the murdered Miss Marshall took place in Torquay. Mrs. Marshall had her daughter's body conveyed to the family vault, so Moorcoombe was not overshadowed by that mournful affair, although the C.I.D. continued secretly and determinedly with the investigation of the mystery of Hope's death.

Moorcoombe temporarily forgot Miss Marshall's death and Jet Saddleman's frightful accident, and turned lightly and more gladly to Miss Marion Grayle's wedding. The Moorcoombe folk were rather proud of the thought that Tom Grayle's daughter was to become Lady Courtland.

Marion, on her wedding-morning, was in the highest state of rapture. She callously laid aside the guilty secrets in her heart, and thought only of Dion . . . of her forthcoming honeymoon abroad.

It had been agreed between them that she should be married quite quietly in her going-away dress. She had bought a grey cloth frock in Torquay, with chinchilla trimming, and a little grey hat with a diamond and sapphire ornament on the brim. Dion's present to her was a beautiful silver-squirrel coat in which she could travel luxuriously, and her father had given her a small but charming necklace of pearls. The soft grey of her toilette softened the brilliant colouring of her red-gold hair. She looked truly lovely; never more gentle and charming, and her real, absorbing love for the man she was about to marry had brought a tender light to her eyes.

Dion was waiting for her at the Church. Marion came out of the inn with her father, preparing to drive to the little Church in the old Ford, driven by Charlie Hodges for the last time.

Just as she was about to step into the car, with a laughing word to Hilda Jessop who was with her friend, on this bridal morning, a man came running toward the little group. Marion paused and stared at him with sudden misgiving. She recognised him as a certain Eddy Trenance, a Cornishman who was in charge of Jet Saddleman's cattle.

'What do you want, Eddy? I'm in a hurry now,' she said, all fever and impatience to reach the church and get through the important ceremony of marriage with her lover.

'This be from t'master,' he said, with a foolish grin.

Marion's heart gave a terrible jerk. Old Grayle stared at Eddy.

'But I thought poor Jet was a paralysed man and couldn't write,' he said.

'T'master recovered use of his fingers s'morning,' said Eddy Trenance. 'Mrs. Pollock she was telling him Miss Marion was bein' married to Sir Dion s'morning, and he sudden-like lifted his hand and signalled for pencil and paper.'

'Why, how splendid,' said Marion's father, beaming. 'Now that's really a nice thing to have happened on your wedding morning, my girl—a bright spark. It shows Jet's going to get better.'

A really nice thing to have happened! Marion's eyes looked stricken. She opened Jet's note. The writing was scrawly, weak, but it was Jet's handwriting. She realised to her horror what this meant to her. He had recovered the use of his hand and he could write . . . oh, heavens! By pen and paper he could destroy her!

The words he had written danced like mocking demons before her sight:

'Marry D.C. this morning and I at once tell what I know. My life is worth nothing to me now I am disabled. But if you will marry me and look after me, I will keep silence.
You must make some excuse to put off this wedding, or I act at once.
Jet.'

Marion's face blanched. Oh, God, was this thing possible? What could she say to Dion? How could she put off her marriage at the eleventh hour? It was cruel . . . cruellest luck that Jet should have recovered the use of his fingers on this morning of all mornings. But she knew, even as she stood there, that she dared not disobey . . . dared not defy him . . .

She was sick with disappoinment, with futile rage and despair. But she was forced into the finest piece of acting of her life. Calmly she

113

tore Jet's note into tiny pieces and scattered them to the wind, then began to climb into the car.

'That's very nice of Jet to write congratulations,' she said loudly. 'Quite the nicest thing that could have happened.' Then she stopped dead, put a hand to her heart, and dilated her eyes. 'Father . . . oh, my God . . . my heart!' she shrieked.

She fell forward on her face upon the ground.

Tom Grayle gave a cry.

'Marion—my girl—what is it?'

He turned her over. Her eyes were shut. Her face was livid, her very lips looked blue. He took it for granted that she had had a heart-attack. Agitated, scared, the poor man, with Charlie's help, lifted Marion into the inn and laid her on her bed.

Then Dion was sent for.

When he came, his face puckered with astonishment and distress, he was told that his marriage with Marion could not take place to-day. She had had a heart-attack. She was very ill—too ill even to see him.

'But I don't understand,' said Dion to Marion's father, who looked very worried. 'She was radiant last night when I left her.'

Old Grayle described the scene that had taken place outside the inn just now; the letter from Jet; the sudden fainting attack which had resulted in this serious illness.

'But she absolutely refuses to see a doctor,' he ended. 'Perhaps you could send up a note and beg her to see Dr. Seymour from Moorcoombe, my boy. She is very obstinate. She says she can treat herself—that she has a horror of doctors.'

Dion pursed his lips. This was ridiculous. If Marion was so ill that she must postpone her wedding, she must see a doctor.

'I will ask her to send for Seymour,' he said. 'Won't she see me?'

'She is sleeping now, I think,' said Grayle. 'I looked into her room as I came down, and she was asleep.'

How could he know that the guilty girl was far from slumber . . . that she lay there, her face buried in the pillows, her face ghastly, convulsed with hatred and disappointment. It was frightful to Marion to be robbed of the prize just as it was being handed to her . . . to have had the cup of joy, of security, dashed from her very lips.

While Dion and her father sat downstairs discussing this serious illness, she fought with her wild feelings, every fibre of her being calling for her lover . . . yet she dared not see him . . . and dared not let a doctor see her— tell her father that her heart was absolutely sound.

Dion was perplexed by the story about Jet's message.

'I wonder if he wrote anything to upset

Marion?' he suggested to Grayle.

'Surely not,' said old Grayle, puffing at his pipe. 'Marion said it was a congratulatory message.'

'Marion is very sweet and brave,' said Dion. 'She might conceal the fact that there was something in that note to have upset her. Saddleman is a rejected suitor—is he not? He might have written spitefully . . .'

'I doubt it,' broke in the old man, shaking his curly white head. 'Marion smiled after she'd read it—it was just as she stepped into the car her heart seemed to give her sudden pain . . . she called out "Oh, God, my heart" . . . then fainted clean off.'

'Well, I shall take it upon myself to send for the doctor,' said Dion. 'And I am also going over to Double-Styles Farm to see Saddleman and ask him if he wrote anything to upset my darling.'

Dion spoke firmly. He was genuinely upset and disappointed that his wedding to Marion had been put off at the last minute, like this. He thought of her as he had seen her last night, their wedding eve. She had been charming . . . as she had rested in his arms when he had kissed her goodnight, she had said: 'When I am your wife, my dearest, I shall be able to help you all the more, I think, to bear the shock and grief of poor Hope Marshall's death . . .' and he had thought that very understanding and sweet of her. For he was still considerably shaken by Hope's terrible end.

He left the Travellers' Rest, distressed because Marion refused to see him, and walked to Moorcoombe to cancel the arrangements for the wedding, and tell the proprietor of the Moorcoombe Arms, where he had been staying for the last two nights, that he would be staying on for a few more days.

He did not get to Saddleman's farm until later that day . . . after tea, when it was cold and misty on the moors. He felt that he must see Jet, and find out if the paralysed farmer had written in a friendly way to Marion, or sent some malicious note to frighten or annoy her.

At Double-Styles Farm, a young village girl opened the door to him.

'Mrs. Pollock is down at Moorcoombe,' she told Dion. 'And Miss Grayle is with t'master.'

'Miss Grayle!' repeated Dion, astounded. 'You don't mean Miss Marion Grayle?'

'Yes, sir,' said the girl, twisting a corner of her apron. 'She come five minutes ago.'

Dion was nonplussed. What was Marion doing here when she was presumed to be seriously ill, in bed with a heart-attack. He confessed himself mystified and slightly annoyed.

'Show me to Mr. Saddleman's room,' he said.

The girl took him upstairs and they reached Jet's bedroom. The door was ajar. Through the gap Dion could see Marion, muffled up in an old plaid overcoat, with a scarf twisted about her head. And she was on her knees beside the bed, sobbing convulsively. The farmer was lying motionless, his eyes fixed on her. And Marion was saying:

'Don't make me do it . . . for pity's sake. Don't make me do it, Jet!'

For a moment Dion was too dumbfounded to move or speak. What was Marion doing here? Why was she beseeching Jet Saddleman not to 'make her do it'? Do what? Why was she sobbing and moaning by his bed, like this?

Then Marion turned her head and saw her lover . . . the last person she had expected to see . . . certainly the last one she had wanted there at the moment. And now it was her turn to be stunned by the turn of events. Why was Dion at Double-Styles Farm?

She sprang to her feet, her handkerchief to her lips, her whole body quivering. Her eyes stared affrightedly at Dion, who was coming toward her, with a stern, surprised look on his young face.

'Marion!' he exclaimed. 'What does this mean? What are you doing here? I thought you were in your own room at the inn, too ill to get up or see anybody.'

She tried to answer him but could not. Words failed her. For one paralysing instant, she thought that all was over . . . that she was done for.

Dion reached her side, looked from her to the man in the bed. His expression altered from amazement to one of acute annoyance.

'Has Mr. Saddleman been worrying or frightening you Marion?' he said. 'What can he make you do that you don't want to? My dear, this is all very extraordinary, and I must say that I want an explanation.'

Jet Saddleman lay motionless, his vivid blue eyes narrowing to slits of fire. He burned to speak . . . but he could not . . . he was voiceless. But at least he had regained the use of his hands. He raised the right one, very slowly, and pointed at Marion . . . a suggestion of accusation in the gesture which made the girl tremble.

'Oh, oh, my God, what can I do now?' she inwardly cried.

She had been a fool to come, secretly like this to Double-Styles Farm. She might have known she would be discovered by somebody. She had waited for dusk, keeping to her bedroom. But at last, tortured and agonised by her guilty thoughts, her fears, she had been driven to do a desperate thing . . . to come to Jet and plead with him; beg him not to make her give Dion up. Fortune had favoured her, insomuch as Sarah Pollock had been out, at Moorcoombe village, but it was nothing less than a catastrophe that Dion should have followed her here. She presumed he must have followed; did not suppose he had come of his own accord to speak with the farmer.

Dion grew impatient. He examined Marion's face critically. She certainly looked ill—deathly white—her eyes fevered, distended under their black, curling lashes, her usually scarlet lips pale and quivering. His heart softened toward her, and he took hold of her arm quite gently.

'Marion, my dear . . . speak to me . . . what is this all about? Why did you leave your room to come to this man?' he asked.

His sudden kindness gave her courage. She made an effort; pulled herself together, and answered him:

'Oh, Dion, Dion . . . I had to come . . . I *was* frightened, it's true. But take me away—take me away now.'

Dion was frankly perplexed.

'But, my dear, I must have some explanation. I came to speak to Mr. Saddleman. Your father and I rather thought your heart-attack had been brought on by some shock—something in that note from Mr. Saddleman. You are my future wife, Marion, and I can't allow this sort of thing . . . I must inquire into it.'

Marion gripped his arm tightly. She tried to smile. She dared not look at Jet . . . dared not speak to him.

'I'll explain, Dion . . . only take me home

120

now . . . I feel terribly ill,' she said in a smothered voice.

He felt her against him, shivering as though with ague. Certainly in this moment she might be a person suffering from heart, with her bluish lips and wild, anguished eyes. He put an arm right round her.

'My dear, of course I'll take you home. But you ought never to have come. I'll take you home, then come back to the farm later on and speak to Mr. Saddleman.'

That was the last thing in the world Marion wanted him to do. She had to bite her lower lip to keep herself from screaming aloud. The net was tightening . . . tightening around her. She was hysterical and unnerved . . . she seemed to hear old Emm's prophetic voice cackling in her ear: 'The Dark Death for you . . . the shadow of the gallows.' . . . Dion's strong arm supported her, half carried her to the door.

'It was most unwise of you to come out like this when you have had a heart-attack, Marion,' he said. 'I cannot think why you did it and kept it from us all. Surely I, your future husband, could have dealt with this man . . . or your father! Marion, I can't pretend to understand your conduct.'

Never before had he spoken to her so severely. She was frozen with misery and fear.

'Dion, Dion, don't be cross with me—I am the unhappiest girl in the world!' she said in a heart-rending voice.

'My dear, I don't understand,' repeated the perplexed man as he led her to the door.

In the big, four-poster bed, Jet Saddleman silently cursed the Fates that had tied his tongue, rendered him so dumb, so helpless. He could write his thoughts, but he could not act in this case as he would like to have acted. He frothed a little at the mouth; mentally writhed with chagrin as he watched Marion being led from his room by her lover. He hated Sir Dion Courtland; he hated Marion who had been the cause of his frightful accident and paralysis. Yet he wanted her still. His desire for her beauty outweighed his hatred and his contempt for the callous murderess which he knew her to be. He had asked her to give up Sir Dion—to marry him, Jet. He wanted her youth and beauty at his side, forever . . . wanted to tie her down; make her compensate him for the terrible suffering he endured through her.

He would like to have sprung from his bed in this moment and torn Marion from Dion's arms . . . beaten Dion by superior strength, if by nothing else. Ah! In the old days he had been so strong . . . he could easily have felled an ox.

Marion allowed her lover to take her right down stairs. But by the time they had reached the lowest stair, she had formed a fresh plan of action. She was forced by her very fear to stamp on her weakness. She released herself from Dion's arms.

'One moment, darling, please,' she said in her most seductive voice. 'I won't keep you waiting a second . . . but there is just one word I must say to that unfortunate man.'

'No, please Marion—' began Dion.

But Marion had already sped past him up the staircase to Jet's bedroom again. Her heart beat violently. She *must* speak to Jet . . . she knew that all would be lost unless she capitulated.

She rushed to his bedside. His eyes, scornful, yet hungry, stared up at her wonderful face . . . they seemed to speak . . . to say: 'Well, what have you come back for?'

'Jet,' she said breathlessly, 'listen quickly. You must give me time. I will break with Dion . . . but not at once. I have reasons. If you drive me too far, I shall refuse altogether and let you tell everybody that you know. I shall be so mad, so desperate, I shan't care whether I'm hanged or not. But if you give me time, I'll work things . . . I'll marry you in the end. Now listen . . . give me a week to make up my mind. I'll make things right with Dion, about today . . . but if he comes to you, promise you will keep silent . . . that is, if you want me! I swear, Jet, if you don't give me a week, I'll let everything go to the winds.'

He twitched slightly but remained dumb. It was a terrible silence that seemed to rend him. But he considered what she said. He saw that she was desperate; that she might indeed defy him, accept the justice of the law, if he drove her too far. Better give her a week . . . perhaps.

'Will you give me time . . . keep silence for a week?' she whispered, panting. 'Close your eyes for "yes".'

One tense moment. Then Jet's terrible eyes slowly closed.

The relief to Marion's feelings was exquisite. She gave a long sigh.

'Thank you, Jet,' she gasped. 'I swear I'll make up my mind to break with Dion and marry you. But I must have time. It's a compact then. By today week, I will come to you.'

Jet's eyes closed again, silently saying 'yes'.

Marion hurried down to her waiting lover. He was pacing up and down the wide hall of the farmhouse, his brow stern and puckered. His eyes rested on her with very little love or trust as she came toward him.

'Now, Marion,' he said, 'I want an explanation of this.'

'Take me home first—please,' she said. 'I am—very ill.'

'If you are ill, you had no right to come here. What hold has this man over you? Answer me, Marion,' he said sternly.

She shivered and averted her eyes.

'Oh, Dion, Dion, don't speak like that—I can't bear it,' she whispered.

He put an arm about her, more for support

than in affection. He was thoroughly disturbed by her strange behaviour.

'You can't expect me to be very pleased, my dear,' he said as they walked out of the farm into the purple dusk. 'A few minutes before our marriage was to have taken place you put me off by having this heart-attack, and then you leave your bedroom and rush off to Saddleman in this extraordinary way. I can't understand it, and you must explain.'

Marion grew calmer. Jet's promise to keep silence for a week gave her courage and self-confidence again. But she took refuge in tears. She began to sob. Dion could not bear to see a woman cry . . . and it must be remembered that, although some of his illusions had been shattered today, he still loved Marion Grayle . . . her beauty, her fascination were still in his blood, driving him to wild passion for her. He hated to see her cry like this.

'My dear!' he said more softly, 'my dear, don't . . . please. Try and tell me about it . . . trust me. Marion, you don't know how you've hurt me over this business. You have shown a complete lack of trust in me.'

'No, no—I love you—adore you!' she sobbed, stumbling down the road over the moors toward the Travellers' Rest, leaning against him. 'I trust you with my life, Dion. But I didn't want to hurt you or worry you about Jet.'

'It is my duty—my privilege to help you over

any difficulty, Marion,' he said. 'My dear, do stop crying and explain.'

But she did not stop the torrent of tears until they reached the inn. Then she allowed him to lead her into the parlour, and once they were alone in front of a cosy fire, she took off her plaid coat and scarf, and curled up on the rug before the fire at his feet. She put her arms about his knees and leaned her head on them.

'Oh, Dion, Dion!' she sighed.

His heart was softening toward her every moment. He laid a hand on her head.

'My dear . . . my own Marion . . . there should be nothing between us,' he said. 'Tell me all about Jet. But don't you think you ought to be in bed?'

'I will go presently . . . but just now let me stay like this . . . I love you so,' she whispered.

He sighed, torn between doubt and love. She was so like a child . . . a rather guilty child at this moment, sitting at his feet, confessing a wrong . . . she was so sweet, so lovely . . . and this was to have been their wedding-day. How could he go on being angry and severe?

Marion blurted out her story . . . made up on the spur of the moment . . . and one which answered the purpose very well for just now. She reminded Dion that Jet had once been in love with her.

'Perhaps I flirted—led him on too much,' she said in a shamed voice. 'Gave him hope where there was none. It was cruel . . . but it was before I met you, my Dion. So forgive me. I wrote him some letters . . . foolish ones . . . and he refused to give them back. Then this morning, when he recovered use of his fingers and could write, he sent me the most bitter, malicious note, saying that he intended to tell you what a flirt I had been, and that he would send you the letters I had written him. I was excited about our wedding . . . my heart has never been strong . . .' she told this lie smoothly with her beautiful eyes looking beseechingly up into her lover's face. 'It brought on a heart-attack. Then when I felt better at tea-time, I decided to run over to Jet's house and implore him to give me back my letters. You . . . you found me there. That is all, Dion.'

She had spoken every word with apparent sincerity. Dion was relieved by this child-like confession. So that was the trouble. This girl, in her younger days, had been stupid . . . written foolish letters . . . made Saddleman promises . . . well, what girl had not done the same? Marion was lovely and had been much petted and courted in Moorcoombe. He could not expect her to have had no affair before he met her.

He put his arms around her.

'My darling,' he said. 'So that is all! Why, if only you had trusted me—asked me to get your letters back, I'd have done it! But you were saying, "Don't make me do it". What was the fellow trying to make you do?'

'Tell you—about—the—letters,' she sobbed, hiding her face in his knees. 'Oh, Dion, darling, I never cared for Jet. You know that. I've never loved any man on earth but you. I was a stupid kid when I wrote to him. Dion, Dion, forgive me . . . say you understand'

'Of course I do, darling one,' he said in his generous way. 'You never concealed the fact that Saddleman was once keen to marry you. I'm sorry you led him on—it was very unkind. But so far as the foolish letters go, I'll soon get them back.'

She raised a tear-wet face.

'Oh, thank you, thank you, Dion darling,' she said. 'But don't go and see him. It's so frightfully difficult and beastly, dealing with a paralysed man who can't speak. He'll probably send the letters to you as he threatened—then you can tear them up.'

She knew that there were no letters; that the whole story was a fabrication of lies. But to Dion's unsuspecting mind it was all quite feasible. He was a little hurt that Marion should not have trusted him . . . that was all.

'Damned impudence of that fellow, threatening you on your wedding-day,' he growled. 'By jove! if he were a well man, I'd deal with him quickly enough. Now, Marion, you look very white and tired, and I'm going to send you straight to bed. Seymour must see you in the morning and put that heart of yours right, then we'll get married and get away from Moorcoombe.'

The 'weak heart' was very heavy at this moment. Marion saw nothing but trouble ahead. But she was thankful for temporary respite. She rose to her feet and Dion took her into his arms. She clung to him in the old wild way.

'I love you—I love you—I was so terribly disappointed when my illness prevented our marriage,' she whispered.

'And then you go out into the cold and walk miles on top of it because you didn't trust me to get back the stupid letters. Oh, Marion!'

'I'm sorry,' she said, throwing her arms about him. 'Kiss me, kiss me, Dion, and say you love me!'

'Of course I do,' he said, stirred by her ardent beauty. And their lips met in a long kiss.

CHAPTER TWELVE

During the next few days, things did not go very well for Marion Grayle. Perforce she remained in her room, assuring everybody, including the Moorcoombe doctor, that she had a weak heart and could not think of getting married. Dr. Seymour examined her and retired perplexed. He could find nothing wrong with Miss Grayle's heart. She was in a nervy, hysterical condition, yes . . . but her pulse was splendid; that of a normal, healthy young woman.

Dion taxed Marion with this. She then scorned the local doctor's advice.

'He is an old fool, Dion. I *know* my heart is bad,' she persisted. 'Any decent doctor in Torquay would say so.'

Dion grew a little impatient. He loved this girl, and was anxious to marry her and take her away.

'Well, darling, if you don't feel better by the end of the week, you must see a man from Torquay,' he said.

The end of that week! Marion was tormented by the thought of it. She was playing for time. But she knew that she must do something by the end of this week, or lose the game and pay a dreadful penalty for her sins. Jet was silently waiting . . . like a horrible vampire, she thought, just waiting . . . to suck her very blood. He would keep to his word . . . betray and ruin her . . . if she refused to give up Dion.

Before the week ended, Dion arranged for his mother to come down to Moorcoombe to meet his future wife.

'The mater is a darling, and will be a good influence on my wild bird, Marion,' he told himself, thinking tenderly of the girl. 'I'll get her down here.'

He told Marion of his plan. She had no alternative save to agree to it.

'Of course, I'd adore to meet your mother,' she said.

But Lady Courtland was the last person she wanted at Moorcoombe to criticise her . . . a fresh one to spy, to condemn . . . And what about the girl who was living with Lady Courtland . . . this Pat Westby about whom Dion had spoken? If she came, too . . . Marion ground her teeth at the thought. Hope Marshall was dead . . . gone . . . out of Dion's life. Marion could not bear the idea of any other girl entering it.

Unfortunately for her, however, Patricia Westby was just the person whom Lady Courtland brought down to Dartmoor as her companion.

The two women motored in a beautiful touring saloon car from London, and arrived at the Travellers' Rest one misty November night . . . two days before the fateful week ended for Marion.

Marion was now assuming the rôle of convalescent 'getting stronger.' When Dion's mother arrived, she was on the couch down in the sitting-room, covered with a rug; just that touch of wistful sadness in her eyes which made her look so appealing and innocent. She wore the black velvet frock which Dion loved, and had wound a lovely Spanish shawl of fine black lace, which had been one of her lover's gifts, about her beautiful shoulders.

Dion's mother came to Moorcoombe feeling distinctly hostile. She was in deep mourning for her late husband, and not at all in the mood to welcome a future daughter-in-law, especially one whom her son had chosen from a Dartmoor inn, and about whom she knew nothing. She had always wanted Dion to marry well . . . a girl like Patricia Westby, for instance. But she adored her boy, and as he had begged her to come down here and be nice to Marion, she had done so.

Marion was her sweetest and best tonight. She held out both hands to Lady Courtland, and said:

'Oh, dear Lady Courtland, I do so want you to love me!'

Dion's mother gave one look at the beautiful face, then sighed and kissed the girl.

'I hope to be very fond of my son's wife,' she said, in her usual gentle, courteous way.

She tried to console herself that Dion's fiancée, although not the aristocracy, was very lovely, and quite refined and sweet.

Marion, although she had not wanted Lady Courtland to come, now conceived one of those wild, inordinate affections which rose in her ungoverned young heart for people, from time to time. Lady Courtland was a handsome, white-haired woman—with fine hazel eyes like Dion's—and Dion's lips. Marion wanted to love her. And she meant that Lady Courtland should love her, too. She would defeat Jet . . . defeat all the Fates that were leagued against her. She would be Dion's idolised wife, and be beloved of his people, his friends, in spite of everything.

Patricia Westby was the thorn in her side, tonight. She instantly hated the girl, and curiously enough, Pat Westby, who was an easy-going, amiable young woman, instantly disliked Marion. It was not jealousy. Pat admired Dion immensely . . . but she had not known him long enough to be in love with him. It was just that she felt antagonistic toward Marion Grayle at first sight, and felt that something was wrong, somewhere. There was Irish blood in Pat . . . at times she was curiously psychic. When first she looked into Marion's eyes and touched her hand in greeting, she felt a most extraordinary shiver of repulsion. She tried not to attach any importance to it, nor to remember it. But it was impossible for her after that to like or trust Marion. When Lady Courtland asked her, later, what she thought of Dion's choice, she said generously:

'Oh, a very beautiful girl—and they seem very much in love.'

Lady Courtland sighed and said:

'Yes, pretty enough. I hope she won't be delicate. I don't like this heart affair. I'm sorry, Pat, anyhow, my dear, that Dion is rushing into a marriage like this.'

Dion was the happiest of them all, tonight. In his blind masculine fashion, he did not notice what the women were thinking or feeling. He took it for granted that, since they had all embraced and smiled at each other, they were good friends, and he felt pleased with Marion for being so charming and gentle with his mother.

He was very attracted by Pat. He had liked her out in Monte Carlo . . . he liked her more now that he saw her again. She was so frank and friendly . . . there was almost a 'boyish' charm about her. He sat talking to her, absorbed in a discussion about golf which interested them both, not dreaming for an instant that Marion's great eyes were fixed upon him with burning jealousy and fear . . . that ever-present fear which knocked at her guilty heart, that she might lose him for whom she had sinned . . . lose him forever.

Patricia Westby was a tall, slender, graceful girl, not strictly beautiful, although her frank, laughing grey eyes were very attractive, and she had a clear, sun-tanned skin, a charming mouth and a ringing laugh which was infectious.

With Marion, Dion was always strung up to the pitch of impetuous passion and drama It was almost a relief to talk to Pat, laugh with her, feel as one feels in a cool ocean breeze . . . in some fragrant, spring-touched wood where crystal brooks ripple and dimple; in cool, green meadows where thrushes trill and sing. That was how Pat Westby made a man feel.

Before she went to bed, Marion foolishly spoke of Pat.

'Do you like her very much?' she asked, her arms about her lover's throat. 'You scarcely spoke to me at all.'

'My *dear!*' protested Dion. And he was rather shocked and disturbed by the jealousy which seemed to him a lack of self-control . . . Marion's usual fault!

That night Marion lay awake until dawn, tossing, turning, worrying . . . dark thoughts crowding through her brain . . . evil thoughts that refused to be banished.

Jet Saddleman stood between her and her lover. Jet was a barrier between her and her heart's desire. Once, she had tried to send Jet to his death, and had failed. But now she realised, beyond all doubt, that unless Jet was silenced forever, he would either separate her from Dion and condemn her to a frightful existence with him, Jet . . . or send her to the gallows . . .

She awoke, hot, fevered, exhausted by her night of mental torture. But she rose and was down earlier than anybody else in the inn. She had a queer, fatalistic look in her eyes . . . as though she had made up her mind to perform some action either for good or for bad . . . the look one might see in the eyes of a desperate gambler who throws the dice for the last time.

In the garden at the back of the Inn was a little shed where Tom Grayle kept gardening tools. On the shelf there was a small white packet, tied up with red string. It was a weedkiller . . . arsenic.

Marion took this packet and slid it into her pocket. She came out of the shed quietly, unseen. Not even the servants were down. Then she went back to her room.

That morning, Dion suggested a round of golf on the Torquay course with Pat Westby. Marion's heart beat fast with annoyance when the suggestion was made. How she hated the thought that Dion might grow fond of that grey-eyed laughing girl! But she said nothing. Lady Courtland was going to Torquay. She wished to do some shopping. The kindly, gracious old lady had it at the back of her head to purchase a suitable present for her future daughter-in-law, and thus show her goodwill.

Marion was left alone.

She waited until her father and Charlie Hodges were busy in the inn, then she walked slowly to Double-Styles Farm.

Mrs. Pollock opened the door to her and gave her a sour, suspicious look.

'What do you want?' she snapped. 'Every time you come, you upset the master, Marion Grayle. I've been told how you sneaked here the other day when I was out and—'

'How dare you be rude to me?' interrupted

136

Marion, drawing herself up to her full height. 'You be careful, Sarah Pollock. Mr. Saddleman wouldn't want you to be rude to me.'

Mrs. Pollock crossed her arms on her chest. She longed to be rude again. But she knew that Marion spoke the truth. Jet Saddleman was infatuated with the girl. She had better be careful. She adored her master, and the one thing she feared was that he might give her notice if she annoyed him through her conduct toward Marion Grayle.

Marion was shown up to Jet's room. She was far from hysterical today. She was calm with the calm of desperation. She advanced to his bedside, smiling very sweetly. She looked charmingly flushed from the exertion of her walk over the moors, and nobody would have dreamed that any guile lay in her eyes.

'Well, Jet,' she said, taking one of his big brown hands. 'I've come to spend the day with you and make you happy.'

He could not speak. He looked up at her rather bitterly, but after a moment his eyes grew pleased, and a painful, difficult smile contorted his face, which was drawn up on one side from paralysis. Marion took off her hat and coat, and sat down by the bed. She was more adorable and friendly than he had known her for years. She said that she intended breaking her engagement with Sir Dion Courtland on the morrow; that she had had several rows with him, had been working up to a suitable 'break.'

'Then I shall marry you, dear,' she told the man. 'I believe in my heart I care for you best, and I will devote myself to you and make up for all that you have suffered.'

Jet's eyes, pathetically eager now, stared up at her. She nerved herself to bend down and kiss his forehead. But it was the kiss of Judas.

She sat with him until lunch-time. Then Mrs. Pollock, jealous and sour, brought up lunch on a tray for the invalid.

'You going to feed the master?' she snapped.

'Certainly I will. Would you like me to, Jet?' Marion asked, bending over him.

He closed his eyes in silent acquiescence. To him it would be exquisite pleasure to be fed by Marion Grayle's slender hand instead of the bony one of his faithful housekeeper. Alas, such is man!

Marion fed the paralysed farmer with a spoon—giving him soup and a little fricassied chicken. Then she asked him whether he would like anything to drink. He shut his eyes. Marion looked round the room and saw a bottle of burgundy on a table on the other side of the room. Her heart began to beat violently; her brain felt that it was on fire. She rose and walked to this table. It was situated in a corner, so that the man in the bed could not see her. So she was able to pour out a glass of burgundy without being overlooked.

She filled a wine-goblet with the rich, red liquid. Then like a flash she opened the tiny white packet of arsenic which she had brought with her, and emptied most of it into the glass. This she stirred carefully until the powder was dissolved.

She then walked to the bedside of the man who stood between her and Dion and happiness. She knew that the dose she was administering was fatal. But without a qualm she lifted it to his lips, smiling down at him.

'It will do you good, Jet,' she said.

Fascinated by the loveliness of her eyes, the wretched man stared up at her, then drained the glass to the dregs.

CHAPTER THIRTEEN

Marion stared down at her victim. She watched the expression in his eyes change from admiration and longing to piteous astonishment, then to acute pain. He screwed his features up; his lips writhed; a froth came from the corners. Little, dreadful, grunting noises issued from that twisted mouth, and suddenly his knees hunched up, as though in the frightfulness of the agony which he suffered from the arsenic administered, his paralysis was cured.

The dose Marion had mixed with the

burgundy had been sufficient to kill two or three men. Just for a few seconds he writhed and groaned in horrible pain; his rolling eyeballs turned to the girl, concentrated on her with a look of awful condemnation. He spoke one word . . . the first he had been able to say for weeks; the last he would ever say on this earth:

'MURDERESS!'

Then his head fell back on the pillows . . . he lay still, eyes staring at the ceiling, mouth open.

Jet Saddleman was dead.

For a moment, Marion Grayle was transfixed with the horror of what she had done. That word, hissed at her . . . *murderess* . . . shook her to the foundations of her being. Yet mixed with her horror of herself, was a terrible relief, because Jet was silenced for ever . . . he and his knowledge no longer stood between her and Dion Courtland.

Not for long did she ruminate on the possibilities of this thing. It occurred to her that she must act now, act for her very life . . . that either she must deceive everybody into thinking her innocent of the dreadful thing she had done, or she would be ruined forever.

She gave one shuddering glance at the tormented, ghastly thing in the bed, then ran to the door, shrieking . . . shrieking.

Sarah Pollock came rushing up the staircase, her sallow face pale. She had never heard such awful cries. She was met at the top of the staircase by Marion.

'Mrs. Pollock—oh, my God—Mrs. Pollock!' Marion sobbed.

'What is it? Heavens alive, girl, what is it?' gasped Sarah.

'Jet . . . Jet . . . he's *dead!*'

'Dead?' repeated the housekeeper. 'It's impossible.'

Marion pointed a shaking finger at the door.

'Go and look,' she panted. 'I gave him a drink of burgundy . . . then he started writhing and foaming at the mouth . . . go and look.'

Mrs. Pollock did go and look. For a moment she stood by the bedside, looking down at her dead master, her features convulsed with grief. She had loved Mr. Saddleman and served him for years. She saw at a glance that he had gone beyond human reach. Her grief, however, speedily changed to horror and suspicion. She picked up the emptied burgundy glass and smelt it. Bitter . . . a queer, bitter smell . . . and at the bottom of the glass a whitish powder.

Mrs. Pollock drew herself erect. She knew in one word the answer to the mystery of her master's sudden death. *Poison.* Mr. Saddleman had been poisoned. And by whom? By whom, save this girl who had given him the drink?

She walked out of the room to the landing where Marion clung to the banisters, sobbing. She held out the glass with a dramatic gesture.

141

'This is your doing, Marion Grayle!' she said in a harsh voice. '*Poison* . . . and you've given it to him . . . my poor master!'

Marion stared at her.

'Poison . . . you mean he has been poisoned?'

'Yes, that's what I mean, and you're responsible.'

'You're crazy, Mrs. Pollock,' said Marion, growing calm and quiet. 'You're off your head. What reason could I possibly have for wishing to poison poor Jet?'

'I don't know,' said Mrs. Pollock. 'But you've done it. I've always suspected 'twas you that pushed him over the quarry and well-nigh sent him to death, then.'

'You're certainly mad, my good woman,' said Marion, passing a handkerchief across her lips, which were pale and quivering. 'I rather think the cap is on the other head . . . that you are responsible for this. Everybody knows Jet made a Will in favour of you. He told everyone so—that he meant to leave his farm and money to you unless he married, because you had served him all your life. Perhaps you were in a hurry for the money and the house, eh! Perhaps that is why *you put the poison in that burgundy, and got me to give it to him!*'

Mrs. Pollock stared at the girl, aghast.

'Almighty God! she said in accents of horror. 'That you should suggest such a thing.'

'I do more than suggest it,' said Marion,

pursuing her diabolical plan of action with composure and cunning. 'I accuse you of murdering your master and I am going straight to the police.'

She could not have acted more cleverly. She literally took the words out of Sarah Pollock's mouth. Sarah had been going to the police . . . to accuse Marion Grayle. The housekeeper was no longer young. She was a woman of sixty, and could not stand what a young, strong girl could stand. The sight of her murdered master, followed by this girl's terrible accusation, took the wind out of her sails. She tottered to the banister-railing and caught hold of it, one hand to her heart.

'Oh! she gasped. 'Oh, you wicked, wicked girl!'

'Don't dare to leave this house until I've brought back the police,' said Marion. 'You shall pay the penalty of your vile crime, you hypocrite!'

Mrs. Pollock gave a heart-rending cry.

'Master . . . master . . . you know 'twas never me that did it . . . I loved you too well!'

But Marion had gone, fled down the stairs, out of the farm on to the moor. It was a fresh, sunny morning. The sky was clear blue, save for one or two fleecy white clouds scudding across the heavens in the breeze. The moorland was a study in gold and purple and green. Such a fair morning; it seemed like late summer today, rather than the approach of stern, cold winter. Marion Grayle should have been out in all this beauty on a more innocent errand, in tune with the fresh beauty of Dartmoor. But instead, her heart, her very body surged with evil, terrible thoughts and desires. She raced across the moors to Moorcoombe Village. She did not stop until she reached the cottage wherein dwelt her good friend and admirer, Patterson the constable.

Patterson came out to meet her, pulling his brown beard in a pleased fashion.

'Why if it b'ain't my Miss Bubbles—good morning . . . !' he began, then saw her beautiful little face was distorted and white, and his smile faded. 'Why, what on earth—'

'Patterson—Patterson!' she gasped. 'A most terrible thing has happened. Jet Saddleman has been murdered—poisoned!'

'Miss Bubbles, are you serious?' gasped the constable.

She fell into his outstretched arms. Like a child, hysterical with grief and terror. She sobbed on his shoulder, while he patted her curly head and soothed her; gasped out a story of visiting poor Jet . . . of being given burgundy by Mrs. Pollock to give Jet . . . of his subsequent death.

'That wicked woman has murdered him!' she said, her slim body quivering from head to foot. 'I've never trusted her, Patterson. Only the other day she said she wished he'd hurry up and die instead of lying there paralysed, because she wanted her freedom and his money.'

Patterson's bearded face went a shade paler.

'Moorcoombe's bewitched, Miss Bubbles!' he muttered. 'Murders 'olesale . . . first the young lady from Torquay . . . now Jet Saddleman. But come, we must go back to Double-Styles Farm, at once. Wait for me, miss, while I telephone Torquay headquarters.'

Marion wiped away her tears. Her heart beat violently with excitement and nervousness, but her cheeks had regained some normal colour and her lips actually curved into a smile. All the Moorcoombe people were her friends . . . loved and admired her. Nobody had cared for Mrs. Pollock, with her sour tongue and critical ways. Marion believed that she was safe . . . that nobody would ever dream of accusing *her* of the murder of Jet Saddleman.

CHAPTER FOURTEEN

Two hours later Moorcoombe was in an uproar, and the news of the death of Jet Saddleman from arsenic-poisoning had spread like wildfire from house to house.

Folk shared Patterson's belief that the

village was 'bewitched' . . . that some evil spell had been cast over it. Whoever had heard such happenings? Two murders since last month! It was an outrage. First Miss Marshall's body, found in Linton Wood, dead from drowning. Now Farmer Saddleman had been poisoned.

Sir Dion Courtland, his mother and Patricia Westby returned from Torquay after a pleasant game of golf, to be plunged into the chaos.

An inquest was being held on the body of Jet Saddleman, and Sarah Pollock and Marion Grayle were at Double-Styles Farm, both detained by the Torquay police while investigations were being made.

Dion was almost stunned by the turn of events. He went to Marion's side at once. He found her quite cool and collected, and, in fact, smiling, with just a touch of pathos in the smile. She had done with tears and hysteria. She was quite composed. She gave Dion both her hands, and said:

'My dearest—I'm terribly sorry that my name has been dragged into this frightful thing . . . but that fiendish woman, Mrs. Pollock, deliberately chose me to give poor Jet the fatal dose. Can you imagine anything more awful? I shall never, never get over it.'

Dion looked down into the girl's lovely eyes without speaking for a moment. They looked back without flinching . . . they seemed such innocent, sweet, loving eyes . . . how could they

146

belong to any but a good, true woman? Just for the fraction of a second suspicion had torn at Dion's mind . . . then it passed and he loathed himself for that moment's disloyalty to Marion.

'You poor darling,' he said. 'It must have been perfectly frightful for you. You look as white as a sheet.'

'No wonder,' she said, her eyes wearily closing. 'It's all so terrible. I went to see poor Jet . . . to ask for my letters . . .' her voice sank to a whisper. 'He was much more human and generous, and had just promised to give them back. He answered by opening and shutting his eyes for "yes" and "no." I found the stupid letters in a drawer and burnt them in that fire in his grate. Then I asked him if he would like a drink, and he said "yes". Mrs. Pollock came up and poured out the burgundy behind a screen and gave it to me to give Jet. He drank it . . . and that was his end.'

'I see,' said Dion.

He believed every word she said. She had got back her letters . . . burnt them, in fact. The last thing *she* would want, poor little girl, would be Saddleman's death. But this woman, Pollock . . . yes, she would have motive for murder . . . it was said that she was to inherit her master's property, as he had neither kith nor kin.

He pressed Marion's slim, soft hands to his lips.

147

'My poor Marion,' he murmured. 'You seem fated to be connected with troubles . . . you have had nothing but horrors lately. But cheer up, darling . . . I will stand by you . . . nobody will hurt you.'

She clung to him gratefully. Ah, this was worth all the crime, the fear, the horror . . . this warm, strong clasp of her lover's fingers . . . the love-light in his eyes.

'Mrs. Pollock is trying to put the blame on me,' she said with a forced laugh. 'But of course that is too absurd for words.'

Moorcoombe thought it absurd, too. What reason could Miss Grayle have for wanting poor Farmer Saddleman out of the way . . . she who was engaged to Sir Dion Courtland; had everything a girl could want? Besides, she had been so frank, so sincere . . . telling the police she had given Saddleman that drink.

'I helped him take it—actually poured it down his throat,' Marion said at one part of the inquest, the tears pouring down her cheeks. 'How could I *dream* Mrs. Pollock had poisoned the wine?'

'What reason have you for suggesting that it was Mrs. Pollock who did so?' she had been asked by the Coroner. And she had answered:

'Last time I visited Mr. Saddleman, Mrs. Pollock muttered something to the effect that she wished the man would hurry up and die,' said Marion.

Sarah Pollock's iron nerve gave way under

148

the proceedings. She appeared old and feeble, and could only mutter: 'Marion Grayle killed him . . . she's a liar . . . a liar . . . she killed him.'

But Marion appeared confident, cool, naturally distressed by the terrible thing that had happened, but laughing at the mere idea that she, personally, was responsible for Jet's death.

The police were baffled.

The beautiful young daughter of old Tom Grayle was obviously not guilty. Mrs. Pollock had motive for the murder, yet stoutly denied her guilt. Before that terrible day ended, however, Marion had won the game she had set out to play; had successfully shifted the blame from her own shoulders on to another's. While nobody was looking she had transferred the little white paper, marked 'Weedkiller,' from her pocket to a drawer in Mrs. Pollock's bedroom. The investigating detective from Torquay discovered that paper, and it was the strongest evidence against the old woman. She denied all knowledge of it. Appalled by the whole affair, she was not her usual caustic-tongued self. She could only keep repeating that she was innocent and that Marion Grayle had poisoned Mr. Saddleman. Yet when asked what reason Miss Grayle could have, she was dumb. She knew no reason. And nobody could see any reason why Marion should have done it.

Then, after the finding of that paper in her

drawer, Jet Saddleman's Will was read. He had left Double-Styles Farm and a large sum of money to Sarah Pollock who had been with him over twenty years.

There lay the motive for the crime . . .

Sarah Pollock was arrested for the murder of her master, and Marion Grayle was sent home. The poor old woman went with the police; dazed and broken. She was not very highly educated; not very capable of fighting for herself; she was just a simple, God-fearing Devonshire woman. She continued to protest her innocence but things were black against her.

Marion was the heroine of the moment. Everybody in Moorcoombe sympathised with her. It must have been so terrible for a young, gentle girl like Marion to have unwittingly given Jet Saddleman that fatal glass of wine. She, with tears in her beautiful eyes, and a pale, weary face, shook hands with her friends and thanked them for their sympathy.

'I can't forget the horror of it,' she said. 'I shall never forgive myself for giving that poor, paralysed creature his death-drink. Oh, that wicked, unspeakable Mrs. Pollock!'

'Don't think about it—for God's sake try not to brood over it, you poor darling,' Dion said. He was the most ardent sympathiser with Marion. 'Mrs. Pollock will get what she deserves. I think it's a ghastly business, and I'm afraid you'll be dragged into it a good bit more yet—have to give evidence at the trial and all that.'

'I know, Dion,' she said piteously, 'but I don't mind that. What I can't get used to is the thought that Mrs. Pollock made *me* give him that fatal drink!'

He felt her shiver in the circle of his arm, and kissed her curly head.

'I know—I know, sweetheart,' he said tenderly. 'It must have been frightful . . . but try to forget it.'

Marion received an incredible amount of love and tenderness that night at the Travellers' Rest. Lady Courtland was as sweet to her as though she had been her own daughter, and even Pat Westby, who did not like Marion, was sympathetic and kind.

'Enough to upset any delicate girl,' Lady Courtland exclaimed. 'Poor little Marion!'

'Poor girl!' echoed Pat Westby.

'It's high time we married, Marion, and got away from all these horrors,' Dion remarked seriously. 'I'm beginning to dread this place.'

'So am I. It's full of darkness and death,' said Marion.

She was, however, happy and exultant. Everything had gone off splendidly—much more successfully than she had dared hope. Sarah Pollock was in custody, accused of the murder, and everybody, including Dion and his mother, were on her, Marion's side.

She drank in all the sympathy and

tenderness; basked in it. She went to bed, her head whirling with excitement. Dion had suggested that they should get married at once.

'I want to take care of you, and I can protect you so much better if you are my wife,' he had said. 'Your heart is stronger again now, my Lovely One. Say you will marry me at once?'

And what reason had she for refusing? She was not afraid of anybody now. The man who had known the grim secret of Hope Marshall's death and had tried to separate her from Dion, lay stiff and cold in his shell. She saw no reason for saying 'no' when the one thing she most desired was to become Dion's wife.

For effect she prettily suggested, in front of Lady Courtland and Patricia Westby, that they should wait until Sarah Pollock's trial was over.

'I don't want to drag the name of Courtland into it,' she said. 'Wouldn't you prefer to wait?'

Lady Courtland agreed with this. In her heart of hearts, she still deplored Dion's engagement to the innkeeper's daughter, although she admitted Marion's charm and beauty. But Dion was firm.

'The name of Courtland will be "dragged in," as you call it, anyhow,' he said. 'You are my fiancée now. No—marry me, darling, and let me take care of you.'

Marion gave a great sigh, and whispered 'yes.'

And who was there to notice that Pat

Westby's charming face went just a little pale, and that she turned away lest Dion should see the wistful, regretful look in her bright grey eyes.

That next day, when Moorcoombe was still buzzing with excitement over the murder of Jet and the arrest of Sarah Pollock, Dion made arrangements to marry Marion Grayle. This time there would be no hitch . . . no heart-attack, he hoped. He was still blindly infatuated with Marion. Her touch, her voice had power to stir him to hot passion. When she was in his arms, with his lips on her mouth, he could forgive all her too-impetuous ways and lack of self-control. After all, he reflected, she was only a wayward, passionate child . . . adorable at that . . . he would teach her as his wife to take her place with dignity as Lady Courtland.

Tom Grayle came to his daughter that day and had a few serious, whispered words with her.

'Marion, gal,' he said, 'after reading up all this about poor old Saddleman's death in this morning's paper, I thought of that arsenic I bought months back for weedkiller. I thought I put that in the shed outside, but seems I didn't. It isn't there.'

Her heart seemed to stop beating. But she gave him an innocent, questioning smile.

'Isn't it, Dad? Well, that's funny. No—now I remember—you gave it to poor Jet, who asked for it one day last Spring. I remember. No doubt Sarah Pollock stole it from him.'

Tom Grayle scratched his curly white locks.

'Don't remember that, my gal.'

'Well, I do,' she said firmly. 'But let's forget about it, Dad. We don't want to say any more in the witness-box than we need . . . it's all so horrible.'

Marion's father agreed with her. But he was still worried about that packet of weedkiller. He could have sworn he had put it in the tool shed, and he did not recollect the incident that Marion spoke of . . . giving it to Saddleman, last Spring.

He was not a talkative man, however, and he kept his thoughts to himself. The last person in the world whom he could suspect was his own daughter; such suspicion never crossed his mind.

That afternoon a young man called at the Travellers' Rest to see Miss Grayle.

He gave his name as Sidney Pollock.

'I am Mrs. Pollock's nephew-by-marriage,' he said grimly, when Mr. Grayle inquired his business. 'The only relation she has left in the world. I know Aunt Sarah, and I know she ain't the sort to murder no one. She always had a sharp tongue, but she was kind to all. I've had a talk with her in the prison cell, and she's just broken up over this business. She says Miss Marion Grayle's the one and—'

'Here,' broke in Tom Grayle, sharply. 'If

154

that's what you got to say, you clear out o' here. I'm Miss Grayle's father . . .'

'Wait, Dad,' said a sweet voice from the doorway. 'I'll see the poor young man.'

Sidney Pollock clenched his hands. His interview with his aunt had left him certain that this girl, Grayle, was a murderess and a foul liar, and he had come to tell her just what he thought of her.

Marion calmly walked into the bar-parlour.

'You go out, Dad, and leave Mr. Pollock to me,' she said.

Mr. Grayle reluctantly departed.

Sidney Pollock faced the girl whom his aunt accused. He had come from Torquay, where he lived, to speak to Marion in defence of his aunt.

The words of abuse died on his lips as he faced Miss Grayle. Her appearance left him dumbfounded. He could only stand there, twirling his tweed cap in his fingers, staring . . .

Marion had risen from her after-lunch nap. She wore a dark blue georgette frock with a scarlet patent belt about her slender hips, and ivory georgette frilling at the throat and wrists. Her cheeks were flushed from slumber, rosy like a child's; her red lips smiled at the boy; her great dark eyes were like pools of mystery and beauty.

'You poor lad,' she said, holding out her hand. 'I'm so dreadfully sorry for you.'

He found himself taking that hand, being

155

thrilled by the contact with her soft, warm fingers. Her eyes, which looked at him with tender pity, might have been the eyes set in the face of a Madonna.

'Sit down,' she murmured. 'I quite realise how you feel. You are fond of your aunt, eh? It is terrible for you. I can't think what induced her to do such a terrible thing.'

That stung Sidney Pollock. He grew very red in the face. His honest blue eyes flashed. He began to talk very rapidly and thickly. Aunt Sarah wasn't guilty. He knew her. He was mortally wounded by the catastrophe—that his aunt, wife of his dead uncle, Ted Pollock, should be in gaol, accused of murder. He had often see her at Double-Styles Farm. She had been a devoted servant to Mr. Saddleman— didn't want his property, etc., etc.

Marion listened in silence, thick lashes hiding the irritation, the nervousness she felt. Drat this boy for coming to interfere. He was a big, hulking lad with shaggy, curly fair hair, a weather-beaten face and nice blue eyes. A motor-engineer in some big motor-works . . . a simple, hard-working fellow. She could see that he believed firmly in his aunt's innocence.

'She's that broken up—it was pitiful to see her,' he finished, drawing a finger across his eyes. 'Honestly, miss, it's gone to her brain— the horror of it—she weren't herself at all.'

Marion's wicked heart leaped. Gone to her brain, eh? All the better if Sarah's brain gave way under the strain. But she continued to be gentle and charming to Sidney Pollock.

'I'm so sorry—it's all awful for you. But if you don't believe she did it—whom do you suspect?'

He looked at her. Her lovely eyes looked straight back into his. He was masculine enough to feel the heady charm of her, to let his senses master his reason.

'It couldn't be you—it couldn't,' he stammered, his face fiery red. 'Honest to God, miss, when I come here, I wondered if it was you—Aunt Sarah accused you—but now—'

'Now you don't think so,' she finished for him, gently.

'No,' he muttered. 'I don't . . . how could I? . . . you've the face of an angel!'

Her pulses leaped. The expression in her eyes changed from pity to contempt, although Sidney Pollock saw it not. Poor fool—poor man-fool so easily deluded by a woman's charm and beauty. Sidney Pollock left the Travellers' Rest that day convinced that Marion Grayle was not the guilty one. Poor Aunt Sarah's brain was going . . . no doubt about that, now.

Marion, certain now that she had Sarah's nephew on her side, bade him come and see her again.

'I'm so sorry for you, Sidney,' she said. 'I'd like to be able to do something for you. I am being married tomorrow to Sir Dion

157

Courtland. I'm sure he would like to help you, too.'

Young Pollock returned to Torquay in a maze, bewitched by Marion's lovely face, and the sweetness of her.

That next morning, at eleven o'clock, Marion reached the very summit of her ambitions. Whilst Sarah Pollock languished in gaol, half off her poor head with the strain and horror of her unexpected fate, Marion was married to Sir Dion Courtland at Moorcoombe Church.

All Moorcoombe turned out to see the popular young daughter of Tom Grayle united to the young baronet who had also gained popularity during his sojourn in Moorcoombe. It was a pleasant change from horrors. Moorcoombe had been sunk in gloom and tragedy after the murder of Jet Saddleman, following so soon upon Miss Marshall's mysterious violent death. It was an agreeable change to flock to Moorcoombe Church and see a wedding.

Marion walked up the aisle on her father's arm, her bearing like that of a triumphant princess. No 'heart-attack' this time; no necessity to lie or act or deceive. She was free of suspicion; she need be afraid of no man's tongue. She wore the pretty pearl-grey dress she had put on once before; the little grey hat with the diamond arrow, on her red-gold head, and the silver squirrel coat which Dion had given her. She carried a bouquet of exquisite flowers—from Dion—sent early that morning by special car from Torquay . . . a great mass of dewy, hot-house roses—red roses—Marion's favourite flower. Across her breast was a magnificent diamond and ruby bar . . . a wedding-present from her mother-in-law, Lady Courtland. And amongst the many presents given by Moorcoombe folk, was a charming Russian leather bag from Pat Westby.

Pat knelt in a pew beside the bridegroom's mother, and watched the marriage ceremony with very mixed feelings. Marion looked lovely—like one of the perfect roses in her bouquet—and the face she turned to Dion as he slid the wedding-ring on to her finger was ecstatic. As Sidney Pollock had said, it was the 'face of an angel.'

Yet Pat could not feel happy about this wedding; could not get rid of the queer, psychic feeling that something was wrong.

Marion walked out of the Church on her husband's arm, a triumphant, radiant being. She was Dion's wife at last. She was Lady Courtland. She had gained her heart's desire. What penalty she might have to pay *one day* for her sins, she neither thought of, nor cared about.

'Marion, my darling, my own wife,' Dion whispered, as he led her into the sunshine. 'I love you so!'

'I adore you,' she said.

'If only we could get right away from everybody—to the other side of the world,' he sighed. 'It's a rotten shame having to wait for that beastly trial.'

Marion shivered slightly. It was like a cold sponge being thrown at her hot, flushed face . . . the mere mention of the forthcoming trial. She wanted to forget that on this day of days.

Old Grayle had insisted on holding a wedding breakfast at the Travellers' Rest. To this meal—generous and homely—many Moorcoombe folk were invited by the old innkeeper. Marion secretly chafed against it. She wanted to get away . . . right away from Moorcoombe, with Dion . . . to be with him, her darling, her Love, alone.

During the wedding-breakfast—sitting at the top of the long table which Mr. Grayle had decorated gaily for his daughter's benefit—she forced herself to be gay and good-humoured with her relations and friends. She was her sweetest and best with Lady Courtland, and even to Pat Westby, whom she disliked. When one of the guests leaned across and addressed her as 'Lady Courtland,' she thrilled and flushed. Oh, the pride of it . . . Lady Courtland . . . she, who had been just Miss Grayle.

In the middle of the meal, an unexpected visitor arrived at the inn. A servant announced him . . . 'Mr. Sidney Pollock.'

The very name cast a hush, almost a chill on

160

the wedding-party. Pollock! Nephew of the wretched woman now awaiting her trial for murder of poor Saddleman. Marion's beautiful colour faded and her heart gave a little leap of fear. What did young Pollock want? Why had he come, now of all times? But she acted with rather foolish bravado and nonchalance.

'Better ask him in to drink my health,' she said, her brown eyes flashing proudly round the table.

Sidney Pollock walked into the room. The moment Marion saw him, she regretted that invitation. He was not the admiring, cringing youth who had left her presence a day ago. He looked sullen, strained, almost defiant. He marched straight up to Tom Grayle.

'I'm sorry to interrupt a wedding breakfast,' he said in a gruff voice. 'But I thought, Mr. Grayle, as perhaps you'd tell me if you know this photo . . .'

'What photo?' asked Grayle, as he took the tiny piece of paper Pollock handed him.

'I've been making a search all round Hunter's Hill Quarry,' said Pollock, fixing his eyes on Marion now. 'I saw my Aunt Sarah again last night, and she said one or two things that made me want to investigate a bit closer than the police did. I found this bit of photo amongst the stones there . . . scratched and torn . . . but you can see the face. You know folks about here. Who would you say that was?'

Tom Grayle examined it closely. Then he gave an exclamation.

'Why, surely to goodness, it's my dead wife, Lucy! Marion . . . it's the miniature of your mother, girl. You always wear it in your locket round your neck. How did it come to be up at the quarry?'

CHAPTER FIFTEEN

The old man's innocent inquiry had a paralysing effect upon the whole party. Marion sat staring at the tiny faded photo in her father's hand, her cheeks blazing hot, her eyes bright with terror. Sidney Pollock looked at her through the spectacles of suspicion. His last meeting with his wretched, agonised aunt had decided him against Marion Grayle.

At the first meeting with Marion, he had been stirred to passion—to a youth's admiration for a beautiful young woman. He had thought her an angel, incapable of one evil thought! But since then he had been thinking . . . investigating . . . listening to his aunt. Now he was suspicious. He glowered at her. He then glowered all round the table, at everybody as though challenging the party to say one word against Mrs. Pollock.

At last Marion spoke:

'I can't understand it,' she said weakly. 'I

thought mother's miniature was still in my locket.'

'Look—look and see,' said her father.

Her hand went up to her throat and pulled at the slender gold chain from which was suspended a gold locket which she had worn ever since her mother died, under her frock. Her heart pounded and her hands felt ice-cold as she opened the locket. She was *beginning to remember* . . . details of that day on the edge of Hunter's Hill Quarry when she had tried to push Jet Saddleman over to his death. Hurrying back from that grim spot, she had noticed her locket hanging out over her dress, half open. Without looking inside, she had just snapped it to. Fool that she had been! The photo must have come out . . . the glass been loose . . . and it had been half buried in the sticks and stones of the Quarry. The police had passed it by. But young Pollock, bent on securing his aunt's innocence, had found it . . . had probably in his stupid, yet dangerous mind, connected the person who had pushed Jet into the quarry with the one who had given him his death-draught a few days ago.

With trembling fingers she opened her locket. Her father leaned over her shoulder and looked with her. The miniature was gone . . . the glass, too.

'So it *is* the one that belongs to you, girl,' said Tom, in a slow, puzzled voice.

'Exactly,' said Sidney Pollock behind them.

'Now what I want to know is, how did it get in the quarry, unless Miss Grayle was there—*and what was she doing there?*'

Marion did not answer. Her tongue was dry . . . her throat was hot. She dared not look at anybody, although she felt that she was the cynosure of all eyes. Then Sir Dion Courtland rose to his feet.

'Look here, Pollock,' he said curtly, 'I am extremely sorry for you and your aunt's trouble, but I see no reason why you should come here and interrupt this wedding-breakfast in such a fashion. Also, I'll thank you to remember that Miss Grayle is now my wife—Lady Courtland.'

Marion gasped with relief. It was glorious to be defended by Dion. Mutely she gave him her hand and he took it, pressed it warmly in his own. Sidney Pollock looked at Marion with the same smouldering suspicion in his eyes.

'Begging Lady Courtland's pardon,' said he, with slight sarcasm, 'I still want to know why that photo, if it belongs to her, should ha' been found in Hunter's Hill Quarry, where Mr. Saddleman was found half-dead and—'

'That will do, Pollock,' interrupted Dion. 'If you wish to cross-question us and to investigate matters, do so at a more suitable time. Your aunt's trial will be coming up very shortly, and you will have every opportunity of saying what you wish in Court. At the same time, I warn you to be careful what you do say.

There is such a thing as *libel*.'

Young Pollock flushed crimson, and muttered something under his breath. It was not that he disliked Sir Dion. He rather liked the look of the handsome young baronet—and was sorry for him. In his heart, Sidney Pollock shared his aunt's belief that Marion was responsible for all the frightful trouble . . . and he pitied the man who had married her this morning. At the same time he burned with eagerness to cross-question Marion about her mother's miniature, and was angry because Dion thwarted him.

'I agree with you, my boy,' Tom Grayle said to his newly-made son-in-law. 'This is no time for inquiries. And the finding of my girl's miniature has got nothing to do with Jet Saddleman. As if Moorcoombe folk don't often go up to Hunter's Hill Quarry for walks!'

'Of course!' said Marion's friend, Hilda Jessop, who had been listening to the little drama in horrified silence.

'Of course!' echoed Charlie Hodges.

And now the tension was broken and a buzz of conversation broke out round the table. Sidney Pollock was regarded with resentment, and his nasty insinuations angrily stamped upon. All these people were the Grayle's good friends.

Marion, herself again, laughed lightly about the matter.

'The poor young man is half off his head

with worry and grief,' she said in her sweet, sympathetic voice. 'I can't blame him for saying terrible things. You see . . .' she gave a tremulous sigh, and a slight shiver . . . 'I was the one to give that fatal drink to *poor* Jet and—'

'Don't talk of it,' interrupted Dion. 'I won't have you upset about this thing on our wedding-day, Marion dearest.'

She wiped away an imaginary tear and pressed his hand. Her pulses were leaping and her heart beating more normally. Sidney Pollock had marched out of the room. The terrible moment had passed. Dion had defended her magnificently. She was still cold and nervous, because Pollock had insisted on taking the dirt-stained miniature away with him, and she knew that he would bring it up as evidence in the trial . . . against *her*. But she tried to forget it . . . to forget everything except that this was her wedding-breakfast and that she was Dion's bride.

She behaved so naturally and sweetly that she put everybody at their ease, and none of the Moorcoombe folk thought of allowing young Pollock's hideous insinuations to disturb them.

Three people at the table failed to regain composure, however. They were Dion, his mother, and Patricia Westby . . . the three clever, well-educated brains of that party.

Lady Courtland and Pat exchanged looks

which were eloquent. They shared the same feeling of dismay. If only Dion had not insisted upon marrying this girl . . . it was so dreadful to think that she would be brought into the trial . . . that, as Lady Courtland, she would be the chief witness . . . have crazy youths like Sidney Pollock accusing her of having had a finger in the pie. Was Marion as innocent as she appeared?

Dion's thoughts were more mixed. He sat beside his bride, smoking hard at his cigarette and trying *not* to think. He did not want to. He wanted only to be happy, because Marion belonged to him now, and soon he would be taking her away for their honeymoon. He gave her a quick look, and the passion in him burned for her beauty . . . she was laughing now, her great dark eyes full of light and sparkle . . . her cheeks hot and pink . . . her red-gold hair a nimbus of glory about her beautiful, vivid face. He was ashamed of one suspicious thought concerning her. Yet he was not a blind fool, and he could not help remembering that Marion had gone to see Jet Saddleman on that day when he had been found in the quarry; that she had been in the thick of a quarrel with him, trying to secure her love-letters. Then she had been at his bedside when he had died and . . .

But he snapped off the thread of his own dreaded reflection with a shudder. He dared think no more. Such thoughts were

167

hideous and disloyal. He loved Marion. She was his wife . . . the victim of unfortunate circumstances not in any way her fault.

He seized a glass of champagne and drank it down thirstily. He plunged into conversation with various people at the table. Finally toasts were drunk . . . speeches made . . . congratulations were poured upon the bride and bridegroom. Dion responded. Marion sat beside him, the picture of innocent, shy beauty . . . and thus ended that wedding-breakfast at the Travellers' Rest.

The relief to Marion when she drove away from Moorcoombe in the new two-seater Sunbeam touring-car which her husband had bought for her was overwhelming. She waved a hand to the good-natured crowd who flung rice and confetti after them, then snuggled down under the rug beside her husband, and pulled the rich soft collar of her squirrel coat well over her ears.

'Thank God that's over, Dion,' she said.

'Thank God,' he echoed grimly. 'I loathe crowds. And that fellow interrupting our party spoilt everything.'

Marion's beautiful eyes narrowed.

'Oh, I'm not worrying about him,' she said.

'But I am. I wish he hadn't found that miniature in the quarry,' said Dion, gloomily, as he steered the car round a sharp bend in the road, out of sight of Marion's old home. 'He'll make trouble at the trial, you know, darling.'

She bit her lips hard.

'Pooh—I'm not afraid,' she said with bravado. 'Now, please, dearest, don't let's spoil this hour by worrying about anything.'

'No, we won't,' he said, only too glad to be lifted from his own mood of depression and worry.

The car ran swiftly and quietly on its great tyres, over the winding, hilly roads across Dartmoor. As they passed the little wood fringing the Suicide's Pool, Marion pressed both her hands convulsively to her breast and stared straight ahead of her, a kind of sick horror in her eyes. If only she could wipe out the past . . . wipe out the terrible crimes she had committed in order to win this man who sat at her side. But nothing could wipe them out, and nothing could silence the voice of Conscience. Dion's thoughts instinctively turned to Hope Marshall as they drove past that gloomy spot. It was commonly believed, now, that she had been drowned in the pool before she had been buried in Linton Wood. Poor little Hope! Once he had contemplated marriage with her. What terrible fate had befallen her? He felt almost callous that he should be setting forth on his honeymoon with Marion so soon after Hope's frightful death!

Not until they were well out of Devonshire did the bridal pair cease to be tormented by their own gloomy thoughts . . . his, puzzled and frightening . . . hers, guilty—remorseful . . .

The November day was short, and they did not get much further than Bath before dusk. Dion had suggested they should spend one night in the historic old city, then go on the next day to London, cross over to Paris for a few days . . . Paris, the city of Marion's dreams and ambitions. So long as Marion was back in time for Sarah's trial, it did not matter much where they went. Dion had consulted his solicitor on that point, for at first he had imagined it impossible for them to leave England.

To a great extent, Dion and Marion found forgetfulness and the happiness they craved in each other that wedding-night. They were passionately in love, and for once Dion welcomed the unrestrained, almost tempestuous love that Marion gave him . . . taking it as a narcotic . . . to make him forget other things. She surrendered to his arms, his kisses, feeling everything worth while in the rapture and triumph of this hour.

When they were alone in the bedroom of their suite at the Grand Pump Hotel, late that night, Marion sat before her dressing-table, brushing her glorious hair and revelling in the luxury of it all. It was delicious to be Lady Courtland . . . to be rich . . . to have a husband like Dion, charming, handsome . . . a man at whom other women looked enviously. The bedroom was full of flowers—flowers he had ordered for her. And although the November night outside was sharp and cold, in this room it was hot and perfumed like a bower.

Dion stood by his wife and looked down at her . . . thrilled by her extreme beauty. She wore a white velvet wrapper with a huge collar of white fox fur, and under it a filmy nightgown of white georgette—both presents from Lady Courtland. In this moment she looked exquisitely young and pure, and it was impossible to believe that sin had ever laid a finger on her.

He suddenly put his arms about her, drew her to her feet and held her close.

'Marion,' he said huskily. 'Marion . . . my own . . . at last . . .'

She shut her eyes and surrendered to his lips, her arms curving about his neck.

'Oh, Dion,' she said, 'Dion . . . promise you will love me like this forever . . .'

He promised . . . poor fool . . . intoxicated by her loveliness . . . thrilled because she was his bride . . . his very own. How little he guessed at the ghastly secrets locked in her heart . . . the ghastly doom that hung over her lovely head!

CHAPTER SIXTEEN

The honeymoon of Sir Dion and Lady Courtland was by no means a success. It did not last long because the trial of Sarah Pollock for the murder of Jet Saddleman came off at the Exeter Assizes rather sooner than expected, and Marion was forced to return to Devonshire.

She had loved Paris, and Dion had been generous—given her everything within reason which she asked. But as the days had sped by, the atmosphere between these two had become strained. Dion could not totally annihilate the reasoning of his keen brain, and nasty, suspicious little thoughts gnawed at him incessantly. Passion is swiftly sated, and before Marion had been his wife for a week, he found it difficult to find absolute oblivion in her kisses and the possession of her. She was so closely connected with Saddleman's death . . . it was impossible to separate her from it. Her manner with regard to the affair, puzzled him, too. She was either callous and indifferent; or like a shivering, hysterical child. To the man who had married her, she never appeared to be normal. She was a creature of extremes. Sometimes she would burst into laughter when she spoke of young Pollock's discovery of her mother's miniature . . . sometimes she would cling wildly to Dion, and beseech him to take her out of the country before the trial because 'her heart wouldn't stand the strain of it.' Of course, he could not do that. She had to go through with it. And the next instant she would recover herself and laugh again . . . strive to distract him from the subject by all her woman's wiles.

Her caresses and the tempestuous passion she bore him commenced to lose their hold, and she knew it . . . secretly went in terror of losing his love altogether and making him suspicious of her.

She had thought that once she was his wife, it would be so easy to forget the shadows of crime that hung over her; that she would be happy and carefree again. But she soon discovered her mistake. Remorse continually tore at her . . . wrecked her nerves and her joy in her new position as a wealthy, titled woman. Coupled with remorse was the terror of being found out . . . of old Emm's dark prophecies coming true.

She strove wildly and in vain to take command of herself. But as the time drew nearer to the day when she must return to Devon and attend Sarah Pollock's trial, fear and shame gripped a tighter hold and made her more nervy and unhappy.

The last night they spent in Paris was the unhappiest of all for them both. They had been to a revue, then on to a cabaret, returning to their hotel in the small hours of the morning. Dion looked haggard and strained. He was sick of Paris and sick of Marion's feverish search for gaiety. He could not help remembering Pat's cool restful personality. He would like to have gone with her on to some sunlit, wind-swept golf links and played a peaceful, healthy game.

He stared at his wife, who was lying in bed, smoking a cigarette, her beautiful white arms behind her head. She looked a wreck . . . tired, nervy, white . . . violet circles under her eyes, and lips too brightly painted with vermilion lipstick. She was lovely enough, but in some extraordinary way her beauty had begun to repel him; to make him feel that she was a siren—luring him to ruin. He tried to laugh at that, to tell himself that he was an idiot and that there was nothing wrong with Marion. But deep in his heart of hearts lay the one thought he dared not voice or confess even to himself . . . that he bitterly regretted his marriage.

Marion held out her arms.

'Dion darling,' she murmured. 'You love me still, don't you?'

He forced himself to smile and say 'yes.' But even while she lay in his arms, his kisses warm on her lips and her hair, she felt a difference . . . a Something between them. The burden of guilt lay heavy on Marion's soul that night.

She had a terrible dream . . . a nightmare . . . in which evil spirits pursued her . . . amongst them the terrible face and form of Jet Saddleman . . . the pale, drowned corpse of Hope Marshall. She woke in a cold sweat, shrieking in terror.

'Keep away from me . . . keep away . . . oh, God . . . forgive . . .'

Dion, wakened from his sleep by her screams, started up and switched on the light. She sat bolt upright, her face distorted with fear, the perspiration pouring down her cheeks, her eyes rolling . . .

'Good God, Marion—what is it?' he gasped.

She fell into his arms, sobbing, panting, refusing to be comforted.

'It was only a bad dream,' he told her.

She could not speak, but she was frozen with the terror of her imagination and her thoughts. He was tender and protective, but even while he stroked her head, his own thoughts chilled and frightened him. What was there in this girl's mind that she should be so terror-stricken, so wild and unnatural? Why had she screamed 'Keep away from me . . . God, forgive me . . . !' Forgive her—what?

She slept at last, worn out and sick with sobbing. But Dion Courtland did not sleep again. He paced up and down the bedroom, smoking, hour after hour, trying desperately *not to think.*

The day of Sarah Pollock's trial arrived.

The court at Exeter was packed out; indescribably hot and stuffy, in spite of the cold weather outside. Old Lady Courtland, now at Torquay, did not attend the trial. It was altogether too unpleasant for her, and she shrank from even hearing the name of Courtland connected with the murder. But Patricia Westby was there. Somehow Pat had

175

been drawn to that Court against her will. And by some strange coincidence she sat next to a little grey-haired woman in deep mourning . . . Hope Marshall's broken-hearted mother.

At the beginning of the trial, Mrs. Marshall spoke to Pat about some odd incident in Court, and thus introduced herself.

'I had to come,' she said in a low voice. 'It seems so terrible . . . a second murder in the Moorcoombe district, so soon after the murder of my darling child. I feel positive the same criminal is responsible for both.'

Pat regarded her with pity.

'It must be dreadful for you,' she whispered.

'Do you know Marion Grayle . . . now Lady Courtland?'

'Yes,' said Pat, flushing slightly. 'She married a—a great friend of mine.'

Mrs. Marshall raised her lorgnettes and looked through them at Marion, who sat wrapped in her silver squirrel coat, beside her husband, waiting to be called as witness for the prosecution.

'It is strange how that girl has been connected with both the Moorcoombe crimes,' said Mrs. Marshall. 'At least, I mean she knew my poor Hope . . . Hope was with Dion Courtland when they had the accident outside the Travellers' Rest. And she seems even more mixed up in the Saddleman affair.'

Pat Westby nodded but made no response. But her heart was strangely heavy when she looked at Dion. How pale, how quiet he had grown since his marriage! Both she and his mother noticed the alteration in him. He was not the boyish, happy Dion who had driven away with his bride. He was a haggard, worried man. What had happened? Was he unhappy? Had he already found out his mistake?

Pat had never loved any man in her life. But lately she had come nearer to loving Dion Courtland than was good for her peace of mind. Since his marriage to Marion, she had striven to put him out of her thoughts. But she had found it difficult, and as she looked at him in the Court today, she found herself wishing that she could spare him the sorrow, the gloom which were already shadowing his life.

Sarah Ann Pollock, the accused woman, and one-time housekeeper at Double-Styles Farm was not long standing in the dock. She said the words 'Not Guilty' in rather a faint, quavering voice, then sat down again. It was obvious to all those who had known her that her sojourn in gaol had changed her from a domineering, capable woman into a pathetic, broken creature. Everyone's hand seemed against her. She had nobody but her nephew, Sidney, to stand by her, and Sidney had done his best. But she was too old to stand the strain and horror of being wrongfully accused of murdering her beloved master, and she seemed nervous and feeble, which demeanour unfortunately went against her.

When the name 'Lady Courtland' was called in Court, necks were craned to get a view of the girl who had been Miss Grayle of Moorcoombe, and pressmen and artists got busy once she was in the witness-box.

She looked her loveliest in her rich fur coat; a big bunch of violets pinned on her shoulder; a smart little black satin hat, with a paradise plume (one of her Paris purchases) on her red-gold head. She turned a face of exquisite innocence on the defending counsel who cross-examined her, and answered every question in a firm, clear voice. She roused the admiration and interest of the entire Court.

Dion sat with folded arms, listening to every word; his gaze fixed on his young wife. But his expression was gloomy and harassed, and now and then he stirred uneasily and brushed his forehead with a silk handkerchief, as though he found it hot and breathless in Court.

Marion rose to the occasion grandly. A few hours before the commencement of the trial, she had been agonised, terrified, almost ready to fling herself at Dion's feet and confess . . . beg him to save her. But that had passed. She played to the gallery now . . . fighting for very life . . . without an ounce of pity for the poor old woman who stood a very good chance of being condemned to death for the crime which she, Marion, had callously planned and committed.

On her oath, she lied coldly and with

cunning, to suit her own ends. She described, when asked, how she had unwittingly given the deceased man his death-draught . . . and here she put a charming quiver into her voice, and held a little lace-edged handkerchief to her eyes.

'It was so dreadful,' she said. 'He was thirsty . . . asked for that drink . . . and I gave it . . . I gave it . . .'

A murmur of sympathy buzzed round the Court. Only Sidney Pollock stared at her, unmoved, sullen, suspicious . . . and Mrs. Pollock, herself, watched Marion with a kind of wondering horror, mumbling to herself between the wardress and policeman who were with her in the dock.

'Who poured out that glass of burgundy?' asked the counsel for the defence.

'Mrs. Pollock,' said Marion, at once. 'I called her and asked her to give Mr. Saddleman a drink. She went behind that screen in the bedroom and poured it out.'

'That's a lie!' Sarah's quavering voice broke the silence in the Court.

She was promptly silenced by the Judge, and the cross-examination of Marion continued. Mrs. Pollock sank back in her chair, with a hopeless, bewildered expression on her face.

Marion described the death of Jet Saddleman; then, with a glance at Sarah, she shook her beautiful head and added that so

179

many times she had heard Mrs. Pollock wish for the death of her master so that she could get his property.

'It isn't true!' said Sidney Pollock in a loud, fierce voice. 'Aunt Sarah never . . .'

'Silence!' said two voices from the back of the Court.

'If there are any more interruptions, I shall clear the Court,' said the Judge, sternly. 'Now, Lady Courtland, please continue.'

Marion continued. Pat Westby listened with a growing feeling of horror. Her psychic instinct never led her astray, and she had the most acute feeling that every word Dion's wife uttered was a lie.

When Lady Courtland was allowed to leave the box, she did so gracefully, her beautiful eyes flashing a proud, rather defiant look round the Court. Sidney Ernest Pollock was then called as a witness for the defence.

The young motor-engineer made a brave attempt to help his old aunt. He had known her all his life, he said; she had always professed love and respect for Mr. Saddleman. He was positive she neither wanted his money, nor knew, for a certainty, that she would inherit it. He believed that somebody did exist who had wanted Mr. Saddleman's death, and that same person, had, no doubt, pushed Mr. Saddleman into Hunter's Hill Quarry.

Young Pollock pointed an accusing finger at Marion, who flinched but smiled disdainfully

180

at him.

'Lady Courtland, then Miss Grayle, visited Mr. Saddleman on both occasions; he stated. 'On the day when he was found in the quarry and on the day he died. And I found a photo belonging to her—one that had fallen out of her locket—at the quarry . . .'

The counsel for the prosecution rose.

'My Lord—I protest—this is not in order—'

Sidney Pollock was informed that he was in the witness-box to speak in defence of his aunt, not in accusation of Lady Courtland. He was asked what motive he imagined Lady Courtland could possibly have had for the murder. She was about to marry Sir Dion . . . she had nothing to gain . . . only a lunatic would commit a murder for the sake of murdering.

The jury smiled. The Court yawned. Obviously, Lady Courtland had no motive for murder. Sidney Pollock was wasting time. Sarah Pollock had strong motives. She wanted Mr. Saddleman's money—and her freedom. The empty packet marked 'Weedkiller' had been found in her drawer, etc., etc.

The Counsel for the Crown continued on these lines. Then finally, Mr. Walter Collins, K.C., Counsel for the prisoner, Sarah Pollock, made his closing speech. Pointing out the long years of faithful service which Mrs. Pollock had given Mr. Saddleman, and the insufficient evidence against her.

The Judge solemnly charged the Jury, and the Jury retired.

As the Court emptied, Marion edged closer to her husband. He looked down at her and saw that she was very white now; no longer 'playing to the gallery'—her slender fingers were tearing her handkerchief to bits.

'Why are you so nervy, Marion?' he asked, almost irritably. 'You have nothing to be afraid of, surely!'

'Naturally not!' she said. 'But it is all—so frightful!'

Dion glanced at the unfortunate woman in the dock. Poor old Sarah was bowed, her head on her hands, as though she could not bear the weight of her thoughts.

'It would be frightful if Mrs. Pollock were being wrongfully accused,' he said.

'Of course she is guilty,' said Marion, in a sharp tone.

The Jury returned.

The Clerk of the Court asked the members of the Jury if they had agreed upon their verdict. The foreman stated that they had, and that they found the prisoner, Sarah Pollock, guilty.

Marion gave a deep sigh of almost agonised relief. It was smothered by a piercing scream from Sarah.

'It isn't true . . . I'm not guilty . . . I'm not!'

The Judge put on his black cap, and solemnly passed sentence of death upon Sarah

Ann Pollock. Marion stared at him as he spoke the dreadful words, and as she stared, everything swam before her . . . she put a hand up to her throat as though she were being stifled . . . as though she, not Sarah, felt the grim noose already about her neck. She gave a gasping moan, and fell suddenly across her husband in a dead faint.

CHAPTER SEVENTEEN

Dion put both arms around his wife, and clicked his tongue in a worried way as he saw what had happened. His young wife's face was ghastly—marble-pale. Quite obviously she was very ill. Her forehead was wet, and her lips had a queer, bluish tinge.

'She has had another heart-attack,' was his surmisal. And there followed more tender thoughts of Marion. Poor little woman—she was not strong—not nearly as strong as she looked. This was the second time she had been ill lately. She had gone through a terrible ordeal. Once, Jet Saddleman had been a friend of hers; even a lover. To have had to come here to a Court of Justice, and give direct evidence against the woman who had murdered Jet, was a dreadful thing for any delicate, sensitive woman. And Dion knew so well that Marion was more than ordinarily sensitive—she was highly-strung, neurotic. The trial and the frightful sentence of death just passed upon Sarah Pollock, had been too much for her.

Instinctively, Dion's eyes turned toward Patricia Westby. She was just the sensible sort of girl to help him. Pat's grey eyes met and answered his. She saw the drooping body in his arms, and guessed that Marion had fainted. She whispered a hurried good-bye to Hope Marshall's mother, who had been discussing the verdict against Sarah, and hurried to Dion's aid.

By this time a man sitting near Dion had also seen Marion's collapse, and was assisting him to get his wife out of the Court. Once outside the stuffy, crowded room, it was simple enough to send a policeman for Sir Dion Courtland's limousine, and put Marion into it.

During the drive through the crowded Exeter streets to the hotel wherein Dion and his wife had taken rooms for the period of the trial, Marion lay in her husband's arms inert and unconscious. She was in a very heavy swoon. With her brilliant eyes shut, she looked colourless—piteous enough to rouse even Pat's pity.

'Poor Marion has had a lot to bear,' Pat murmured, as she put out a compassionate hand and stroked the damp red-gold curls back from the other girl's forehead. 'It has been too much for her, Dion.'

'Yes,' said Dion, listlessly. 'Too much for us all. A beastly business, Pat. Thank God the trial was so short and over so quickly. Do you think Marion is very bad? Oughtn't she to have recovered consciousness by now?'

Pat had been a V.A.D. nurse all through the War; had done some excellent work at one of the Base Hospitals, and she was thoroughly capable and proficient. She bent over Marion and examined her gravely, her third finger on the pulse that beat faintly and irregularly in Marion's delicate wrist.

'H'm—she is rather bad, Dion,' she said. 'I don't know that it's a heart-attack. In fact, I don't think it is. To me it is more like a severe fainting-fit brought on by overstrain. She may be ill for days after this. As soon as you get back to the hotel, take her upstairs and I'll get her into bed while you 'phone for a doctor.'

Dion looked at her gratefully.

'What a dear you are, Pat,' he said. 'Marion has a splendid friend in you.'

Pat suddenly flushed scarlet all over her nice, sun-browned face, and she turned her head quickly away lest Dion should see the sudden hunger in her eyes. A 'splendid friend' . . . was she that? To Dion, yes. She knew, to her bitter cost, that she loved him . . . would have gladly lain down her life to spare him pain. She had seen how he had cared for Marion, and had realized that it would be heaven itself to be loved by Dion. But such thoughts must not come into her head. She must keep them locked away. Dion belonged to Marion, and she would try, for his sake, to be a friend to his wife. But how could she avoid the unpleasant feeling that always gripped her when she saw or spoke to Marion? . . . how could she get rid of that awful, psychic sensation that Marion was not as innocent, as pure, as guileless as she appeared to be?

'I shall always be glad to do anything I can for you or Marion,' she said, in a low voice, without looking at the man she loved.

He looked down at Marion, and sighed heavily. Even as he sighed he felt guilty of disloyalty to the woman in his arms. For he knew he had made a terrible mistake in marrying Marion Grayle . . . in connecting his name . . . his mother's name of which they had always been so proud . . . with the murder trial which had just ended. Pat Westby, at his side, cool, capable, charming and sympathetic, was the sort of woman he should have made his wife. Marion roused passion in him; could still stir him to some semblance of passionate love when she lay in his arms, intoxicating his senses with her perfumed kisses, her wonderful allure. But Pat was his friend . . . his consoler. He felt an incredible desire at this moment to lay his head against Pat's shoulder and cry . . .

But instead he said:

'Thanks, my dear . . . what would we do

186

without you? Mother said you have been her greatest comfort since the pater died, and now you are mine . . . ours . . .'

He added the last word out of loyalty to Marion. But Pat—through many weary and difficult days to come—remembered the first spontaneous thing that he had said. She was *his* comfort. Ah, that helped! To know that she helped him would console her for the pain she had endured since the hour she had opened her heart and taken him wholly into it.

Later, in the big bedroom of the hotel from which one could glimpse Exeter cathedral, and which was Marion's room, Pat undressed Marion with the assistance of a chambermaid.

Then she sat on the edge of the bed, while Dion paced up and down the room, waiting for the doctor. She bathed the insensible girl's forehead with water and *eau-de-cologne*. Brandy, poured with a spoon between the dry, bluish lips, had brought a gasping moan from Marion, and no more. She remained unconscious.

'I'm afraid she's seriously ill, Pat,' Dion remarked, pausing in his restless walk and standing at the foot of the bed. 'I hope to God she's all right.'

'I hope so, Dion,' said Pat, quietly.

'She's been through a ghastly time, poor girl!' she added.

'Yes,' agreed Dion. 'When she's well again, I must take her away . . . right away from

England, I mean. I think I'll try and persuade her to come to Egypt.'

Pat winced, but she smiled her frank, brave smile at the man she loved, and nodded.

'Yes, that's a good idea. Now the Pollock trial is over, there will be no need for you to remain in England.'

Dion sat on the other side of Marion's bed and took one of her slender hands. It had grown white since her marriage. She had blanched much of the sun-tan with Parisian cream. It was a beautiful hand, with it tapering fingers and rosy filbert nails. Who would have dreamed that that lovely hand had pushed Hope Marshall into the Suicide's Pool . . . had callously poured the poison into Saddleman's burgundy! It looked as though it were made to hold a bunch of flowers . . . or to be kissed.

Dion did kiss that hand, now . . . his heart smote him as he felt its softness, and looked at her, lying there on the big square pillows. Her face seemed shrunken and dreadfully white . . . and the thick lashes were so very long and beautiful and appealing, curving on her cheeks.

'Poor little nervy thing,' he thought. 'This rotten business has done her in, and I ought not to feel annoyed or impatient with her. She worships me. I must make up to her for my irritability when she is better.'

He felt that perhaps he had been irritable; lacking in understanding of her; that he had
188

had no right to feel suspicious; to attach any sinister meaning to her fits of depression. Was it not natural that she should have been sunk in gloom?

By the time the doctor arrived, Dion had worked himself into a state of love and real anxiety for Marion. Pat Westby stood quietly by, waiting to offer her services.

The doctor, a pleasant, intelligent young physician who had recently bought a practice in Exeter, informed Dion that Marion was suffering from a severe nervous breakdown, and ordered her complete rest and careful nursing.

'She ought to have both a day and night nurse, this week,' he informed Dion. 'Lady Courtland is really very ill. When she recovers consciousness, she will probably be extremely weak. We may expect delirium and a high temperature tonight.'

Dion's handsome eyes were deeply troubled now. He forgot all that had recently transpired to make him regret his marriage; remembered only his first wild love for Marion, and what it would mean to him to lose her. Whatever she had done, she loved him . . . it would be terrible to lose her . . . never again to feel the splendid, vital beauty of her in his arms, to feel her thrilling to his kisses . . . to hear her say, 'Dion, Dion . . . I love you!'

'Look here, Dr. Greenway,' he said. 'Money is no object. For God's sake send in two of the

189

best nurses procurable.'

'Gladly,' said Dr. Greenway, nodding, scribbling something on his memorandum pad. 'But the trouble is, Sir Dion, there is a bad 'flu epidemic in Exeter, as perhaps you have heard, and nurses are at a premium. I spent a hair-raising day yesterday trying to get a nurse for an important fever case, and could not find one Lady Courtland ought to go into a nursing-home when she is strong enough to be moved. But I don't advocate a move for a few nights at least, while she is in this sinking condition.'

Dion's face grew white.

'Sinking! Is it as bad as that?'

'I don't want to harass you unnecessarily,' said Dr. Greenway quietly, 'but I think Lady Courtland is seriously ill. It's her head more than her heart that is worrying me. From what you have told me, I think she is in for the thing that novelists love to call "brain-fever". At any rate, I can get you one good nurse . . . Nurse Jennings, who could take day-duty first thing after lunch, but I know of no other for night-duty.'

'Can't you get one from London?' demanded Dion.

'There is more chance of that, although there is a serious outbreak of 'flu everywhere just now,' said Greenway. 'We doctors are off our heads with this difficulty of finding nurses during the epidemic.'

Pat Westby suddenly moved forward. She had been standing by Marion's bed, listening to the low-toned discussion between the men. She looked from Dion to the doctor.

'What about me?' she said. 'I've had a pretty good training as a V.A.D. Couldn't I look after Lady Courtland tonight—anyhow till you get a nurse?'

'My dear,' said Dion, with that look of gratitude that never failed to thrill her. 'It is wonderfully kind of you, but why should you—?'

'I'd like to if it will help,' she broke in swiftly.

Dr. Greenway spoke a few words to her, then satisfied himself that Miss Westby was as good a nurse as many with a hospital training. It was agreed between the three of them that Pat should take duty tonight.

'Are you staying in the hotel?' Dr. Greenway asked her.

'No. I only came in from Torquay for the Pollock trial,' replied Pat. 'But I will 'phone at once for my suitcase to be packed and put on the next train, and I will get Sir Dion's chauffeur to meet it.'

'Pat, how awfully decent of you,' said Dion, boyishly. 'What can I say to . . .'

'Nothing,' she broke in again, her cheeks pink.

Dr. Harold Greenway, meanwhile, stood by the bed of his new patient, looked down at the

191

lovely face with its frame of red-gold hair, and thought, like so many men, that it was the face of an angel. How beautiful she was! How fortunate for him to have secured this case! He had read all about young Lady Courtland in connection with the Pollock murder trial, but had never dreamed he would attend her.

Later that same day, Marion recovered her senses. After her prolonged faint, she was heavy, drugged; and her whole body burned and throbbed with fever. But she was sufficiently awake to see her husband's face bending over her, and in the background, the face of a strange nurse in white cap and gown.

'Oh . . .' she moaned piteously. 'Oh . . . what has happened . . . oh, God . . . my head . . .'

'Hush, darling,' said Dion's voice. 'Lie still. Nurse Jennings is looking after you now, and later, kind Pat is going to sit with you . . .'

The name 'Pat' penetrated the mists in Marion's brain. She shuddered and closed her eyes.

'No,' she said in a frightened voice. 'No . . . Dion, Dion, take her away . . . I'm afraid of her!'

He thought she was raving—took no notice of her words. But Marion, ill though she was, had realized the danger of her delirium and of what she might say . . . when Patricia Westby was with her . . . and it terrified her.

She threw out an arm to Dion, who took it.

She felt him kiss her wrist, and moaned again.

'Dion . . . Dion . . .'

Then a wave of darkness submerged her. She felt as though her head were on fire . . . that she was sinking to abysmal depths . . . sinking. She struggled vainly against it and then lost consciousness again. Her last clear thought was of pure fear . . . an agony of fear that she was dying. For she knew how unfit she was to die . . . she knew that Sarah Ann Pollock sat now in the condemned cell; an innocent creature awaiting a cruel, dishonourable death which she did not deserve. She was afraid . . . afraid of the Trial and Punishment which would await her before a higher Tribunal than the one that had judged Sarah . . .

She was very ill for hours after that . . . delirious, raving at intervals . . . weak and motionless in between the fits of delirium.

At half-past nine, Pat, who had attempted to get a little rest during the afternoon, came on duty. She looked tired, but she was cool and self-confident, and Nurse Jennings had no qualms about turning the patient over to her for the night.

Dion wanted to stay up with Pat, but this Pat refused to allow, much as she longed to keep him beside her.

'You are fagged out as it is, Dion,' she said. 'Please go to bed . . . I'll call you immediately if you are wanted. But Dr. Greenway and Nurse

Jennings both agree that Marion is better, quieter with no one in the room. She seems to sense it when somebody is with her . . . it makes her more restless. She needs extreme quiet.'

That was what Pat said. But Pat, when she was alone with Marion, thought other things . . . queer, difficult things that were the outcome of that dreaded sixth sense which Pat possessed. She did not want Dion in the room *for his own sake.* She dreaded what he might hear Marion say while she lay there, insensible, uncontrolled, raving . . .

Pat loved Dion very truly and sincerely. She wanted to spare him unnecessary suffering and regret. What she had to fear from Marion, she knew not . . . but her ravings would be safe with her, Pat. She did know that!

Marion lay quiet until the early hours of the morning. At two o'clock, Pat, in a loose, warm dressing-gown, sat by her, taking her pulse. Marion stirred and moaned. Her heavy eyelids opened and she looked straight up into Pat's face. What she thought she saw, Pat could not guess, but she cowered back on the pillow in a terrified way, and whispered a name:

'Hope . . . Hope Marshall . . . no, my God . . . don't come near me . . . Hope Marshall . . . go away . . . don't torture me . . .'

'Hush, Marion,' said Pat, taking her hand. 'It is Pat Westby with you.'

Marion wrenched her fingers away, strong

194

for the moment in an extremity of fear.

'Go away . . . oh, God, I'm afraid of you . . . your staring eyes . . . Hope Marshall . . .'

'She has got that unfortunate, murdered girl on her mind,' thought Pat, shuddering.

Dark, terrible thoughts seemed to chase through Marion's demented brain . . . grim, sinister shadows chased and clouded her. She began to shriek . . . this time another name . . .

'Jet, you loved me . . . forgive . . . Jet, you, too . . . torturing me . . . ah, God . . .' this in a tone that froze Pat's marrow . . . *'don't drink that burgundy* . . . it has arsenic in it . . . ah, God! The Dark Death . . . Emm was right . . . the gallows . . . stop . . . stop . . . *don't . . .'*

She had both fingers up to her throat now; her great dark eyes were frenzied, her teeth chattering, her whole body shaking with terror.

Pat Westby sat staring at her in horror. Marion was livid and terrible to behold. And her raving . . . what did it signify? Pat did not know . . . dared not think, but she thanked God that Marion's unsuspecting husband was not in the room. It was obvious that Marion knew *something* and was afraid of the dark and secret knowledge.

Pat was too fine and noble a character to have any wish to delve into the secrets of a delirious sick woman. She had but one wish . . . to stop that dreadful raving . . . stop it . . . and for half-an-hour she fought with Marion, until finally the girl lay spent and still, eyes shut, the terrors chased from her mind; her body drenched with perspiration . . . but her temperature down to normal, at last.

It was the worst night of Pat's life, and when morning came, bringing Dr. Greenway and the verdict that Lady Courtland was better and out of danger, she fell on her knees and wept, in the privacy of her own room. But she did not cry with relief because Marion was saved . . . it was a more passionate and intense prayer that Dion might never lose his faith in Marion; that he might not suffer as she believed he would one day suffer—through his wife.

CHAPTER EIGHTEEN

Two weeks later, Sir Dion and Lady Courtland were back in Torquay in the beautiful furnished flat which Dion had taken on the sea-front for his wife's convalescence. He had made plans for travelling with her to Egypt before Christmas. When he had made the suggestion at first, she had responded to it apathetically, and he had not pressed it. She seemed to have no life . . . none of her magnificent vitality left. She had risen from her bed of illness a nervous wreck . . . a thin, pale, pathetic creature with great, haunted eyes and colourless cheeks. She looked even more beautiful than she had looked before—

etherealised by the new delicacy and slenderness. But Dion had loved her vivid tints, and sighed that only the golden-red glory of her hair and the brilliant brown of her eyes were left.

'You must get the roses back, my Beautiful,' he said to her one day, in their flat at Torquay. She was lying on a couch at right-angles to a big, blazing fire, and he was beside her, smoking, trying to rouse her from her apathy.

She smiled at him. She had nothing left in life but her passionate worship of her husband. Everything else bored her . . . she was indifferent to riches, pretty clothes, all the expensive flowers, fruits, jewels and furs which he lavished on her. She had but one desire . . . to keep him and his love. The fear that he would find her out tore at her, night and day . . . tore at her nerves. She had seen specialists from London . . . they had advised and prescribed . . . but who can 'minister to a mind diseased?' Like Lady Macbeth, Marion suffered from a guilty conscience. Once she turned, grimly, to that mighty play of Shakespeare's, and quoted certain lines to herself:

'Here's the smell of the blood still—
All the perfumes of Arabia will not sweeten
This little hand . . .'

How true that was. Her hands were blood-

197

stained . . . her mind tortured by frightful memories of guilt. They were shadows perpetually separating her from the man for whom she had sinned so unpardonably.

She was unreasonably jealous of Pat Westby. The girl had nursed her . . . was kind and even sympathetic . . . yet behind it all, Marion sensed the fact that Pat mistrusted her. And when she had asked Pat what she had said in her delirium, Pat had unconsciously blushed— a burning red—although her answer had been noncommittal. But Marion hated to be in the same room with her nowadays. It was a sore point with Dion.

'Pat was so ripping to you while you were ill . . . why not ask her to this flat more often?' he continually reproached her. She would throw her arms about his neck and say:

'I want only you—only you, my Dion . . .'

He tried to be satisfied with that and to feel as she felt. But in spite of his efforts to be content and to find the old, delirious happiness with Marion, he was worried and at times, gloomy. He could not understand the nerve-wracked unhappy creature she had become, compassionate though he felt for her.

When she was well enough, he asked her if she wished to know what had become of Sarah Pollock. She had shuddered violently and turned her head from him. Then he told her that the wretched housekeeper had been spared capital punishment because she had gone quite mad in the cells. Her sentence had been commuted to incarceration for life in a criminal lunatic asylum.

The news had made Marion ill again for days. Dion thought it was because she was sorry for Sarah. In a queer way she was sorry . . . haunted by the thought of that poor, guiltless woman locked in a criminal asylum . . . mad . . . mad through *her* . . . that would torment her conscience for her life-time, now. She would almost rather have heard that Mrs. Pollock was dead and gone.

She began to watch for the day when Sidney Pollock would come into her life again. In the Court, during his aunt's trial, he had looked at her with such suspicion, such hatred in his eyes.

On this cold, winter's afternoon when she lay on her couch in the listless fashion customary to her now, Dion strove to rouse her from her depression.

'Come out with me, sweetheart,' he said. 'Let me take you to a cinema or a dance.'

She carried his hand to her lips. They burnt his flesh and made him shiver curiously.

'No,' she said. 'I don't want to go out.'

'Will you forgive me, then, dearest, if I go? I'm getting so stuffed up in this room.'

'Of course,' she said.

'I'll run round and see mother,' he said.

'*And* Pat Westby,' she said bitterly.

His eyes clouded.

'Marion, darling, for God's sake don't be foolish and jealous—it is so unworthy of you—' he began.

She moved her beautiful head wearily.

'Oh, all right—go along, Dion,' she said.

He went—with the horrid feeling that she *was* jealous of Pat, and the equally horrid feeling that although she had absolutely no cause for jealousy, he *did* want to see Pat. Her influence was so soothing, so restful after his poor, unhappy Marion.

That afternoon, while Dion was out, Sidney Pollock called to see young Lady Courtland.

Marion received him because she dared not refuse. What she had dreaded—had come. But when the young engineer marched into the pretty, flower-filled drawing room, cap in hand, blue eyes sullen and morose, she received him with a smile. She had risen from the sofa . . . assumed a careless, happy attitude.

'So it's you, Sidney,' she said, holding out one slender hand on which gleamed a magnificent sapphire. 'I'm glad you've come. I wanted to tell you how sorry I am about poor Mrs. Pollock being in the asylum.'

Pollock refused the hand and regarded her with almost horror in his eyes. How dared she smile and offer that hand which he felt was blood-stained. Yet she looked angelically lovely with her pale, thin face in its frame of glorious hair, her slender form in a frock of deep blue chiffon-velvet with great wide chiffon sleeves through which her arms gleamed like ivory. A rope of pearls hung from her throat which was no less milky white.

The man in Sidney Pollock admired her. The avenging nephew of Sarah Pollock hated and despised her . . . would like to have beaten her with a rod until red marks showed on the transparent whiteness of her neck.

'I haven't come to speak friendly with you, Lady Courtland,' he said roughly. 'But to tell you I haven't forgotten what me and my aunt owes to you. I'm still working . . . still investigating. Aunt Sarah is mad . . . poor creature . . . heart-breaking . . . raving in a criminal madhouse. Through *you*!'

Marion recoiled. Such sheer hatred glowed from the boy's blue eyes in this moment. What little colour she had in her cheeks, fled. She pressed a tiny cambric handkerchief to her quivering lips.

'Sidney . . . you misjudge me cruelly,' she said. 'I assure you that what happened to Mrs. Pollock is not my fault.'

'Oh, yes it is,' said the boy harshly. 'She was sane enough until the day o' the trial, and she told me the truth—she swore it on her mother's Bible, and Aunt Sarah was a woman o' religion. I know it was you that murdered Jet Saddleman, Lady Courtland . . . *and you know it.*'

Marion trembled violently.

201

'No—it isn't true,' she stammered. 'You are wicked . . . unkind to say so . . . I . . . you are half-crazed because of your aunt's trouble and . . .'

'No,' he broke in. 'You are guilty, and you know it.'

Marion swayed a little on her feet. She felt icy-cold despite the warm fire at her back. She looked at the young engineer with agonised eyes.

'Sidney,' she said hoarsely, 'you are making a terrible error. I am innocent. I . . . swear it. W-what are you doing?'

'Using every penny I've saved on a private detective,' he said sullenly, his eyes fixed on the ground. 'A cute chap, too, from the Yard. He's at Moorcoombe now . . . finding out more about you and your movements that day Mr. Saddleman *fell* into Hunter's Hill Quarry.'

Marion stifled a cry. This boy was stirring up muddy waters, and she could scarcely breathe . . . she felt choked . . . terrified. A detective . . . at Moorcoombe . . . investigating . . . and what of that figure she had seen going down the hill that day? The person may not have seen her with Jet, or come forward at the trial . . . but with a detective, nibbling, worrying, following up every tiny clue . . . oh, God . . . what might not come out?

'What's more,' added Sidney, 'I have a friend in Mrs. Marshall. She's helping me pay the detective, and doing a bit on her own besides. She and I have the belief that the person that sent Mr. Saddleman to his death sent her daughter, Hope, to hers.'

Marion's blood seemed to freeze in her veins. Mrs. Marshall . . . Sidney's ally . . . a valuable ally, too . . . Hope's mother, who would like to avenge her child's horrible end.

'Oh, God!' she smothered the cry. 'Why have you come here to frighten me . . . to accuse me . . . you cruel man . . . you utter fool!'

'Because I suspect you,' he said. Then he added in a voice of anguish: 'What do you think it means to me, my fine lady . . . to throw all my savings into this job . . . to have my aunt, the only relation I've got left, in a lunatic asylum? Once I was walking out with a young lady in Torquay, and I hoped to marry her. Now I can never marry . . . with my name tarnished . . . my money gone . . .'

Marion looked at him with distended eyes. She felt no pity for him; only the most acute terror because he was working hard to get *her* convicted . . . because he suspected her . . . had put Mrs. Marshall on her track . . . because he was the type to go on . . . mercilessly . . . until he got her pinned.

She shook from head to foot.

'You do me wrong,' she moaned. And then: 'Oh, Sidney, be kind . . . I have been very ill and I am still ill.'

'I'm sorry,' he said sullenly. 'You deserve it,

203

though.'

'Once before, you were rude and suspicious,' she gasped. 'Later, you begged my pardon.'

'I am surer now of what I suspect,' he said.

'Oh,' she moaned. 'I am falling . . .'

She was acting now . . . assuming faintness . . . keyed up to the situation . . . alive to the realization that she must do something with this boy . . . something to prevent him from continuing his remorseless hunting her down. Instinctively he moved to her side and caught her in his arms. She lay against him with closed eyes. He held his breath as he looked down at her and felt the softness of her body in his embrace. He had never before held a woman so exquisitely fragrant . . . some subtle French perfume which she used, mounted to his nostrils, and her gold-flame hair brushed his rough chin.

Sidney Pollock was young . . . younger than Marion, and essentially masculine. The woman in his arms was the very essence of femininity; a lovely woman, too . . . a creature of heady charm. She let him hold her a moment without moving, then opened her eyes and smiled up at him.

That smile was the wretched youth's undoing. It intoxicated him . . . rendered him blind, deaf, dumb to all else save the wonder, the sheer rapture of holding her in his arms. How light, how delicate she was . . . and she had been ill . . . he had bullied and threatened her.

'If I thought I was on the wrong track after all,' he muttered, 'I . . .'

'What?' she whispered, smiling up into his eyes which were like blue flames now. 'Oh, Sidney, you foolish boy, instead of being unkind . . . why don't you *love* me?'

'*Love* you . . . ?' he stammered.

'Yes, Sidney . . . love me,' she repeated. Her arm stole round this throat and she pressed her velvety cheek to his sun-bronzed young face. She loathed doing it. She loathed him and herself in this moment, for fundamentally she was faithful to Dion and her passion for him . . . she would have died rather than make love to another man while her husband lived . . . had she lived under happier circumstances. But she was fighting for her very life, and incidentally, for Dion. She dared not let this boy carry on his investigation . . . track her down . . .

'You are married . . . you are Lady Courtland . . . are you crazy?' he was stuttering, loosening his hold of her.

But she pressed closer to him. No Delilah ever practised more perfect charms on any Samson.

'I may not be happy,' she said, shuddering at the lie. 'I may dislike my husband, and if you were sensible, Sidney, you would see that I like you . . . that I have always liked you. We could

205

snatch some happy moments, you and I, you dear, blue-eyed, simple lad. We could find a little happiness . . . if you would just be sensible and stop looking upon me as a miserable sinner.'

Sidney Pollock breathed hard and fast. For a moment he thought of his wretched aunt, languishing in her asylum, then the loveliness of Marion overwhelmed him. He was lonely, depressed; had no sweetheart now . . . none of the delights of life which this beautiful woman offered. His arms caught and held her closely, and she buried her face on his shoulder so that he did not see the disgust, the shame in her eyes.

'If I thought you were really innocent,' he said in a hoarse voice . . . 'if I thought you meant it . . . meant you liked me a bit, my God, I'd be tempted . . . you're so beautiful . . . so sweet to love . . .'

She felt utter contempt for herself and for this poor, weak boy. But she raised her lips to his and whispered his name . . .

'Sidney . . .'

He lost his head completely and kissed her.

When that long kiss ended she was sick with misery and dread lest Dion should see or hear or discover this new, enforced sin. But she smiled at the boy, and he, drunk as with new wine by that fatal kiss, stammered passionate words to her.

'You wonderful thing . . . God . . . you can't

be guilty . . . you're too sweet.'

'Will you stop that detective, then, boy?' she whispered, her heart pounding . . . pounding . . . 'Will you tell Mrs. Marshall you don't think me guilty any more?'

CHAPTER NINETEEN

Just for an instant the foolish, vacillating boy hesitated. His heart pounded in his breast, his eyes swam as he looked into the brown pools of Marion Courtland's eyes. He was drowning . . . mentally drowning, only to perish as miserably as Hope Marshall had perished in the Suicide's Pool. His body shook from head to foot. For the fraction of a moment he thought of his unhappy aunt, and of the man who had been murdered at Double-Styles Farm. Then those pictures faded. He saw nothing but Marion; heard nothing but her soft, beguiling voice which was luring him on to ruin just as surely as the sirens of yore lured sailors on to the rocks to their death.

'You lovely thing,' he muttered, straining her against him. 'Oh, God, you're driving me mad! Am I mad? Or are you? Can you truly care for me . . . rough, uneducated fellow that I am . . . you, who are married to a chap like Sir Dion Courtland?'

She clung to him.

'Pooh . . . what does Dion matter? Once I was Marion Grayle . . . a publican's daughter . . . I helped dish up food in my father's kitchen . . . I dusted and swept and did all sorts of things when we were short of staff. I'm not really Lady Courtland, you know. That was a mistake—I mistook the dross for the gold. The glitter of the life Dion offered, tempted me, but I realize now how wrong I was. Love matters . . . nothing else but love.'

The cunning words were just calculated to touch Sidney Pollock's heart. Yes, she was right, he thought, flaming with pity and understanding. She was only a poor girl, really . . . his class. But he found her a thousand times more adorable, more tempting than any girl he had ever met in his own social circle. And he need not be frightened of her or feel ashamed before her. He believed, now, that she had married Sir Dion for money and hated the gilded cage in which she had been placed. How could he dream that her genuine feelings were of hatred and contempt of himself . . . that she adored Dion . . . had sinned for him . . . blackened her immortal soul to gain him, her heart's desire?

Few men could have held Marion in their arms, listened to her sweet, rich voice, and doubted her. Sidney Pollock was weak and passionate. During these last unhappy weeks of his aunt's trial, he had been half off his head with worry and misery. This was the reaction

. . . this wild thrill of desire; this wonderful, intoxicating thing called Love . . .

He covered her head with intemperate kisses.

'My dear, my pet, my Lovely,' he crooned over her. 'To think you ever married a gentleman for money . . . it was a mistake, Marion . . . you're just a human, natural girl, built for loving . . . made for me . . . you Precious!'

She let him ramble on. She kept her face hidden from him, dreading the touch of his lips upon her mouth again. She hated this uncontrolled passion from the boy who held her. It was a triumph for her . . . she had turned her bitterest enemy into a lover . . . it was a splendid triumph of woman's witchery . . . her allure . . . over hard reason and desire for revenge. But she felt sick at her own triumph. The one good, genuine thing in this strange, sinful girl was her love for her husband. No other man had ever mattered. No other man ever would matter to her. For Dion, she had sold her very soul to Satan . . . and it was because she honestly loved him. It was a very terrible love; wicked in its passionate intensity and callous selfishness. Real love is selfless and self-sacrificing. Many people would have called Marion's feeling for her husband infatuation or madness. It amounted to mania, of course . . . it had touched her brain with a kind of insanity, so determined was she to keep Dion . . . to retain his affection and trust. She swept people from her path like flies . . . squeezed out life with those small, pretty hands . . . ruthlessly . . . in order to achieve her own ends. But in her own peculiar way it must be admitted that she loved Dion. This 'affair' with Sarah Pollock's nephew revolted her. She shrank from him, listened to his wild, uneducated endearments with scorn and disgust in her heart. It was the hardest thing she had ever done . . . to make Sidney think she cared for him. But she went on with it. She did nothing by halves . . . and she knew that she *must* be mistress of this man or he would master her . . . send her to the gallows.

'Dion, Dion, forgive me,' she inwardly cried, as she let Sidney cover her face with hot kisses. 'I love only you . . . this *is* for you, my beloved . . . to save myself . . . and you from finding out that which would break your heart.'

With this she salved her conscience and began to turn her fresh wickedness into a kind of martyrdom. When she raised her head, Sidney saw that her eyes were full of tears. He thought the tears were from emotion . . . love for himself.

'You do care for me, my Lovely, then?' he whispered.

'Yes, oh yes,' she lied. 'And you love me?'

'More than love,' he said. 'I worship you. It's like holding a flower . . . something sweet and precious and delicate.'

'You make pretty speeches,' she sneered. But he was deaf to the sneer, and laughed again.

'For you. I ain't made speeches like that to any other girl. The young lady I walked out with was poor stuff compared to you, my lovely. Kiss me . . . kiss me again.'

Marion kissed him. And while she suffered that long kiss . . . blazing with a boy's first wild infatuation . . . she wished coldly and brutally that she could kill him. Never had she wanted to kill a human being more.

'You will stop that detective, Sidney?' she asked again, very softly when he gave her breath once more.

'Yes,' he said. 'At once. I shall say I made a mistake.'

'And you did, of course.'

'Of course,' he echoed. 'I made that error before and admitted myself wrong. I admit it again now. You couldn't have done any harm to Mr. Saddleman or poor Aunt Sally. You're too sweet, too gentle.'

Her lips curled.

'I'm glad you've come to your senses, dearest Sidney,' she said coldly. 'This detective man is working on your behalf down in Moorcoombe, you said. What about wiring him, recalling him? You realize, surely, what an insult it is to me?'

'Of course,' he said. 'I'm sorry . . . I'm terribly sorry. Forgive me, my Pretty.'

She shuddered. Jet Saddleman had called her that . . . she remembered him using that endearment on the day when she had pushed him over the Quarry. Viciously she snapped her small teeth and wished that Sidney Pollock lay in his grave, this day.

How different Dion, her husband, was to such a rough, ill-educated fellow . . . how different the touch of his well-bred hands, the sound of his deep, charming voice.

She felt she could bear no more of Sidney just now. She released herself from his embrace.

'We must be very careful, Sid,' she said. 'Remember that I am married and my husband . . .'

'I don't forget that,' said the boy, more gloomily. 'I wish to God you wasn't married, my sweetheart. I would make you marry me.'

Marion could have laughed aloud. This . . . from the boy who had been cursing her, reviling her for a murderess a few minutes ago!

'I know I'm wicked in loving you,' he added weakly, 'but I can't help it, darling, and I think marriage made for money is wrong. Our love is right.'

'Oh, the fool . . . if only I could shut his mouth forever,' Marion thought, clenching her, hands. But aloud she said, with another brilliant smile: 'Yes, it is right, dear boy. But you must only come and see me occasionally

. . . not rouse suspicion.'

'I've got a room over the garage where I work as engineer,' he said eagerly. 'You can visit me there and nobody would ever see us, my Pretty. God . . . I must see you sometimes . . . alone. You'll come to me, won't you?'

'I daren't—' she began, frowning.

'You can manage it,' he broke in. 'You can't care so little as you won't risk nothing for me, Marion.'

She caught the note of surprise, of disappointment in his voice, and writhed. She must go carefully with the infatuated youth, otherwise he would suspect that she was fooling him . . . blinding him. Oh, how she hated it all!

But she would have to give in to him a bit.

'Yes, yes, I'll come sometimes,' she said. 'Now you must go. My husband may come back at any moment.'

He caught her in his arms. His blue eyes were bloodshot, fevered. To Marion, he was a stupid, rough fool, reeking of the motor-works. But he thought she loved him. He possessed the usual amount of male conceit, and to him she was exquisitely beautiful and a sheer intoxicant.

'I beg your pardon, my blessed angel, for ever doubting you or connecting you with anything beastly or criminal,' he said, hugging her. 'Perhaps poor old Aunt Sally was a bit potty . . . poisoned Mr. Saddleman in a moment of insanity.'

'I think that is undoubtedly the whole explanation of the case,' she said.

'I'll do anything for you to make up for my behaviour,' he added wildly. 'I could die for you, you sweet pet, with your great brown eyes and lovely hair.'

'I wish you would die,' she thought. But her answer to him was a kiss that sent him to her feet.

She reflected morbidly, that she was even worse than Edith Thompson had been. Mrs. Thompson had loved the youth, Bywaters . . . helped to murder her husband for love of her lover. She, Marion, was going to ruin this boy's career and break his heart just because she loved another man . . . her own husband . . . and wished to save herself from the punishment she deserved. Edith Thompson had committed the one crime . . . but she, Marion Courtland, was twice a murderess . . . and had sent an innocent old woman to a lunatic asylum.

She shuddered in Sidney's arms. Why should she think of the Thompson-Bywaters case? She had best not dwell upon it. She had read an account of the woman's death in all the papers . . . that dreadful death . . . the prostrate creature carried moaning and struggling to the gallows . . . the awful mask . . . the rope . . . the Burial Service . . .

She felt her hair rise on her head, and her

whole body shook with sudden terror.

'Go—go!' she gasped to the boy. 'I—I think I hear my husband coming.'

Young Pollock snatched up his cap, and departed, saying he would telephone to her, protesting his love, his belief in her. And after he had gone, Marion threw herself on the couch and buried her face on the cushions, striving to shut out the ghastly visions she had had of that other woman who had sinned for the sake of passionate love . . . whose memory haunted her so strangely today.

'Heaven have mercy on me,' she moaned. 'But I can't look back . . . I must go on . . . go on now . . . to save myself . . . to spare Dion.'

Her fit of terror subsided. She began to feel relieved and pleased that she had brought Sidney Pollock to her feet. She knew he would keep his word and wire to the detective to stop his work. And incidentally he would be sure to influence Hope Marshall's mother in the same direction . . . put her off the scent.

When Dion returned to the flat, he found Marion composed and smiling. She had changed for dinner . . . wore a little black lace frock with a sweet-scented gardenia on one shoulder. She looked lovely; faint lavender stains under her beautiful eyes; and she had pencilled the perfect bow of her lips with a carmine stick. She held out her arms to him as he entered.

'Dion, my darling . . . so you are back? And

did you have a nice time?'

'Very,' he nodded. 'Pat and I and two others had a bit of bridge for a change—that's why I'm late. We had a rather long rubber. Hope you don't mind.'

Ordinarily she would have shown jealousy and annoyance. This evening she astonished him by smiling, saying she was glad he had had a good time, and asking most charmingly after the health of Pat and his mother. He took her hands and stared at her.

'Whatever has come over you, dear?' he asked.

She writhed a little at the question but went on smiling.

'I've been thinking things over while you were out, Dion, and came to the conclusion that I have been behaving very badly . . . I ought to be more grateful to Pat for her kindness to me . . . and more a companion to you.'

Dion's face grew bright.

'You mean that, darling?'

'Yes, I do,' she said, as he put his arms around her. 'I have moped enough . . . it is time I pulled myself together, isn't it?'

He was enormously relieved by this new attitude and delighted with her charming mood. Coming back from his mother's place, he had felt depressed and tired . . . dreaded one of Marion's outbursts of jealousy; a passionate display of morbid fear; or desire for

216

him. It had weighed him down. He had not been able to help comparing Marion with Pat—Pat, who was so fresh, so amiable; like a breath of the sea; a flash of sunshine.

To come back tonight and find Marion not on the sofa, moping and complaining, but exquisite and fresh in the black lace gown he admired . . . a new light in her eyes . . . a new joyousness in her voice . . . astonished and pleased him.

He kissed her with more genuine warmth than he had felt for weeks.

'Why, dearest, how ripping,' he said boyishly. 'I am so glad . . . Pat is such a dear . . . and wants to be friends with you.'

Jealousy tore at her even though she appreciated the unusual warmth of his caresses. But she uttered a little lilting laugh, and, standing on tip-toe, gave him butterfly kisses on chin and cheeks and eyes.

'Let's be happy . . . real lovers again,' she whispered. 'Go and get into evening-dress and take me out to dinner . . . to the Palace Hotel . . . to dance.'

He said 'yes' with alacrity. He stroked his wife's beautiful hair, and his eyes brimmed with renewed tenderness for her.

'You're a dear, brave thing,' he said. 'I can guess how all this past beastliness has weighed you down. But I do love you for making this effort for me.'

She was silent. Pressed against him, eyes

shut, she suffered in that moment the acute, indescribable anguish that only a passionate woman, who feels her man slipping gradually away from her, can feel. She had lost that first mad love Dion had given her at the Travellers' Rest. This was only the shadow of it . . . a temporary ignition that would burn itself out . . . she knew it . . . realized it in agony and bitterness. She was able to coquette with him, charm him—rouse herself from her depression because Sidney had so relieved her mind, because she knew he would no longer work against her. But it was horrible to her to feel that only an hour ago she had been in the boy's arms, letting him kiss the lips that Dion owned.

Dion, however, was happy for this evening. He took his wife out to dine and dance. She was much more like the vivacious, sparkling girl he had met in Moorcoombe in the Autumn, and who had completely enslaved him. He hoped and believed that her gloomy, difficult moods were finished with. He was more her lover that night than he had been for months.

And she, sinful, remorseful, wildly happy, in turns, lay in his arms and laughed up at him with shining eyes . . . but in her heart she wept bitter tears of blood . . . wondering how long her little hour would last!

CHAPTER TWENTY

For a few days following that reunion between husband and wife, Dion was comparatively happy and content. Pat came more often to the flat. Marion went out of her way to be sweet to her husband's friend. But she could never face Pat without flinching. Pat's grave grey eyes seemed always to read into her very soul . . . and she dreaded them. Whatever Pat thought or felt about Marion, she tried hard for Dion's sake to tread on her suspicions and hold out the hand of friendship to the other girl.

But Marion knew very little peace or happiness now save during the hours when Dion was her lover. He allowed her lips and arms to act as a kind of narcotic to him, and she took his caresses as a stimulant . . . to bear her up . . . urge her on to action for herself and for him.

Sidney Pollock worried her incessantly now. He telephoned to her on two occasions when her husband was at home, begging her to to go his rooms. She had to answer very guardedly, and to lie to Dion about the call. The intrusion on her peace enraged her, but she had to keep Sidney happy—that was essential—so she wove a fresh tangle about her weary, crime-stained self . . . wrote letters to the boy to mollify him, and made promises for the future, which she did not intend to keep.

She wanted to fall in with Dion's wish to take her to Cairo for the winter. She would love to have seen Egypt . . . to revel in the extravagant amusements of Shepheard's Hotel, Cairo, where so many smart people lived in the season. And more than anything, she desired to get away from England . . . from memories of the past.

She half promised Dion that she would sail with him in a month's time . . . began to buy a trousseau for the East.

Then, one morning, she came face to face with Hope Marshall's mother in a main street in Torquay, while she was shopping.

Mrs. Marshall stopped dead in front of the girl . . . looked for a moment with a hard, suspicious expression at the slender, beautiful figure in the sable coat and perfectly-tailored, fawn-coloured skirt. A *chic* felt hat on the red-gold head completed the toilette. Very lovely . . . very *distingué* young Lady Courtland, to her fingertips. But Mrs. Marshall looked through that beauty to the real, unlovely creature beneath the mask.

'I suppose you think you are quite safe and sound and triumphant, Lady Courtland,' Mrs. Marshall began in a low, menacing voice. 'But let me tell you that you are wrong.'

Marion blanched and her heart began to pound furiously. She clenched her fingers so tightly over the little brocade bag she held that the delicate ivory clasp snapped in two. But she smiled.

'I fail to understand you, Mrs. Marshall,' she said, gently.

'I may be quite wrong, myself,' said Hope's mother, her lips a thin, hard line; her eyes still fixed on Marion's lovely face. 'But I feel somehow that I am right. You are at the bottom of all the trouble.'

Marion's tongue clave to the roof of her mouth. She stood very still. Mrs. Marshall continued in the same sinister voice:

'Mr. Pollock saw me this morning. He originally shared my belief that you know more than you care to tell about my daughter's death in Moorecoombe . . . and about Mr. Saddleman's murder. Now he has swung round. I suppose you have influenced him! But you won't be able to influence me. I intend to carry on investigations myself.'

Marion found speech.

'You are mad!' she said, in a gasping voice. 'If my husband heard you, he would put you in prison for slander. Be careful, Mrs. Marshall.'

'It is you who had better be careful,' said Hope's mother. 'My poor little girl's body lies under the ground, now . . . but her blood cries out for vengeance, and she shall have it.'

'You are mad!' repeated Marion, white to the lips. 'What have I got to do with it?'

'That's what my man at Moorcoombe is trying to discover,' said Mrs. Marshall, with a

221

freezing smile, 'and if I am mad, Lady Courtland, *you*, if I may say so . . . are *afraid*.'

'It isn't true,' panted the girl.

'Oh, well, time will tell,' said Mrs. Marshall. 'But *new* facts are coming to life. Somebody in Moorcoombe saw you with Jet Saddleman near Hunter's Hill Quarry that day he was injured . . . somebody who has been too afraid to come forward about it before, but who is willing to testify to that now. And if it can be proved that you *pushed him in* . . . it will prove a few other things. Perhaps you pushed my girl into the water and drowned her because you wanted Dion Courtland!'

It was all wild surmisal; the hysterical cry of a mother who had been brutally robbed of her only child. But Marion, as she listened, felt the blood congeal in her veins. She knew that there was little the woman could prove . . . nothing about Hope. But the bald truth, flung at her wildly, like that, terrified her. Her heart sank when she realized that the person she had seen on Hunter's Hill that fatal day had been discovered by Mrs. Marshall's detective.

'God . . .' she said to herself. 'God . . . this investigation must end, or I am done for!'

But she held her head erect, and without another word, passed Hope's mother by.

That same afternoon, when Dion went down to Cook's to make inquiries about the boats to Egypt, Marion for the first time visited Sidney Pollock's room at the garage.

The winter noons were short, and it was dark by the time she reached the place . . . a big motor-works and hire garage owned by a firm called 'Walker's,' where Sidney was head mechanic.

She had telephoned her intention of coming, so he expected her. She dressed very quietly in a black walking costume and small black felt hat; a stone-marten stole about her neck. She was very pale and nervous, but she put on a bold front when the boy met her in the cobbled yard of the garage by the petrol-pump. He conducted her up a narrow staircase to his room.

'Nobody can see us here, and if anyone does see, they'll only think I've got a young lady for a bit of courting,' he said.

He grated on her horribly . . . she was so used now to a man of Dion's breeding. But she clung to Sidney's arm and laughed.

'That's right. You and I are courting, aren't we?'

'I've lived for this moment,' he said, closing the door behind him. He stared at her with blue eyes aflame.

She looked round her distastefully. The bed-sitting-room was hideous. A screen hid the bed. There was a table beside it, bearing a pot of cheap flowers; cheap oil paintings on the flower-papered walls. Yet the wretched boy had spent an hour tidying it up for his lady . . . bought those flowers to welcome her . . . lit an oil-stove to warm the room. The stove gave out a fierce heat and smelt vilely. Marion felt sick at the atmosphere. She could not bear it for long. She allowed Sidney to take her hat off, and her fur, and coat, showing the thick silk jumper with its girlish black bow at the throat. She allowed him to play with her hair, kiss her passionately, then she sat down by the table, and began to talk to him seriously.

'Sidney, do you really love me?'

'You know I do . . . my heavens . . . too much,' he said. 'Since I last saw you, I ain't slept or eaten properly, Marion.'

She noticed that he was paler, thinner, already a wreck . . . already a pitiable lunatic, in his passion for her. She put out a hand and patted his with contemptuous pity.

'Poor Sid . . . but never mind . . . one day . . .'

'One day what?' he finished eagerly. 'Oh, my Lovely, if on'y that husband of yours didn't stand in the way.'

'He isn't in the way,' she said, gritting her teeth.

'Who is, then, my Pet?'

'Mrs. Marshall,' she said, in a cold, harsh voice.

'Mrs. Marshall!' he repeated, astonished.

'Yes,' she said. 'Listen, Sidney—'

She repeated, word for word, her meeting with Hope's mother in Torquay this morning. She simulated both anger and fear.

224

'Fancy the horrible woman threatening me like that,' she ended, putting a handkerchief to her eyes. 'Oh, Sid, I was so frightened.'

He rushed to put his arms around her. He couldn't bear to see her tremble and cry.

'Duckie, don't—don't,' he said. 'Why should you be frightened? You're innocent enough. I know that now. I told her so myself.'

'I know,' she said, with a little sob, clinging to his arms. 'But, Sid, don't you see what harm she can do, just bringing in that person who saw me on Hunter's Hill? It would mean any amount of unpleasantness. I'm innocent . . . I swear it, Sidney . . . but I can't bear any more trouble.'

He believed her. He was ready to accept her slightest word, now . . . to fight for her . . . die for her . . . he was torn with longing for her.

'She shan't scare you no more, my Pretty. Why, of course you're innocent, and I was a fool ever to doubt you.'

Marion snuggled in his arms.

'You dear, Sidney. But what will you do to stop her speaking about me and going on with that horrid "tec"?'

'Don't let it worry you,' he soothed.

'But it does.'

'I started it, too,' he said, remorsefully. 'You are sweet to forgive me'

'I love you,' she said, averting her gaze from him.

He kissed the tears from her thick lashes.

'You angel of joy . . . I'll do any mortal thing for you now . . . If Mrs. Marshall worries you and threatens you, I'll kill her.'

'You don't mean that,' she said, her eyes narrowing to slits.

'I don't mean it,' he said, with a sheepish laugh. 'No . . . but I am really prepared to do in anyone who worries you, my beautiful.'

Marion sat silent in the circle of his arm. Dark and desperate thoughts crowded into her mind, so burdened already with thoughts of crime. She knew she was getting more and more entangled in the consequences of her own misdeeds, and that she must fight on and on, wildly, before the net closed about her and rendered her helpless. This boy was mad with love for her. He was weak . . . it would take little to unhinge him . . . he was the hysterical breed calculated to do anything in a moment of passion. If she worked on his feelings . . . kept on quietly making statements to the effect that Mrs. Marshall stood between them . . . who knew but that he would turn that grim jest he had just made into a terrible truth.

She thought of Edith Thompson again. She had worked on Bywaters . . . on his affections . . . until he had stabbed her husband, for her sake. She, Marion, could do likewise.

'Sidney,' she said, breathlessly. 'I'd almost be inclined to run away with you if we could stop that woman's scandalous tongue.'

The boy flushed.

'You mean it, Marion?' he said. 'You'd come to me . . . altogether . . . you . . . so lovely . . . so much the lady?'

'Yes,' she lied. 'I don't mind giving up my title and riches for you. But first of all, you *must* stop that woman's tongue. I can't run away with you while she is spreading terrible reports about me, otherwise people would think I was trying to escape the law, which would be a vile untruth.'

Sidney saw the reason in this.

'I'll see to that woman,' he said. 'And don't you worry no more, dear, sweet thing.'

She felt her heart leap with triumph, and hid her face on his shoulder. For a moment there was silence while he held her, caressed her shining hair. Then suddenly, through the half-open window, came the sound of a voice that sent the blood receding from Marion's cheeks.

'Sid,' she breathed. *'Listen . . .'*

Sidney raised his head—held his breath.

From the courtyard came a man's voice . . . and it was the voice of Dion Courtland.

'Is Mr. Pollock in?'

'Yes, sir,' came the reply from one of the young motor-drivers employed by Walker's. 'Up in his room, sir . . . first door on the right, there.'

'God!' said Marion, her cheeks ashen, her eyes wild with fear. 'It's my husband . . . he has come to see you about something . . . and he'll

227

find me here . . . !'

CHAPTER TWENTY-ONE

Sidney took her right hand, and pressed it with a nervous grip that made her wince with pain. 'What the devil has he come here for?' he whispered.

'God knows,' said Marion. 'Unless he has found out I am here.'

'Can't you make any excuse?'

'None—for coming to see a young man in his bed-sitting-room at this hour of the day,' she panted. 'You fool, Sidney! . . . be quick . . . do something . . . say something . . . he is coming up the stairs, now.'

Young Pollock, crimson, distracted beyond words, put a hand to his head. He did not know what to do. He had never in his life been put in such a desperate position. But he was forced to realize that this beautiful young woman, who had just embraced him so passionately, was *another man's wife*—the wife of the man who was coming up these stairs now. He gulped hard.

'But look here, Marion darling . . . if he's found out . . . why not tell him now, and here, that we—we love each other?'

For an instant her cloak fell from her. She looked at him with eyes that blazed with fury and contempt for his stupidity and ignorance.

'Idiot!' she said. 'You want to spoil everything. If he finds out now . . . and Mrs. Marshall on my track, too . . . what do you think will happen to me?'

He fell back, abashed and disconsolate. He only half understood her meaning. And he completely failed to understand the look on her face. This was a very changed girl from the soft-eyed, gentle creature who had wound her white arms about his throat and played Delilah to his Samson. He was a dull-witted, slow-thinking fellow, and he could not begin to analyse her. He presumed she was half off her head with anxiety, and that she did not wish to be found out by her husband, just yet. He took her arm.

'Hide . . .' he muttered. 'Get into that cupboard—quickly—I'll put Sir Dion off.'

She was shivering and wild-eyed. This was a moment as bad for Marion as though the police themselves were marching up here to arrest her. It meant more . . . everything to her, to lose Dion's love and esteem. She had done so much—too much!—for the sake of winning him. She picked up her gloves and darted to the cupboard, which was a kind of wardrobe let into the wall. It was dark, stifling, full of clothes, but she welcomed the security of it, and stood with her back pressed to the wall, her cheeks livid. She prayed that the 'imbecile of a boy' would act properly . . . put Dion off the scent. She could not imagine why Dion had come here to see Sidney. The cupboard-door was almost shut, but she was forced to leave a crack open, so that she could get air to breathe.

There came a knock at the door.

Sidney pulled himself together, smoothed back his hair, and choked out a 'Come in!'

Dion walked into the room.

He looked haggard and distressed, and as he entered, his eyes roved round the little hot, stuffy room with suspicion. His nose wrinkled as he smelt the vile odour of the oil-stove. Then he looked straight at the boy who was half-sitting on the edge of the table.

'Pollock,' he began, in a stern, abrupt voice. 'I want an explanation from you.'

Sidney's ears burned and tingled.

'F-from me, s-sir?' he stuttered.

He had felt a fine fellow when he had held Marion in his arms. But face to face with Sir Dion . . . Dion could be extraordinarily dignified and strong at times like these . . . he wilted and became instantly conscious of his ignorance, his lack of breeding, his sinfulness in the love in which he had been indulging.

'Yes, from you,' said Dion. He drew a piece of paper from his pocket and held it out to Sidney. 'What does this mean?'

Marion held her breath. Her heart had sunk as she had heard her husband's stern voice. What had Dion discovered? What, in heaven's name, was 'this'? She could not see—dared not open the cupboard-door wider.

Sidney took the paper handed him. He gave a little exclamation of dismay when he realized what it was. It was a note—a very foolish note—bearing his address, and signed 'Your adoring Sidney.' He had written it to Marion last night. It must have missed the post. Marion had not got it. And it had fallen into Sir Dion's hands this afternoon while she was out. It was a stupid letter, written against all her orders, and gave away the fact that they 'loved each other' and that there was an affair in progress.

He was utterly taken aback—could only stare at the note, fearful of raising his head and looking the injured husband in the face.

'Well?' exclaimed Dion. 'Can you explain that note? I do not as a rule open my wife's correspondence, but when I got home this afternoon and saw that letter waiting for her, written in a man's illiterate hand—if I may say so—I got it into my head that somebody was worrying her. She had had enough worry from the Pollock murder trial, and I did not wish her to be annoyed any more. So I opened it. I wish to God I had not done so. It was the most crashing blow I have ever had. It stunned me. A love-affair between Marion, my wife . . . and *you*! Good God! If it were not in black and white, I should still refuse to believe it.'

Sidney kept silence. He was flummoxed,

albeit a little exalted, secretly, because he thought Marion preferred him to this rather splendid gentleman. But in her hiding-place Marion felt sick and burning with rage. The fool . . . the utter imbecile to have written to her. She had forbidden it. And he had ruined things completely now. Dion had had his eyes opened . . . just as things had been so nice . . . just as he had begun to care for her again in the old passionate way. What was to be done now?

Dion began to pace up and down the little room, lighting a cigarette.

'Can you offer any explanation, Pollock?' he demanded. 'I don't understand it. How long has it been going on? When and where have you seen my wife? I thought she hated you—never wanted to see you again—and that you were against her all the way through your aunt's trial! What does it mean?'

Sidney pulled at his collar. He began to stammer out words, trying to save Marion's face because she had asked him.

'I—look here, sir—I'm terribly upset about it. I can't help it. I f-fell in love with M . . . Lady Courtland, and realized she had nothing to do with Mr. Saddleman's death . . . I . . . she was kind to me . . . but it isn't her fault . . . it's me . . .'

'Stop all that stuttering,' broke in Dion. 'What are you trying to tell me? That my wife doesn't care for you?'

232

'No, no, sir . . . she . . . loves you . . .' stammered the boy. 'I am the offender, sir . . . not Lady Courtland . . . of course.'

'Yet in this note you intimate that she has seen you often, and that you have kissed . . . pah!' Dion broke off with a savage gesture. His blood was beginning to boil. When he had first read Sidney Pollock's letter, it had robbed him of all reason. He had been bewildered . . . incredibly hurt and astonished. Marion—and young Pollock! But why? What was the explanation? She had professed such dislike of him, and he of her. And she had seemed in all sincerity to adore him, Dion. He had come straight here to have things out with Pollock. Marion was out. He could not question her.

Suddenly his gaze became fixed on a little curled-up furry thing on the floor by the side of the table. For an instant he stared at it. Then he leaned down and picked it up and regarded it in silence. It was a stone-marten tie! It was only too familiar . . . and from it came an equally familiar scent . . . a Parisian perfume of which Marion was very fond.

Dion looked at young Pollock with frozen eyes.

'This is my wife's fur,' he said. 'She has been here?'

'I—no . . .' stuttered Sidney.

In her hiding-place, Marion's nerves gave way. She uttered a gasping moan. This was the end of all things. She had forgotten her fur in

233

the haste, the fever of the moment when she had darted into the cupboard.

Dion heard that stifled moan. He walked straight to the cupboard and flung open the door. Marion half walked, half stumbled into the room. She was piteously white, and her eyes held an expression of anguish and despair. But Dion looked at her without mercy ... with only a kind of incredulous horror.

'You!' he said. 'Oh, my God! Am I going mad, or dreaming? You, *my wife* ... hiding in a cupboard in the bed-sitting-room of a boy like Pollock!'

Her teeth chattered. She grasped his arm.

'Dion, Dion ... you don't understand ...'

'No ... I ... it's my fault—' began Sidney, desperately. 'Lady Courtland was kind to me, and ...'

'Extraordinarily kind, it seems,' said Dion, with a hard little laugh. He picked up his hat and put it on his head. 'I've no more to say here,' he added. 'I'd better go, before I lose my self-control.'

'If you want to f-fight . . .' Sidney stammered, trying to swagger a bit before Marion, 'I'll fight as good as any chap, Sir Dion.'

Dion, who had been walking to the door, swung round and looked at him.

'Fight? Good God, no—I couldn't fight a poor weakling like you,' he said, with cold contempt. 'And now that I know where we all

234

are, it is with my—wife—I have to deal . . . not you.'

Marion rushed after him.

'Dion . . . wait . . . wait . . .' she said, frenziedly.

But he had gone and shut the door after him. She heard his footsteps going down the stairs.

She put a hand to her whirling head, then walked back to Sidney.

'Oh, you fool . . . you utter fool!' she wailed. 'I told you not to write me letters of that kind. Now what can we do?'

He tried to take her hand, but she shook him off.

'Marion—my Pretty,' he said. 'I'm terribly sorry. But it had to come sooner or later if we care for each other, hadn't it?'

She clenched her fingers to keep herself from screaming curses at him, like a hag in a fish-market. She was seething with anger. But she was forced to control her rage. Care for him . . . the poor, idiotic mutt! . . . stuttering, jibbering before Dion! God, hadn't it shown him up? And Dion had been so splendid. Dion, her Dion . . . whom she had lost, now! . . .

'Listen, Sidney,' she said between her teeth, 'I do care for you, but I can't afford to give my husband up, just yet. I've told you why. I'll have to go home and patch things up as best I can, now. But it's ruined everything.'

235

'Come away with me—now, Marion darling!'

'No,' she said passionately. 'I tell you it isn't time. I must try and make it up with my husband. When Mrs. Marshall has been silenced . . . then I'll come away with you.'

'You mean that? the boy panted.

'Yes,' she lied. *So see to it, Sidney.*

He was maddened by her words . . . by the sight of her there, so beautiful and desirable; seemingly within his grasp. When Mrs. Marshall ceased her investigations in Moorcoombe, Marion would leave her home for him. Not until then. She worked on his emotions, his mind, in the most insidious fashion. He began to feel that he must do what she wanted, at all costs, in order to win her.

'I'll manage to see you, somehow . . . or write to you,' she said hurriedly, putting on her hat and fur . . . the fatal stone-marten tie which had given her away. 'If you see Mrs. Marshall, and want to communicate with me, write to me under the name of Mrs. Sidney . . . X. Street Post Office, W., and I'll call for letters there.'

He caught her hand and covered it with mad, feverish kisses.

'I adore you,' he panted. 'Say you love me and I'll do anything for you, Marion.'

She uttered the lie without conscience. She saw to her satisfaction that Sidney Pollock was completely enslaved by her. But her one idea at the moment was to get back home and patch things up with Dion.

She allowed the boy to kiss her lips, then with another promise which would fire him on to work on her behalf, she left him and took a taxi home.

She found Dion had not come back. She changed her frock for the prettiest one she had in her wardrobe, rubbed a little rouge into her ghastly cheeks, tried to make herself beautiful ... then waited for him.

It was a terrible waiting, fraught with sick anxiety and suspense. For hours she paced up and down her boudoir, reviling Fate ... strung up to concert-pitch with the strain of suspense. Where had Dion gone? What was he thinking ... doing? Had she lost him forever?

At midnight Dion came home.

He had walked the streets aimlessly, trying to clear his head, to regain calm before he saw his wife again. He had had no food, and he was mentally and physically exhausted. But he was quite calm. He walked into the drawing-room, where she was sitting, haggard, wretched, waiting for him.

'Now, Marion,' he said, quietly. 'Let us have this thing out.'

CHAPTER TWENTY-TWO

The unhappy scene between husband and wife lasted till the grey finger of dawn touched the deserted streets with its cold and weary light.

Again and again Dion cried from the bitterness of his soul: 'I always thought you loved *me* . . . why did you start a sordid, low intrigue with a rough, common boy like that?'

Again and again she assured him that she did love him . . . that the affair with Sidney Pollock had been a passing madness. She wanted to tell him the truth . . . tell him that she never cared for Sidney . . . that she loathed and despised him. But she could not . . . *dared not.* How could she explain that she was pretending to love Pollock in order to stop his tracking her down, in league with Hope's mother? That would give her away altogether . . . show him her guilt, her fear of discovery. She was in a ghastly position . . . a net of her own weaving. Neither truths nor untruths could disentangle her now. The only thing she could do was to assume deep contrition and shame; say she had been momentarily infatuated with the boy.

'It's over now. It didn't go very far . . . I only kissed him once or twice,' she said, on her knees, her golden-red hair bowed on Dion's lap. She was sick with shame, with impotent fury that she must say such a thing. But she was between the devil and the deep sea. This confession was the least of the evils.

Dion covered his face with his hands. Worn out after the long hours of pacing the streets, and of arguing and reproaching Marion, he felt nothing now but shame for her, and the bitterness of disillusion. Last night he had been happy, convinced that Marion loved him. To discover this sordid intrigue between herself and a common working-lad not only amazed him, but was a sore blow to his pride. She was Lady Courtland. Already she had dragged that name through the Criminal Courts. Now did she want to break his heart by dragging it through the divorce courts?

He was ready, however, to let her convince him that the affair had not gone far enough for him to think of divorce . . . that it had ended with those few shameful kisses. Now she was sobbing . . . begging him for forgiveness.

He looked down at the beautiful curly head on his knees. But he felt no softening toward her. To-night, Dion Courtland's passion for Marion had died . . . utterly. She heard him say in a cold, detached way:

'I will try to forgive it, but I cannot forget it, Marion. We must go to bed, now—it is nearly four o'clock; and you must stop crying or you will be ill again.'

She raised her face; caught his arms.

'Dion, Dion!' she cried in a heart-rending

voice. 'You don't understand, but I *do* love you.'

He sighed wearily. No—he did not understand. He could only suppose that this girl whom he had made his wife had forgotten her new station, and reverted to her class . . . he had to remember she had been a publican's daughter, ill-bred, half-educated under that veneer of brilliance and beauty. Perhaps she had grown tired of him . . . wanted to flirt and amuse herself with a boy of her own class. He did not know—scarcely cared—so complete was his disillusion, tonight!

Marion seemed to read his thoughts. She grew agonised. It was as though she was on the rack, being pulled asunder . . . tortured . . . powerless to put an end to the agony. She dared not tell the truth. And although she had saved herself in one way, she had lost everything for which she had sinned in the beginning. She read the indifference, the coldness on her husband's face, now. Perhaps he would turn to Pat Westby on the rebound, she thought.

This was her punishment. She was, actually, in heart and soul, faithful to Dion—loved him. And she must allow him to think otherwise.

The tears poured down her cheeks.

'Dion . . . Dion . . . try and forgive me, and love me again!' she said with a moaning cry.

He put her arms gently but firmly away.

'Please spare me that, Marion. To have

found that you could stoop to an intrigue with young Pollock has killed all my love for you.'

'No, no . . .'

'Yes,' he said. 'We will go on living like this . . . here . . . for the sake of appearances. I don't want to bring any more sorrow to my mother. But don't ask me to love you. Meanwhile I put you on your honour neither to see nor communicate with Pollock again. He is only a lad . . . oh, Marion, it was not very decent . . . the fellow is probably crazy about you . . . it wasn't fair—'

He broke off with a gesture of disgust. Then, without another look at her, he walked out of the room.

Marion stared after him. She heard him move his things from their bedroom. He was sleeping in his dressing-room tonight.

She crouched on the floor, her face in her hands. Not only had she lost Dion's love, but she realized she would have to go very carefully in the future, otherwise she would find herself branded as a murderess . . . come to a horrible end.

She remembered old Emm's prophetic words. Her head sank lower, lower, till it touched the floor. Hope . . . Jet . . . poor, mad Sarah . . . they all gathered round in that hour and jeered at her; pointed ghostly fingers of derision. The hour of vengeance was at hand. Marion Grayle's punishment had begun.

CHAPTER TWENTY-THREE

Those next few days were sheer hell for Marion.

Dion treated her with icy politeness, and went out of his way to avoid her. That nearly broke her heart. He saw her follow him about with great, agonised eyes, but was indifferent to her pain. She could not love him, he told himself, otherwise she would never have had one unfaithful thought. She was only piqued because he would not pander to her whims.

When she saw Dion go round to his mother's flat for consolation, she grew desperate. She imagined he was comparing her with Patricia. It was almost more than she could bear. He did not tell old Lady Courtland, or Pat, of the rift between himself and his wife—he was too ashamed of it. But he found himself wondering why he had married Marion . . . why he had made such a dreadful mistake. He found himself looking at Pat's charming, boyish face and picturing her as his wife. He tried not to give way to such feelings, but could not banish them. Every time he shook hands with her . . . looked into her steadfast grey eyes . . . he was sick with misery. The time had come when Dion realized where real love, real happiness might be found. And it was forever barred from him by his own folly, his blind infatuation for Marion.

Pat knew that he was unhappy—she was sure that there had been some serious quarrel between him and Marion. She asked no questions—treated him in the usual friendly fashion—was charming to Marion when she saw her. But in her heart, she yearned over Dion; longed to comfort him . . . tell him of her deathless love.

But neither of them spoke.

After the sharpness of pain, during those first days of mental and physical separation from Dion, had passed, Marion became obsessed by the thought of Hope Marshall's mother and the detective who was hounding her down. She temporarily gave up the struggle to regain Dion's love, and devoted her thoughts to Mrs. Marshall and Sidney.

She had received several wild letters from the boy, at the post office, addressed to 'Mrs. Sidney.' All implored her to run away with him. She tore them to bits and answered guardedly, intimating that she would join him as soon as she was certain that Mrs. Marshall would leave her alone.

The difficult days dragged by. Sidney Pollock grew maddened with longing for Marion . . . to see her exquisite face again . . . hold that perfumed, adorable being in his arms . . . bury his face in the rich, scented masses of her hair. In his excited imagination he visualised her as a wronged and suffering angel. He grew thin, nervy, hectic . . . a wreck of himself. He went about his work with a half-crazed look in his eyes. Marion's influence was gaining a stronger, more deadly hold every day.

One morning they spoke on the telephone.

'I must see you . . . God, I must see you . . .' he said hoarsely. 'Be kind to me . . . be merciful . . . I'm nearly mad, my darling.'

'You're not the only one . . . so am I,' she lied. 'And I am having to act a part . . . be the repentant sinner . . . and my husband is treating me abominably.'

'You poor little thing . . . why not come away with me?'

'I will . . . when you have silenced Mrs. M.,' came the usual significant answer.

Sidney clenched his teeth.

'I can't do anything with her, Marion. I've seen her three times. I've implored her to withdraw that tec, and leave your name in peace.'

Marion's hand, holding the receiver, shook.

'What did she say during the last interview?'

'That I was crazy . . . merely taken in by you because you were lovely and had a plausible tongue . . . that she meant to go on thinking the worst of you.'

Marion's eyes held the look of a hunted creature.

'She's carrying on with the investigation, then?'

'Yes. She believes all sorts of horrible things about you which I know ain't true, my Pretty.'

Marion swallowed hard. She was thankful the boy could not see the terror, the guilt in her eyes.

'Of course they aren't true. But she can do me a terrible lot of harm . . . spreading false reports . . . and if I bolt with you . . . people will wonder . . . be suspicious.'

'I understand . . . I know,' he said.

'Sidney—Sid—do something for me,' she panted the words down the telephone.

'I'm mad for a sight of you. I must see you,' he returned.

'I'll come away with you as soon as you've got that woman to shut up,' she said.

She went home in a fever of impatience, of dread.

Sidney Pollock returned to his garage right off his head . . . temporarily insane with his blind, dreadful love for Marion. Most crimes are actuated by passion . . . and this boy's weak brain had been turned by the strong, subtle influence of a very dangerously attractive woman. He wanted her to run away with him. The only way he could get her was by obeying her command . . . silencing Mrs. Marshall. He had pleaded, argued, threatened Hope's mother, and she had seemed all the more obstinate in her determination to prove that Marion was a murderess.

All that night, Marion's sinister influence

worked on the boy's maddened brain.

'I must see Marion . . . must do what she wants.' He turned that thought over and over in his mind. 'I must *make* Mrs. Marshall give up her investigations . . .'

That afternoon he went to Mrs. Marshall and demanded violently that she should leave Marion alone.

Hope's mother stared at the boy. His deathly face, his burning, abnormal eyes frightened her somewhat.

'I don't know what all this is about,' she said, stepping back a pace. 'First of all you were with me in my suspicions—you believed that Lady Courtland knew more than she cared to state, about Jet Saddleman's death . . . just as I have grown to believe that she knows something about my poor Hope. Now you come here twice a day to bully and annoy me because I refuse to withdraw my detective.'

'Never mind why I've changed,' the boy said between his teeth. He was shivering all over. 'You've *got* to stop it.'

'Look here, my young fellow, I've had enough of this,' said Mrs. Marshall. 'I shall give you in charge for trying to intimidate me . . .'

Something seemed to snap in the unhappy boy's mind. Sleepless nights . . . little food . . . mad, terrible longing to see Marion Courtland, had all driven him crazy. He saw Mrs. Marshall only as a barrier between him and his desire . . . an obstinate, maddening woman who would not share his belief that Marion was an angel. Suddenly he pulled a heavy clasp-knife out of his pocket, and sprang at her.

'You'll have to keep silence . . . to stop your dirty work . . . you'll have to!' he snarled.

The unfortunate woman screamed before she went down before that murderous-looking knife . . . screamed twice . . . shrilly, in mortal terror.

But it was not really the boy, Sidney Pollock, who attacked her. It was Marion . . . the murderess . . . Marion, through the boy whom she had used.

CHAPTER TWENTY-FOUR

That same evening, just before dinner, Marion sat before her dressing-table, preparing for the theatre. Dion had bought tickets for all of them . . . his mother and Pat included. His one desire was to avoid *tête-à-têtes* with his wife . . . difficult, embarrassing scenes. Better to go out and see a show, no matter how heavy his heart.

Marion was deeply depressed. She took a long time over her toilette, and when she went downstairs, she was not satisfied with her appearance. She was getting really haggard.

She had put on a white dress tonight, a

clinging creation of ivory, delicate georgette with exquisite lace . . . and wore an ermine stole. She looked very young in it . . . pathetic, with dark cirlces about her magnificent eyes . . . red mouth drooping. When Dion, who was waiting for her in the drawing-room of their flat, saw her enter, he felt a vestige of compassion.

'Sure you feel well enough to come?' he said. 'You look very white, Marion.'

Her heart pounded and her eyes swam as she heard the kindly note in his voice, and saw that his handsome face was softer than she had seen it for days.

'I'm alright, Dion . . . only I . . . oh, I do not implore you to forget . . . to give me another chance,' she said, with a break in her voice.

He flushed and sighed.

'Marion—please . . .'

'Ah, Dion . . . be kind . . .' she implored, and flung herself into his arms, wreathed her lovely white ones about his throat. 'I love you . . . I do love you . . . I'm terribly sorry for that moment of craziness,' she added with a sob. 'Don't shut me out of your heart forever, my dear . . . my dearest one . . .'

He held her mechanically. Her beautiful hair brushed his chin. She was attractive enough in her delicate white gown to appeal to any man. Love for her had died in that hour he had discovered her in Pollock's room. But even now the subtle fascination which always

248

emanated from Marion stirred him to pity for her. Ought he to go on being hard and cruel? He must not judge her as he would judge an ordinary girl. She was a little abnormal.

Marion clung closer to him.

'Dion, Dion, love me again!' she panted. 'Love me and forgive me, or I think I shall kill myself.'

'Hush, hush,' he said, shocked.

'Then love me . . . kiss me, Dion . . .'

He bent his handsome head. Almost his lips touched her mouth. She shut her eyes, expectant, trembling with dizzy delight, with the belief that she had won him back. Then the telephone bell rang sharply . . . breaking the spell of that moment.

Dion released her. She felt insensate fury against the telephone. Dion walked to the instrument and answered the call. She watched him . . . saw his face change . . . redden . . . grow incredulous . . . then he said in a voice of horror:

'What . . . are you sure? Good God . . . yes . . . at once . . . if it is necessary . . . of course.'

He hung up the receiver. He was not soft now. He was hard—pitiless again.

'What is it? Why do you look so strange?' she gasped.

'God!' he said. 'It is too awful. First Hope . . . now her poor mother . . .'

Marion smothered a cry . . . backed from him . . . her face as white as her gown.

'What has happened?' she asked, hoarsely.

'Sidney Pollock has been arrested for attempted murder of Mrs. Marshall,' he said. 'He stabbed her in the side this evening at six o'clock, and was prevented from escaping by two servants who heard her scream. The 'phone call is from the Inspector at the police station where they have detained this young murderer to whom you gave your affections. You are to go round at once. *Sidney Pollock has asked for you.*'

'Asked for *me*!' repeated Marion. 'But how ridiculous—he couldn't have asked for me. How absurd . . .!' She began to laugh hysterically.

Dion strode forward and took the girl's arm. He literally shook her.

'Be quiet,' he said, sternly. 'Stop laughing at once!'

His harsh voice and his fingers, hurting the soft flesh of her arm, brought Marion to her senses. She sobered at once. She flung a hand up to her forehead.

'My God!' she said. 'My God!'

'Oh, stop all this hysteria!' said Dion, in a low, hard voice. He felt suddenly that he hated her . . . was cruelly impatient with her . . . this beautiful, wicked creature whom he had worshipped in the blindness of youth, and made his wife. 'Pull yourself together, please. Facts are facts. Pollock has stabbed poor Mrs. Marshall—he is at the police station, and he wants you. You must come with me at once.'

'No—no!' gasped Marion.

'Why not?' demanded Dion. 'What have you got to fear, my charming wife?'

'Dion!' she wailed, 'don't speak to me like that. It is *you* who frighten me—you!'

He clenched his teeth. He scarcely knew what was prompting him to be so brutal with Marion about this affair. Perhaps it was because, once again, she had brought the precious name of Courtland into public gaze . . . once again, this very night, the 'specials' would have the name of the 'beautiful Lady Courtland' in large, glaring headlines. An attempted murder had been committed and the young man in the case had asked for Lady Courtland . . . a pretty story for the press!

Dion tried to swallow his anger . . . to look at his wife with more sympathy and understanding, but could not. It was bitter and terrible to Dion Courtland to realize that not only had Marion dishonoured him by starting a sordid intrigue with a working-lad younger than herself, but that they had been—must have been—so intimate, that Pollock dared ask for her when he was arrested for a crime!

Marion's long, slender fingers clung to his arm.

'I'm not afraid of going to the police station,' she sobbed. 'But you frighten me— you look at me so strangely. Dion, Dion, be kind to me—don't hate me—ah, don't!'

251

He moved his head impatiently.

'Come, Marion—get on your coat and hat—quickly. This is no time for scenes.'

She drew back from him, cold in every limb. Her large dark eyes held a hunted expression and her lips quivered. She had lost Dion's love—utterly. She knew in this hour just how completely she had forfeited it. He was a hard, cold stranger. He looked at her with hatred in his eyes.

She tried to collect her thoughts—to concentrate on Sidney. So the poor fool had tried to do her bidding—and bungled it! He had not done it quietly, secretively, as she had done things . . . he had been mad and stupid; committed that most heinous of all offences in Marion's eyes—he had been found out!

'The idiot,' she inwardly reviled the wretched youth. 'The fool!'

There seemed but one bright spot in the whole business—that was the fact that Mrs. Marshall had been effectively silenced.

But even that hope was dashed to the ground by Dion's next words.

'You will at least be pleased to hear that poor Hope's mother is not dead,' he said, walking up and down the room, an unlighted cigarette between his fingers.

'N-not d-dead!'

'No. But dying, poor thing. The Inspector said she had been trying to make a statement and was unable to speak plainly enough. But

252

the doctors are watching her, and have hopes that she will be able to speak before she dies. The wound in her side is terrible.'

Marion's knees shook.

Mrs. Marshall not quite dead . . . and they were waiting for her to speak! God alone knew what statement she would make. But she would be certain to implicate her, Marion. Sidney had bungled things even more badly than she had imagined.

By the time Marion had dressed and was on her way to the police station with Dion, she had grown more composed. And she felt a cruel, cold rage against the boy who had sinned for her sake, and made a mess of things.

Dion did not speak on his way to the station. With arms crossed on his chest, he sat staring out of the taxi at the passing traffic. He was an unhappy man this night. He could not trust himself to speak to the woman at his side. So she, too, sat silent, brooding, guilt-stricken, her pale, beautiful face like a mask under the little green velvet hat which she had crushed down on her red-gold head. Her delicate white evening gown was covered in her silver squirrel coat. Her nervous fingers toyed incessantly with the little evening bag which she had snatched up from her dressing-table just before she came away from the flat.

Dion wondered wretchedly what his mother—and Pat—would think when they saw the papers. He wondered, too, what lay at the back of all this crime and mystery . . . what manner of woman Marion really was, under her mask of beauty and charm.

Once, she stole a glance at his set profile, and felt sick with despair. The one sincere thing of her crime-stained life was her love for Dion. And she had lost him—forever. Before the news of Mrs. Marshall's assassination had come through the 'phone tonight, she might have won him back with sheer physical allure; very nearly his lips had touched her mouth in that instant when she had rested against his heart. But now that spell had broken for Dion Courtland . . . all love, all tenderness for Marion had died within him tonight. Alas! the death of passionate love, which has no friendship for foundation, is of all deaths the most complete. It can never, never live again!

Marion braced herself for the forthcoming scene at the police station. She must act now— act for all she was worth.

When at length she stood by Dion's side and faced the unfortunate lad whose life she had wrecked, she ought to have pitied him—any tender woman's heart would have ached to see the ravages of her handiwork. But Marion felt neither compassion nor remorse. She was thinking only of her own safety, tonight.

Sidney Pollock stood between a warder and a policeman by the Inspector's desk. He had the appearance of one who has been drunk

254

and disorderly. But he was stone-cold sober. He was ghastly white. His curly hair was roughened, dishevelled; his clothes seemed to hang upon him loosely. He had grown pitifully thin these last few days, for he had eaten nothing—slept scarcely at all. His eyes, bloodshot, ringed with purple, fixed upon Marion as soon as she entered the Inspector's room. Like a poor, starving creature in a burning desert, he looked at her as though she were the oasis, the cool water, the rest he sought. She was as lovely as his dreams of her. Yet she seemed cold, aloof, utterly beyond his reach. He held out his handcuffed hands. He was a little crazy. He seemed not to see Dion at all.

'Marion,' he said pitifully. 'Marion!'

'How dare you address me like that?' she said in a voice of ice. 'And how dared you send for me, Mr. Pollock?'

The Inspector frowned and coughed. The warder and the policeman looked at the beautiful young woman in her rich fur coat and green velvet hat, and admired her.

But Sidney Pollock stared at her with almost grotesque dismay spreading over his ghastly face. She had come to him—his Marion—the siren of his dreams—and she spoke to him like that . . . called him 'Mr. Pollock' . . . looked at him as though she loathed him. What did it mean? He had done everything she had asked. At least he had done his best. He had tried to silence the woman who wanted to ruin her.

'Now, Pollock,' said the Inspector, curtly. 'Lady Courtland has very kindly come here, because you sent for her. What is it you wish to say?'

'Yes, what is it?' seconded Dion, feeling it his duty to act on Marion's behalf, although he alone knew the disgraceful affair that had existed between these two. 'My wife has recently been very ill, and I cannot have her brought here like this, at your request, for nothing.'

Sidney's eyes went on staring at Marion. They were glazed and dreadful now, and he licked his dry lips as though in torment.

'Marion,' he said. 'I did it for you . . . !'

She went scarlet—then as white as her gown.

'How dare you—' she began. Then she turned to the Inspector: 'The poor fellow is crazy, of course,' she added. 'I came because I thought I might be of help, but if that is all he has to say, my husband had better take me home.'

'One moment, Lady Courtland,' said the Inspector, courteously. 'If you—'

But Sidney interrupted him. The glazed look left his eyes and they became brilliant, feverish. The colour rushed darkly to his sunken cheeks. He made a movement toward Marion, and was prevented by the policeman at his side. He began to gasp out a stream of hysterical words:

'You aren't going to desert me now, are you? Oh, my God, I did it for you—Marion, you said you loved me—you said you'd go away with me—you don't mean you're going to chuck me over, now—because I made a mess of it—oh, my God, my God, Marion, smile at me—be kind—say one kind word—say you thank me—I tried my best for you—for you!'

'Quiet!' said the Inspector.

Marion remained white and rigid and unbending. Dion felt physically sick.

'The poor devil!' he thought. 'What frightful work has Marion done here?'

'Marion—Marion!' Sidney lost his self-control altogether and began to cry like a child. He clasped his handcuffed hands together and held them out to her; the tears poured down his cheeks. 'Marion—look at me—say you don't mean to desert me now—I sent for you because I wanted to hear you thank me for doing as you asked. *Marion!*'

The last word—her name—was a frenzied cry. It made Dion shudder and turn away. Even the officials, hardened though they were—raised their eyebrows and moved uncomfortably.

Marion, of all of them, seemed the most composed. Her beautiful face was frozen; her large brown eyes rested on the half-crazy youth with cruel scorn. Inwardly she was nerve-wracked and terrified, and she cursed the hour she had ever placed her confidence in the weak-minded boy before her.

'Poor fellow—quite mad,' she said. 'How dreadful! And how is *poor* Mrs. Marshall?'

'Still breathing,' answered the Inspector. 'But sinking rapidly, I'm afraid. The doctors hope that she may be able to make a statement before she dies.'

Marion shivered and drew her furs closer about her.

'There seems no object in my remaining, if all this poor fellow wants to do is to say these mad things,' she said.

'Pollock,' said the Inspector to the young assassin, 'pull yourself together. Lady Courtland is here at your bidding. Do you want to say anything of importance?'

Sidney, trembling and sobbing like a demented creature, suddenly tore at his hair with his finger-nails. His eyes rested on Marion, now, with bitterest reproach.

'You liar!' he screamed. 'You traitress—you fiend! You said you loved me—you egged me on to silence Mrs. Marshall—you said you'd quit the country with me if I did it—you tortured me till I did do it—now you're pretending to be ignorant—you're deserting me Damn you—damn you—*damn you!*'

He was shrieking, choking with sobs. His voice broke on the last curse—his knees gave way and he sank into the warder's arms, his eyes closing, his lips frothing a little.

Marion shrank back in horror, and clutched her husband's arm. Somehow the wretched boy's curses struck real terror in her guilty heart. She knew that she had ruined him; that she had made a murderer of a once simple, clean-minded lad; that she stood morally guilty of the assassination which he had perpetrated. His words . . . *'damn you—damn you!'* rang in her ears. She felt already damned. She breathed into her husband's ear:

'Take me away—take me home!'

Dion supported her trembling form because he felt it to be his duty. But he literally shrank from touching her. He felt her to be polluted. To his dying day he would not forget Pollock's terrible outburst. He had cursed Marion, and well he might, if indeed she had encouraged him to the extent he suggested.

'The accused has had some kind of fit, I think, sir,' the warder observed, holding up Sidney's sagging body. 'He had best be taken to his cell, hadn't he?'

'Yes,' said the Inspector. 'Let him be taken away.'

The last glimpse Marion had of the boy whom she had treated so vilely was of a ghastly face, with closed eyes and hanging tongue, as the warder and policeman carried him to his cell.

Once he was gone, Marion breathed more freely. She looked round the bare room, with its whitewashed walls and deal benches and

259

high desk—all very severe and ghostly in the glaring electric light—and shuddered. She, herself, might have been brought here before this bench . . . committed to the cells to await her trial. Was she not thrice a murderess, now?

But she advanced to the Inspector, on Dion's arm, and gave him her sweetest, most pathetic smile.

'How very terrible it all is,' she murmured. 'So sad that the poor youth has gone off his head.'

The Inspector looked at her gravely. He was not certain what to make of this affair. Pollock had addressed this lovely, distinguished lady by her Christian name, and hinted at unspeakable things. Undoubtedly, yes . . . he was insane . . . like his aunt, Sarah Pollock, now incarcerated in Broadmoor. The case was too recent to be forgotten or ignored.

'Sorry you were dragged out for nothing, Lady Courtland,' he said gruffly. 'Pollock seems to have had a fit. No doubt he'll recover, and he'll be able to make what statements he wants, at his trial.'

Marion's throat felt dry and hot.

'But I can't understand why he should try to kill poor Mrs. Marshall,' she forced.

'He offered no explanation,' said the Inspector.

'His intimation that he did it for me was nonsense, of course,' she said, with bravado.

'You are unfortunate, Lady Courtland,' said

the Inspector. 'The aunt accused you at the Pollock murder trial . . . now history repeats itself—the nephew accuses you.'

A rather ghastly smile wreathed Marion's lips.

'The same sort of insanity runs through the family, apparently,' she said. 'Well, good night, Inspector. You don't want me any more now, do you?'

'No thank you, Lady Courtland.'

Dion, like a man in a bad dream, walked out of the police station with Marion clinging to his arm.

After they had gone, the Inspector leaned his arms on his desk, and stared at nothing, his bushy brows contracted.

'Funny business, this,' he thought. 'Darn funny. Seems to me some mighty queer things will come out, when young Pollock is tried for murder. And darn me, *if ever I've seen guilt in a livin' being's eyes . . . I saw it in Lady Courtland's—this night!'*

CHAPTER TWENTY-FIVE

Sir Dion and Lady Courtland reached home.

Marion made a futile attempt to treat the affair lightly. She took off her coat and hat, balanced herself on the edge of the drawing-room table, and pulled a cigarette from a silver box beside her.

'All very dramatic and stupid,' she said. 'I always thought Sidney Pollock was cracked—like Sarah.'

Dion stood before her, not attempting to smoke.

'I don't think for a moment that the boy is insane,' he said.

She dared not look at him.

'Why not?'

'All those things that he said . . . my God . . . they were true. You encouraged him—promised to run away with him!'

She swallowed hard, her eyes still averted lest her husband should read the agony of guilt and fear that lay in them this night.

'Rubbish, my dear Dion.'

'It isn't rubbish,' he retorted, goaded by her seemingly callous attitude. 'My God, how can you sit there so calmly, and smile about it—call him a lunatic—when I know there has been a love-affair between you—found you hiding in a cupboard in his room!'

She applied a match to her cigarette. But her fingers shook so that the match went out. She lit another . . . and another . . . until the cigarette was alight.

'I admit there was an affair . . .' she felt forced to go on with that maddening lie. 'But it went no way. He is crazy—he tried to kill Mrs. Marshall for heaven knows what reason—then he accuses me of encouraging him to do it.

Why should I want the poor woman to die?'

Dion put a hand to his burning forehead.

'I don't know. I don't profess to understand this business—it is all too horrible and mysterious. But why was Hope so foully murdered . . . then Jet Saddleman . . . now Hope's mother? The same hand, the same influence, is at the bottom of it all.'

Marion's teeth chattered. The room spun round her. But she strove desperately to ward off the faintness.

'Sarah's influence—no doubt.'

'Sarah would not have wished Hope to die. And Sarah is in Broadmoor, so could not have encouraged her nephew to kill Mrs. Marshall.'

'She isn't dead yet,' said Marion.

'No—and we may hear more about it when she speaks,' said Dion.

Then he covered his face with his hands. A picture of Hope rose before him . . . her sweet, innocent face; her fair hair and gentle eyes. Once he had loved little Hope, and she had adored him. Now she was dead—foully murdered. And he was tied to Marion . . . Marion whom he had thought so enchanting, so sweet. And God—what was she? What had she done? He dared not think.

Marion's gaze rested on his bowed head with anguish and terror. She extinguished her cigarette, rose and walked to his side—laid a hand on his hair.

'Dion,' she said, in a beseeching voice. 'I

263

assure you—'

'Oh, don't touch me!' he interrupted, lifting his head. 'Go to bed—go away from me!'

'Dion—what are you thinking?' she asked, in a smothered voice.

'I don't know,' he said slowly. 'I—don't want to think!'

Morning came.

Marion did not sleep all night. She presumed that her husband had not slept, either. He was like herself—pale and nervous—eyes heavy with shadows. They avoided each other's gaze when they met at the breakfast table. They did not even say good morning. Dion was thinking of nothing now but his mother and his good name. He had ceased to think of Marion—to even pity her. He knew nothing definite. He was only certain that whatever lay in store for her she deserved.

She was suffering acutely. The expression on her beautiful face was piteous in the extreme. Oh, her punishment had indeed begun . . . and would be long-drawn-out. Half of Emm's prophecy was fulfilled.

As soon as the maid brought in the papers, Marion snatched one up. Dion took another. They read the headlines:

'Echo of the Pollock Murder Case . . .
Sarah Pollock's nephew, Sidney Thomas
Pollock, arrested for the attempted

264

murder of Mrs. Marshall, whose beautiful young daughter, Hope, was found murdered under mysterious circumstances in Linton Wood, Dartmoor, a few months ago. Strange sequence of events. Mrs. Marshall still breathing . . . expected to make a statement at any moment . . .'

One after another the hideous headlines focussed within Marion's gaze. Her feverish eyes searched the columns . . . details of Jet Saddleman's murder . . . a photograph of herself . . . an embroidered description and account of the unpleasant outburst of young Pollock at the Torquay Police station last night.

She licked her dry lips as she read the half-veiled insinuations of the press as to her influence over Sidney Pollock, and her connection with the past murder case. She dared not look at Dion. But she heard him speak to her, after a few moments.

'You see—it is all in the papers—our name dragged through the mud—stinking mud—God, Marion, how could you have done it?'

She forced herself to look at him.

'I—I'm sorry—but it—isn't my fault,' she muttered. 'You're terribly hard on me, Dion.'

He closed his eyes wearily, then opened them again and stared at his wife as though at a stranger who mystified him. He failed to understand her—did not want to stir up muddy waters for fear of what he might find at the bottom—yet he was forced to see and realize as much—and more than the papers dared hint.

How beautiful Marion looked—even now, with her pallor, her shadowed eyes. She was exquisitely dressed in a grey tailored suit and creamy silk georgette jumper with a black floppy bow and Eton collar. With her red-gold curls brushed into shining ringlets about her head, she might have been a child of eighteen—innocent—made for love. Yet he looked upon her this morning without one spark of desire or affection. His spirit recoiled from her. He felt that she was like some beautiful witch-creature . . . waiting to ruin those upon whom she laid her white hands . . . that within her were unplumbed depths of cruelty and wickedness. How could he forget that wretched boy's cry . . . 'Damn you—damn you!'

The door-bell rang. Marion started violently. Her nerves were all on edge. It was Patricia Westby, who was shown into the dining-room by the maid. Pat was pale under her healthy tan, and her grey eyes roved quickly from Dion to Marion with undisguised anxiety. She carried a morning paper in her hand.

'Forgive me for coming so early,' she said, 'but your mother sent me, Dion. She wanted me to get some—some sort of explanation.

The news in the paper has horrified her. She is in bed—quite prostrate'

Dion, standing up, turned his face from the kind, questioning eyes of the girl whom he knew to be his friend.

'I was afraid it would upset her,' he said. 'But—I have no explanation—and neither has—my wife.'

The last words were spoken with such bitterness that Pat bit her lip and looked at Marion. Marion sat silent at the table, her chin resting on the palm of her hand, her dark eyes brooding, haunted.

'I—then perhaps I—had better get back to Lady Courtland,' Pat stammered. She felt intensely embarrassed. She wanted so much to stay and comfort Dion. How ill, how haggard he looked. This must be a dreadful shock for him. It was impossible for her to look upon Marion with compassion. Had she not broken hearts and ruined lives without compunction? Always, always, Pat had had that psychic belief that evil lay rooted in Marion Grayle. Now she knew her beliefs to be only too well founded.

Dion spoke:

'Don't go, Pat,' he said hoarsely. 'Stay and talk to me.'

Marion sprung to her feet.

'Ask her to stay—that's right—let her console you—you hate me now—you're down on me—you want to see the end of me—go on, Dion—let Patricia Westby comfort you—curse

267

her. I—!'

'Be quiet!' interrupted Dion, fiercely.

Marion burst into tears and ran from the room.

Pat's fingers shook as she unbuttoned her short sealskin coat, which she wore over a wool jumper and tweed skirt.

'My dear,' she said in an awkward way, 'I'm terribly sorry. What can I do? Ought I to—go to Marion?'

'No,' he said. 'Let her be. Oh, Pat, Pat, God alone knows what the end of all this will be, but I dread it—for mother's sake. It will kill her.'

Pat took off her little felt hat and smoothed her hair back, boyishly.

'My dear, are things so bad—worse than I imagine?'

He shuddered and turned from her.

'I dare not say. I dare not even think, Pat.'

'I'm sorry,' she said again. 'Anything I can do, I will, Dion.'

'You're a brick,' he said.

Her eyes swam with rare tears. But she said nothing. He saw the tears glisten on her lashes. He came up to her, took one of her hands and touched it with his lips.

'Thanks for staying, Pat,' he said huskily. 'It does help, you know, to have a fine pal like you.'

The touch of his lips thrilled her. She loved Dion Courtland. All her life she would love

268

him. To be his friend; to feel that he needed her in his grief, his anxiety, made her immeasurably proud.

In an adjoining room, Marion Courtland lay on her bed, face pressed to the pillows, body shaking with desperate weeping. She, who had broken hearts, ruined lives . . . taken lives away . . . was passing through the fire of hell now . . . the hell of bitter loneliness and loss. She had lost Dion. She knew for a certainty that she had lost him—that Pat Westby would one day win and hold all that she, Marion, would forfeit so soon.

But gradually her fit of jealousy, of anguish passed; gave place to sterner emotions—to real anxiety. She was no longer safe. At any moment Mrs. Marshall might speak— implicate her—at any moment the whole truth, with the help of Mrs. Marshall's detective, might be unravelled.

She dried her eyes, powdered her nose, put on a quiet dark costume and black hat, and slipped out of the flat unnoticed by Dion or Pat, who were still talking. She had scarcely walked further than the corner of the street when she met a newsboy, with a poster, yelling at the top of his voice: 'Speshul speshul . . . Mrs. Marshall recovers consciousness and speaks . . .'

Marion turned ghastly white. She flung the lad a penny and took up a paper. As soon as she had scanned the column, she knew the worst. Hope's mother was dead. But before she had died, she had informed the police that she knew definitely that Sidney Pollock had been working in league with young Lady Courtland, and had advised the police to get hold of her detective—now working in Moorcoombe—to give them details which he had found out about both Hope's murder and Jet Saddleman's poisoning . . . all in connection with Lady Courtland . . . one-time Marion Grayle.

CHAPTER TWENTY-SIX

Marion's fingers shook so that she could scarcely hold the paper. She glanced up and down the street in a furtive way, almost as though she expected to see servants of the Law approaching her, ready to hold out the warrant for her arrest.

For the first time in her life, she knew what it was to be a hunted creature—a criminal—an outlaw. And when the burly figure of a policeman on his beat appeared round the corner, her nerves went to pieces. She dropped the paper, turned and literally ran down the street back to her home. She let herself into the flat with feverish haste, stood an instant in the hall, listening to the muffled sounds of Dion's and Pat's voices, still issuing from the drawing-room; then fled to her bedroom and locked herself in.

Here, in the charming, familiar room with its rose-pink carpet and rose velvet curtains and beautiful Louis Seize furniture, she felt secure once more. But she trembled in every limb as she sank on to the bed and hid her ghastly face in her hands. The 'game was up.' Sidney Pollock's blundering assassination of Hope's mother had ruined her. Mrs. Marshall had made a disastrous statement. The detective from Moorcoombe would very shortly be questioned . . . and then . . . Marion shuddered . . . heaven alone knew what might come out.

She felt sick with terror, with futile rage against the Fates that had played this final trick upon her. In the beginning everything had gone in her favour; she had felt so safe; she had been so cunning, so clever. It was a sickening disappointment to see her plans go astray . . . her sins brought home to her at last.

She suddenly bit at her finger-nails. Dark furious colour rushed to her beautiful, haggard face. She sprang up and began to pace up and down her room.

'I'm not beaten yet,' she said to herself savagely. 'They haven't got me yet—and they never will get me, either!'

Fresh plans for action crowded into her brain. Even while her conscience struck at her, while the demons of guilt, of terror mocked and jeered, she was still a subtle, resourceful young woman. She reviewed the situation from beginning to end. There was time for her to escape. If she waited here, of course the inevitable would happen—the law would grow suspicious and detain her—she would never be able to clear herself if once they set a mark upon her, made thorough investigations about *her.* Up till now, suspicion had never touched her; everything she said had been believed. But Sidney had ruined her—his wild accusation of her at the police station last night had given away half the truth. The rest would follow.

She must escape. That idea enlarged in her mind every passing second. It would never do to stay here and just wait for Them to come and arrest her.

She pictured herself in prison, denied all the luxuries, the beauty she adored; she visualised the trial, the shame, the horrors crowding down upon her one after another, and last of all she thought of the shame she had brought upon the man she had loved. That mattered more than anything. Even now, she thought of Dion with passionate love and longing. And after today probably she would never see him again.

In an access of passion, Marion plucked at her hair . . . tore some of the glorious, red-gold curls—which he had once loved and kissed— from the roots . . . yet felt no pain. Mental

272

agony far superseded the physical. Scalding tears ran down her cheeks. She beat her clenched fists against her head.

'Dion, Dion,' she moaned. 'Oh, God . . . I loved you . . . whatever I've done . . . I loved you!'

But the spasm of intolerable anguish passed, and she realized the terrible necessity for swift and quiet action. She must leave this flat . . . leave Torquay . . . at once.

She looked round the pretty room, fragrant with the perfume of flowers . . . and her own favourite Parisian scent. In this room she had found heaven . . . the heaven of Dion's love. During her illness, after the Pollock trial, she had lain in that bed and he had sat beside her, holding her hands, smiling down at her with his handsome eyes. Ah, God! To see Dion smile at her once again—like that . . .

He loathed and despised her—shrank from her now. Of all pains, that was the keenest to bear. He was in the next room with Pat . . . Marion writhed at the thought. Yet in the next breath she told herself maliciously that whatever happened between these two in years to come, Dion would never know the extreme ecstasy and delight with Pat that he had known in his most passionate moments with *her*.

She pulled a small suitcase from a cupboard, and began to cram things into it . . . a few necessities . . . an evening gown . . . a change of clothes. She then unlocked a drawer in her dressing-table and pulled out a cash-box. She was afraid to go to the bank and cash a cheque . . . afraid to go anywhere where she was known as Lady Courtland . . . might be detained. She found that she had forty pounds in banknotes, one or two loose £1 notes and some silver. That would be enough to get her away from Torquay . . . over to the Continent where she could hide until she saw how things were going.

Had she paused to think more coolly and sanely, Marion might have realized the stupidity of running away. It was so much a proof of guilt. But she was half-mad with terror and anxiety. She acted on impulse, and wanted to escape.

She put on a black velour hat, and covered the grey tailor-made with her squirrel coat. Then, quietly tip-toeing through the hall, she made her way out of the flat, unseen.

She ached for a last sight of the husband she had adored and for whom she had sinned—stained her immortal soul with blackest crime—in vain! She would have given worlds to rest in his arms once more . . . feel his kiss of forgiveness, of farewell on her mouth. But she was denied even that. Dion was with Patricia Westby—and Marion dared not let him know that she was running away, lest he should try and prevent her from going. She had left a brief note for him on her dressing-table. She walked out of her home alone, a fugitive from the Law, afraid of every face she saw in the street.

She reassured herself as to the fact that, as yet, no warrant had been issued for her arrest. She passed along the street to the taxi-rank, unnoticed . . . found herself in the train speeding up to London, without being questioned or worried. She wondered if, later in the afternoon, officials of the law would be sent to the flat for her?

That journey up to London was the most frightful of Marion's experience. She felt utterly deserted by every human being she had known. Not one who had flattered and cared for her in the past, would smile or offer a friendly hand once they read the papers . . . found out what she really was.

She was thankful to have the first-class carriage to herself. She stared out of the window with feverish eyes . . . her lips nervously twitching, her eyes like those of a creature already in Hell.

One by one the ghosts of the past rose up to accuse and to jeer at her now. Hope . . . her golden hair floating among the weeds of the Suicide's Pool . . . Jet Saddleman, paralysed, terrible, drinking the poisoned wine . . . Sarah, jibbering in her undeserved Criminal Asylum . . . Mrs. Marshall, stabbed—now growing cold in her shroud . . . Sidney Pollock, a murderer through her suggestion, waiting his trial at Exeter.

She shook from head to foot, and put a hand over her eyes as though to shut out the sight of those faces—to ward off that ghastly crew. But she could not escape from them, and in her ears reiterated old Emm's dark prophecies . . . the *Dark Death* . . . the Gallows!

Marion stifled a shriek.

'Oh. God, God, have mercy on me!' she moaned aloud. 'Not that . . . not that . . . let me escape from that.'

But no answer came to her prayer. Why should she expect mercy . . . she, who had shown none to her unfortunate and innocent victims, all sacrificed to her own passions and desires?

Her thoughts turned to her poor old father . . . poor Tom Grayle, at the Travellers' Rest. What would he think when he saw the papers . . . knew the worst? He had adored her dear dead mother . . . he had been so proud of her, his daughter. Soon he would know that she was crime-stained . . . wicked . . . a creature from whom all decent folk would shrink in righteous horror and indignation!

But only for an hour or two did Marion's agonised and remorseful thoughts torment her. Then she pulled herself together, and, taking out her vanity-bag, powdered her face, rubbed a little rouge into her cheeks, and outlined her perfect lips with a vermillion lipstick. She was still beautiful—exquisitely so—still young—still magnetic and fascinating.

And she was not caught yet. She would show what she could do. She would go over to France . . . find some easily-gulled man to take an interest in her—make life worth living for her. With her beauty and charm she would never have to sink to poverty, to starvation, to utter squalor and loneliness.

Reaching London, she did not pause a moment. She went straight to Victoria and took the next boat-train to Folkestone. She wanted to go to Monte Carlo—to the Casino there, where one might so easily lose one's identity and find a companion. So she sailed to Boulogne, and travelled by train down to the South of France. She was thankful now that she had a passport . . . that she had let Dion get her one in preparation for their voyage to Egypt. It was made out in the name of Marion Courtland . . . but she passed the barrier at Folkestone without being detained.

With what bitter pain did she recollect all Dion's plans to take her to Cairo this winter. If things had been different, how happy she might have been with him.

She wondered miserably if, when he found her gone, he would feel a single throb of regret . . . of pity for her . . . or whether he would merely be relieved.

The trip over to France was a ghastly one. She was nervous and afraid of everyone, of everything . . . afraid that at any moment she would feel a hand on her shoulder . . . be taken back to England . . . to degradation . . . to a disgraceful death. The dews poured from her forehead at the mere thought.

Her relief when she reached Monte Carlo was exquisite. But she was exhausted. She had not slept at all in the train. She took a cheap bedroom at the cheapest hotel in Monte Carlo, and signed the register as 'Mrs. Grey'. She would like to have gone straight to bed, to rest, to ease her aching head and limbs. But there was to be no rest, no peace for Marion Courtland . . . hunted criminal that she was. She knew she could waste no time; that if she wanted to meet some foolish fellow who would spend money upon her and take her away to safety, she must get busy at once.

It was all part of her punishment. She really hated behaving in this way . . . she was at heart entirely faithful to Dion. But 'needs must when the devil drives,' and Marion was sorely driven tonight.

The weather was cold for the Rivieria. The cheap continental hotel was draughty and uncomfortable. But Marion set her teeth, made up her face, put on the black sequin dress she had packed, and her squirrel coat, then made her way to the Casino to the Salles de Baccara.

This was for life or for death . . . the Beginning or the End. She knew not which . . . she only knew that whatever happened to her, she had passed through Hell . . . would suffer hideously for her crimes.

CHAPTER TWENTY-SEVEN

Not until lunch-time did Dion discover that his wife had run away. Pat had gone. She had stayed with him for a couple of hours, and had left him in a better frame of mind. She had been sensible, sympathetic . . . had a soothing effect on Dion's jangled nerves. He was ready to face whatever pain and disaster he would be called upon to face, with a courage learned from her. She had shaken his hand with those strong, cool fingers of hers, and said:

'Courage, my friend . . . and at any time, if you want my help . . . send for me!'

He would not forget that, Dion told himself. He might, indeed, need her soon.

Then, when Marion failed to appear for lunch, he questioned the parlour maid. The girl said she had not seen her ladyship personally, but noticed that she had been packing . . . that her bedroom was in disorder, and that there was a note for Sir Dion on her ladyship's dressing-table.

Dion felt his heart miss a beat.

'Bring me the note,' he said.

The maid brought it to him, and left him alone. In the kitchen she told the other servants that 'Poor Sir Dion looked ghastly' and she 'wondered what her ladyship was up to.'

Dion read Marion's farewell note to him. It was short and full of very bitter pain:

> 'Dion, I've run away. I dare not stay and face things. You will never see me again. I don't ask you to forgive me—only to believe that I loved you.
> Your most unhappy
> Marion.'

He read it twice, then folded it and put it in his pocket. He sat down by the window and stared out at the pale, greyish November sky. His face was almost as grey, and he felt physically sick.

Marion had run away because she dared not stay and face things. What a terrible lot that inferred . . . what ghastly facts it disclosed. She was guilty . . . a coward who had run away. Heaven alone knew what she was guilty of . . . Dion could not bring himself to think . . . to dissect his thoughts. But this one truth stared him in the face . . . Marion, his wife, was guilty, and she had run away to escape the law.

Where she had gone he did not know. He could not even visualise the possible consequences of her action, which itself was a confession of guilt. She might have fled to safety; she might be found at any hour and brought back to be cross-questioned and—God help her—condemned.

Dion hid his face in his hands. He was shaking.

'Oh, God,' he said aloud, 'God, what has she done? What has she done?'

Following these emotions, came less terrible, if very painful ones. He had loved this woman once . . . and she had been his wife . . . lain against his heart, thrilled him with her enchanting kisses and caresses. He thought of that exquisite face; that flame-gold head; that magnificent vitality which he had admired so much when first he had met her at Moorcoombe. Mentally, he ran through the many incidents of their early married life . . . the rather trying days in Paris . . . the still more trying days of Sarah Pollock's trial . . . Marion's nervous breakdown.

But as soon as he thought of Sarah Pollock, he felt his very spirit recoil from Marion. It was she who had administered that death-draught to Jet Saddleman. And now he knew the truth . . .

'No, no, no!' he cried the words aloud, hoarsely, as though in contradiction to his ghastly thoughts. He got up and began to pace up and down the room, holding his head between his clenched fists.

What had she done? What had she not done? And she was still his wife . . . Lady Courtland . . .

'It will kill mother,' Dion reflected. 'It makes me feel I want to put an end to myself—it is all so horrible!'

Then he remembered Pat Westby. He felt the need of her presence . . . to soothe, to strengthen, to help him.

He left his lunch untasted. He put on hat and coat, and drove round to his mother's flat. Lady Courtland was in bed, still prostrate . . . and he did not want to see her—to let her see his agony of mind. He went straight to Pat, who was finishing her lunch.

She rose as he entered the dining room, and laid down her table-napkin. She was shocked at the sight of his ashen face.

'Dion—my dear!' she exclaimed.

'Pat—Marion has gone,' he said. 'She has run away. She can't face things. Pat, Pat, it means she is guilty and God only knows of what . . . Pat, I think I am going mad . . . mad . . . I think of Hope . . . Saddleman . . . oh, Pat, help me . . . don't let this drive me crazy!'

His voice was shaking . . . that young, handsome face which had once been so boyish, so happy, was dreadful, livid. Pat stared at him a moment, in silence. Then she realized his condition of mind . . . the shock to his nerves . . . and his utter need of her.

She did not hesitate to give the help and the comfort he needed to keep his sanity through the horrors that were crowding down upon him. She walked straight up to him, put her

282

arms about him, held him to her breast.

'Hush,' she said. 'Hush, my dear. Buck up—don't give way—you've been so splendid—don't give way now, whatever happens.'

He put his arms about her and hid his ravaged face on her shoulder. Something within him seemed to break. He was crying like a child. But she had saved him—and he knew there was no need to apologise for his weakness in that hour.

What passed between those two is too sacred to be described, but at the end of that hour, Dion was brave and composed again, and it was Pat . . . strong, brave Pat, who went to her room and cried and cried.

Later that same day, Dion faced fresh trouble. But he was prepared for it, and when the evening papers were issued and he saw his name, his mother's name blazoned through England, to their unending shame and disgrace, he winced, but he was past breaking down again. He was strong and quiet, and Pat was herself, at his side, waiting to prove the love, the respect she had always felt for him.

There was now a warrant out for the arrest of Marion Courtland. It was a dramatic, thrilling story that the press had got hold of, and they used it to the best advantage. The evening news was full of Marion's photographs, Dion's . . . echoes of the Pollock trial—of the new Torquay murder . . . the death of Mrs. Marshall . . . the death of her daughter, Hope, in Linton Wood. No official announcement had been made, the papers said, with regard to Lady Courtland's hand in these affairs, but grave statements had been made at Scotland Yard, and exciting developments were expected. Lady Courtland was missing—and there was a thrill for the public in that alone.

Dion's lips were set as he read the vivid, merciless paragraphs; and Pat's heart ached for him when she read them, after him.

'We must keep this from your mother, Dion,' she said.

'Yes,' he said. 'As far as possible, Pat. It is all too ghastly.'

'Poor Marion,' said Pat.

'You can pity her?' exclaimed Dion, incredulously.

'Yes,' said Pat. 'Because I feel she must be abnormal, insane, Dion, and must be pitied as a lunatic.'

He shuddered. He could not pity the woman who had brought such hideous disgrace upon his family. There are some things no man can forgive or excuse. Marion was beyond the pale. It was only another proof of Pat's greatness of heart that she could find any shred of compassion for the girl who had done such terrible things. Even now they did not know the full extent of her wickedness. Things were only hinted at, darkly.

That night, officials from Scotland Yard

visited Dion's flat and cross-questioned him as to the whereabouts of his wife.

'You must quite realize that if you are aiding and abetting Lady Courtland to escape the law, you are committing an offence . . . making yourself an accessory after the fact,' he was told. And he replied, coldly, wearily:

'I understand that. But I cannot help you. I do not know, myself, where—she has gone.'

Last thing that night he said to Pat:

'I hope to God they never find her; that she is never brought back. I would far rather she escapes—for her own sake as well as ours.'

'I hope she is never found,' nodded Pat. 'It would be too awful if she were brought back now.'

'Tomorrow I must try and bring myself to drive to Moorcoombe, and see old Grayle,' said Dion, with a long-drawn sigh. 'This will break his heart, Pat. He thought the world of Marion. What must he be feeling, now?'

'I'll come with you, Dion,' she said.

He put out a hand and laid it on hers.

'What would I have done without you, my dear?' he said.

Her grey eyes smiled at him, although her fine lips quivered a little. But the touch of his hand and the deep gratitude in his voice repaid her a hundred-fold for anything she had ever done for this man whom she loved.

CHAPTER TWENTY-EIGHT

Out in Monte Carlo, in the Salles de Baccara, for the next two nights, Lady Courtland—alias Mrs. Grey—staked everything she had in the world at the gaming-table—and lost. She played *Chemin-de-Fer* for the first time, without the beginner's luck. Her little stock of money dwindled down to a couple of pounds, which she dared not spend because she had to live; and in spite of the good exchange, two pounds turned into francs would not carry her far.

The croupier, with his bland smile and swift, sleek movements, raked away her remaining plaques. Marion caught her lower lip with her teeth, her cheeks white under the rouge. She had been disastrously unlucky. Not once had she run a decent bank and won. And now she had lost her all.

She rose from the table, pulling her grey fur coat closer about her. Now what could she do?

A man who had been standing on the opposite side of the table, watching her, extinguished his cigarette and walked toward her.

'You have been very unlucky, Madame,' he said.

Marion looked at him, her magnificent dark eyes quickly taking stock. He was an American from his voice, and a man of means from his appearance. He was well-groomed, and wore a white flower in his buttonhole. He was not young—just past middle-age, but very handsome, with a great stalwart figure, a brown rugged face, curly grey hair, and a pair of twinkling blue eyes. He looked nice—pleasant—easy to please.

Marion experienced an instant's repulsion from this game she had set herself out to play—then she smiled at him.

'Most unlucky, haven't I?' she said lightly.

He thrilled a little under the smile, the gaze of those rich brown eyes. She was 'stunning,' he told himself. He had been watching her the whole evening . . . thinking what a little 'peach' she was, with her prefect face, and that wonderful head of red-gold hair. 'Noo York' would go crazy over her.

'Care to take a drink with me?' he said, with his slight drawl.

'Thanks very much,' she said.

'My name's Harper,' he volunteered. 'Randal Harper. I come from Boston.'

'I'm very delighted to meet you, Mr. Harper,' she said in her sweetest voice. 'My name is Dolores Grey.'

'Say, that's a stunning name and it suits you,' he said. 'You look like a Dolores with those eyes and that wonderful hair.'

She smiled a trifle bitterly. Dolores was the first name that had come into her mind. What did it matter? What did anything matter, now? She was ruined; she had lost all her money. She had lost everything that made life worth while. Now to play up to Mr. Randal Harper from Boston.

An hour later they were good friends. Marion had told him that she was a widow, that her husband had died a year ago in a railway accident; that she was absolutely alone in the world, and very sick of life.

Randal Harper listened with that sympathy and a credulity often found in big, honest, unsophisticated Americans of his type. 'Mrs. Grey' seemed a respectable and charming Englishwoman, and he treated her as such. He told her all that she wanted to know; he was alone in the world; out in Monte Carlo for pleasure; rolling in dollar bills. He had one of the newest American racing cars over here; would take her for a drive tomorrow.

He insisted upon driving her back to her hotel that night, and was shocked because it was such a small, humble one.

'I've kind o' taken a shine to you, Dolores,' he said, holding both her hands when he said good-bye to her. 'I may call you Dolores, mayn't I?'

'Why, yes,' she said, with a look that made his heart race and thrill.

And indeed, with the moonlight shining on that beautiful face which was so fair and deceitful, and which had ruined so many men's lives, it is not to be wondered at that Randal Harper fell completely in love with 'Dolores Grey.'

That next morning, before she met Randal Harper, Marion bought an English newspaper, and saw how far things had developed. She was now wanted by the police. She went cold with terror at the thought. She must act swiftly. She had been lucky to meet a great 'boob' like Harper. She must play the lonely, gentle widow for all she was worth. She must make the American fond of her . . . willing to take her back to America . . . that would be the way to escape the law, utterly.

But it was with anguish in her heart that Marion set forth to meet Harper. She wanted Dion, intolerably. How he must hate and despise her, now that he had read the papers!

That drive up the mountains at the back of Monte Carlo was fruitful. Randal Harper lost his head completely over the 'beautiful little widow,' with her red-gold curls and great dark eyes. He did not bother to read English newspapers. He scarcely glanced at his own 'New York Times.' How could he recognize in the perfect face of his companion, the much-wanted Lady Courtland, of Torquay? He only knew that Dolores Grey was the most attractive girl he had ever met. Hitherto a confirmed bachelor, he suddenly conceived the violent desire to marry. He was 'darn sorry' for the poor little girl . . . she hadn't a blue cent—

he'd marry her, take her back to Boston. My! wouldn't his pals sit up and take notice when he showed them Mrs. Dolores Harper . . .

He proposed to Marion, after a champagne dinner, that night at the *Café de Paris*. He had ordered her a most expensive meal; pressed a bouquet of hot-house roses and carnations into her hands; danced with her once or twice. And she smiled at him and beguiled him with all the allure of Delilah, until he was intoxicated with her beauty and charm. But all the while, the spectres of Marion's conscience sat at that feast and stared at her with hollow, eyeless sockets and gaping mouths, and she shuddered under her paint—her mask of happiness.

Randal Harper took her hands, and said:

'Say, Dolores, you're the most stunning little girl I've ever met this side of the herring-pond. You're all alone, and so am I. What about you becoming Mrs. Randal, and going over to Boston with me, right away?'

At an adjoining table, a boy leaned across to his companion—an older man—and whispered:

'I say, Dad, look at the woman on your left, with the wonderful face and the red hair. Isn't she the living image of that woman, Lady Courtland, who is wanted for murder?'

CHAPTER TWENTY-NINE

The man whom the boy addressed glanced discreetly round the room, then stole a swift, searching look at the beautiful woman with the red-gold hair who was looking into the eyes of the American opposite her.

'Phew!' he said under his breath. 'It is. I *know* it is. I was at the Sarah Pollock trial. You remember . . . that poison mystery—farmer from Moorcoombe, near Torquay. I went into Exeter for the Assizes. Lady Courtland gave evidence. It *is* she!'

The boy grew excited.

'What'll you do about it, Dad?'

'Dad' was not a very nice man. He possessed little kindness—decency of feeling. Under the circumstances, no doubt, most men would have said: 'Let the poor devil alone . . . she'll meet her deserts soon enough.' But he was a self-righteous individual, interested in criminal cases only for the pleasure of seeing the agonies and writhings of the cross-questioned, and condemned. For him, the beautiful Lady Courtland could not be found soon enough. It would be exciting to see her arrested over here in Monte Carlo. Besides, if he, James Holford, assisted the British police, it would bring his name into public notice; and James Holford's soul yearned for publicity. He was a mean little man.

He took another glance at Marion, then licked his lips in a satisfied fashion.

'That's the woman, right enough,' he muttered. 'You were very bright, my boy— spotting her. Now for a discreet wire to the C.I.D. in London.'

The boy—less mean—moved uncomfortably. Marion was a terrible woman—his mother would have called her a 'Daughter of Babylon,' but she was beautiful . . . and it seemed a shame to give a woman away—even a wicked woman.

'I say, Dad—don't—' he began.

'Don't be a fool,' said his father. 'Such creatures ought not to be allowed to rove the face of the earth. Come along. I'm going to the post office.'

The man and the boy rose, and moved away from their table. Marion looked up—glanced casually at the boy. He looked down at her as though fascinated, and blushed bright red. She shrugged her shoulders and smiled at Randal Harper. She imagined the boy was attracted by her beauty. She little guessed that burning flush had been brought to his cheeks for shame . . . because his father was about to betray a woman for the sake of righteousness.

From the moment that James Holford marched to the post office to send an important telegram to the C.I.D., *re* Lady Courtland, Marion's star was on the decline.

But she, careless, unconscious, believing herself safe, accepted the hand and heart of Randal Harper, from Boston, U.S. A.

Dinner over, Harper took her out in his car for a moonlight spin up the lovely mountains at the back of Monte Carlo. He stopped the car in a convenient spot and they looked a moment down at the bay, set like a jewel, flashing and twinkling with lights, in the starry sea.

Randal Harper became emotional. He put both arms around Marion, and drew her slender, supple body close to his. His lips strayed over her hair, found the perfumed scarlet of her mouth in a lingering kiss that intoxicated him.

'Dolores—Dolores—say, aren't you just the loveliest thing?' he said ecstatically.

Marion did not speak, but her eyes filled with tears. Strange, wild, irrational being that she was, her heart was stirred tonight with sadness . . . with a thousand regrets . . . with the bitter hopelessness of remorse. It was not the unsuspecting American who stirred her. Her body was warm and yielding in his arms, but her mind was miles away . . . with Dion. It was for him she longed. She was moved by the beauty of the Southern night . . . she wished passionately that she had never committed a crime, never come down to this ignoble game she was being forced to play. It was shameful to deceive a kind and decent man who thought her a genuine respectable widow.

Randal Harper saw the tears in her great dark eyes.

'Say, honey—why are you crying?' he asked in dismay. 'You do care for me, don't you? You do want to marry me?'

She shivered, but she smiled.

'Yes,' she whispered. 'Of course. I—I'm not crying.'

'Maybe they're tears of happiness,' he said fondly, hugging her. 'My! Dolores, I'll spend the rest of my life making you happy.'

She hid her face on his shoulder. For an instant she clung to him blindly. Her tears fell thick and fast. But they were for Dion . . . Dion, her husband, whom she believed she would never see again in this life. And mingled with her remorse, her sorrow, came overwhelming terror lest this nice, big, strong man, whose arms and affection spelt security, should be snatched from her. She could never love him. But she might get fond of him in time, and if he took her to America, she would be safe forever. The point was, would she ever get across the Atlantic in safety? Or would she be found out . . . stopped . . . like Crippen had been . . . by means of wireless . . . half-way across . . . or detained at Cherbourg . . . or . . . she snapped off the thread of her reflections, shuddering. She dared not think any further. She called herself a fool. Why should she be discovered? She was known in Monte Carlo as

Dolores Grey. Randal was begging her to marry him by special licence the day after tomorrow. She would be all right. She need not fear.

Randall was talking now of a ring for her. Tomorrow they would go to the finest jeweller's in Monte Carlo, and get a diamond that would out-sparkle any of the diamonds in the place. She was his little queen—nothing should be good enough for her.

She thanked him with a smile and a caress.

But when she went back to her hotel that night, she cried bitterly. Even her successful 'netting' of the wealthy American failed to cheer her up. She felt weighed down . . . nervous . . . stupid. She started at every sound . . . felt afraid of every shadow. And she could not laugh herself out of the feeling.

She lay awake, listening to the surge of the Mediterranean; she was sleepless, wretched, filled with forebodings. The room seemed to her full of ghosts. She hid her face in her hands and sobbed aloud.

'Oh, God . . . oh, God! How guilty I am!'

But there was to be no comfort for Marion Grayle, murderess . . . no hope for Marion, now Lady Courtland . . . alias Dolores Grey. 'An eye for an eye' . . . 'a tooth for a tooth' . . . it is written. 'Vengeance is Mine,' said the Lord. And the blood of Hope Marshall, of Jet Saddleman, of Mrs. Marshall, cried out for vengeance.

She believed that all was not yet lost, and she played on . . . played her desperate game with a smile . . . a beautiful smiling mask of a face that hid her terror and guilt.

That next day was spent in reckless gaiety. She was now Randal Harper's promised wife. On the finger from which she had taken Dion Courtland's wedding ring, she wore a huge diamond set in platinum. About her neck hung a rope of rare pearls, and she had moved from the cheap hotel to a bigger, more luxurious one. Randal had insisted upon it. He paid all the bills without feeling it. He was a man of dollars.

On the morrow, by special licence, 'Dolores Grey' was to become Mrs. Randal Harper, and within a week from that date, they were to sail from Cherbourg for New York.

Marion's wedding-day came. Prepared for bigamy—for any other desperate measures to ensure her safety—she drove to the Registrar's to meet the American.

The marriage—which was no marriage—took place at twelve o'clock. At half-past twelve, Marion and Randal were sitting at the *Café de Paris,* having their 'wedding-breakfast.'

Marion was all in white . . . new, expensive clothes, purchased by her 'husband.' She wore a white cloth suit with a smart little cape; a chic white hat with a paradise plume curling from it; a great bunch of dewy violets pinned on her shoulder. She looked radiant, flushed, beautiful enough to make Randal Harper's heart pound when he looked at her, but under it all she was intensely nervous and worried. She kept looking to the left and right of her in a furtive way. But Randal did not notice that. Infatuated, he held her left hand and repeatedly kissed the diamond circlet which had done duty as a wedding-ring.

'My wife!' he kept on saying. 'Gee! What a proud fellow I am, Dolores. My wife!'

She smiled, but she was irritated. She was not his wife. She was Lady Courtland—Dion's wife. Oh, God, if all this had never happened!

Suddenly she said:

'Randal, I'm sick of Monte Carlo. Let's move today. Somewhere else!'

'Why, honey?' he asked, surprised. 'I thought Monte suited you.'

'I'm—sick of it,' she said, her fine brows knit. 'Take me somewhere else.'

'Anywhere you like, my little wife.'

'Why not Algiers?' Marion made the suggestion more cheerfully. In some queer way, Monte Carlo worried her. She no longer felt safe here. Algiers would be new . . . she could get lost there with her 'husband.'

The English papers she had scanned this morning, before her marriage, had terrified her. There was a hue and cry for Lady Courtland. The one definite charge against her was for being an accessory after the fact for the murder of Mrs. Marshall . . . Sidney

297

Pollock had completely ruined her. In the bitterness of his heart against her, he had laid bare the whole disgraceful story of their intrigue . . . of the influence she had used upon him to 'silence' Mrs. Marshall. He had even let the police search his rooms and find her letters . . . some of the mad, guilty letters she had written in the beginning, and which were now being blazoned throughout the country.

Dion must have seen those letters, she thought. Dion must realize the full extent of her shame . . . her wickedness.

There was some suggestion that she might have fled abroad. She wished she had dyed her hair. That tell-tale vivid red would give her away. But now it was too late. Randal adored her hair—would never allow her to dye it.

They arranged to go to Algiers.

Later that afternoon, Marion passed through the lounge of her hotel up to her bedroom, where a chambermaid was strapping up her trucks for her departure. She was going to get her squirrel travelling coat and make the final arrangements for her journey to Algiers, that same day.

As she walked through the lounge in her proud, graceful way, many turned to look at the beautiful woman in white. A boy, half-hidden behind a palm, watched her . . . started forward . . . slunk back . . . then started forward again. Marion saw him, caught his eye—remembered him as the boy who had blushed so violently when he had caught her gaze at the restaurant, two nights ago. She frowned and paused. Why was he staring at her, beckoning her behind the palm like that. Was it impudence . . . or was he mad?

'What is it?' she asked him, haughtily.

'Come here a minute—I want to speak to you—' he stammered.

'Why? What about?' she demanded.

'You are Lady Courtland,' he said, under his breath, staring at her with his frightened, boyish eyes.

Marion stood stock-still, her face growing as white as her attire. Every nerve in her body quivered, then tautened.

'You are mistaken,' she said. 'My name is Mrs. Randal Harper.'

She would have passed on, but the boy caught her by the arm.

'For God's sake listen to me a minute—it's for your own sake,' he said hoarsely.

She came nearer him, tense, fascinated.

'Are you crazy?' she demanded.

'No—listen—we recognized you—my father and I—the other night. It was my fault—I had been reading about you in the papers—I remembered your face—and my father has seen you in Exeter. He has informed the police.'

Marion's nerves went. She stifled a cry with her handkerchief.

'Oh—my God!'

The boy was only seventeen, and tender-hearted. Even now, despite the papers, he could not believe that this lovely creature was guilty, and he would not have known another moment's peace had he allowed her to be arrested—through him and his father.

'I had to warn you,' he said. 'Dad's gone to the station—to meet two detectives from London. You have time to get away—if you go now.'

Marion rocked a little on her feet. Her eyes grew glazed and hot, and her whole body felt racked with nervous terrors. She looked at the boy who had warned her.

'Why have you—done this?' she gasped. 'Or is it a trap—a trick?'

'No—I swear it isn't a trick,' he said. 'I want you to get away. I felt so mean—so guilty about it—because I'd pointed you out to my father—but I'd no idea he'd act like he has done.'

Marion made an effort to pull herself together. She had to.

So a lad's pity had saved her, temporarily. She gave a bitter little smile and put out her hand to him.

'Thank you,' she said. 'Thank you—!'

He gave one of his embarrassed flushes. But the touch of her hot fingers . . . the gratitude in her great dark eyes repaid him for his treachery to his father and to the law. To his dying day he never forgot Marion Grayle.

Even later, when he knew the full extent of her wickedness; when her terrible crimes were laid bare to the world, he did not regret the compassion which had led him to give her that warning.

Ashen, trembling, Marion managed to get to her room, then dismissed the chambermaid, sank on to a chair and tried to collect her scattered thoughts. Her world rocked about her. The warning of the boy downstairs had stripped her of any illusion she might have had that she was safe because she had committed bigamy with Randal Harper.

The police were after her . . . coming here now.

She must get away—at once. She dared not even see the wretched man she had deceived and married this morning.

She was forced to desperate measures. Gone any dream of sailing to America . . . any thought of travelling in peace and luxury to Algiers with Randal Harper, this afternoon.

She tore off her white wedding-gown, her hat. She put her pearls, her diamond rings into her purse, in which there were a few loose notes. She swept her hair back from her forehead and concealed it completely under a small black hat, then put on a black costume. She waited for nothing else. The police were after her. She must be quick.

She left the hotel by the back entrance, whilst Randal Harper stood in the lounge, chewing a cigar contentedly, thumbs in his waistcoat, waiting for his bride to come down and join him.

The hour of retribution was at hand.

Marion fled to the station. Now the boy's father and the two officers would be on their way to her hotel. The train from Boulogne or from Calais had come in. She would conveniently cross them.

She met with no difficulty at the station. She took a ticket for Paris. Her throat was dry, her eyes fevered and distended. She kept her hat well over her forehead, and was afraid of her own shadow. To be hunted, wanted . . . to know herself guilty . . . how ghastly it was . . . and what an end to her scheming!

Once in the Paris express, she felt more relieved. But she sobbed under her breath as the train moved away from Monte Carlo. A blank future lay before her! Friendless, homeless—a few diamonds and pearls to pawn, and after that, starvation or exposure.

At the hotel, a terrible shock awaited the deluded American. 'Dolores' did not join him, but three men came up to him; one of whom introduced himself as Inspector Dawson from Scotland Yard.

'You have been seen about with a beautiful, red-haired woman, posing as Mrs. Grey,' said the Inspector, quietly.

'Posing!' echoed Randal Harper. 'Say, what is this all about? Mrs. Grey became my wife

302

this morning. She's Mrs. Randal Harper, right now.'

'Sorry, sir,' said the Inspector. 'You have been fooled. We believe that woman to be Lady Courtland, and she is wanted in connection with a murder in Torquay.'

Randal Harper's face lost some of its healthy colour.

'Murder . . . Gee! That's an ugly word,' he said. 'You're making some mistake, aren't you?'

'Might I have a few words with Mrs.— Harper?' asked the detective, pleasantly.

'Certainly. She'll tell you to go about your business,' snorted Randal.

It was then that he discovered the flight of Dolores. It was then that he examined the photographs and descriptions of the much-wanted Lady Courtland, and knew beyond all doubt that Dolores Grey and Lady Courtland were one and the same.

It was a smashing blow, and it stunned Randal Harper.

After the two men from the C.I.D. had departed to make inquiries at the station, hot on the track of the missing fugitive, Randal Harper decided to blow his brains out.

Then he had a bottle of champagne and decided not to kill himself, but to play baccarat instead. Cards were safer than women. Dolores! Gee . . . his beautiful bride . . . a bigamist . . . worse . . . a criminal! God! How she had fooled him. His heart was broken. He would never care for any woman again; and to the end of his days, he would loathe women with red hair.

Having abandoned all thoughts of suicide, he got very drunk and lost a great deal of money at the tables, and retired to his hotel, weeping maudlin tears. And that was the end of Randal Harper's wedding day.

CHAPTER THIRTY

Marion reached Paris.

Once there, she decided *she dared not pawn her jewels.* She was certain that once the men from Scotland Yard discovered her flight from Monte Carlo, they would find out that she had taken a ticket to Paris, and be on her track in that city. It would be too dangerous to attempt to pawn the jewels. Every pawn-broker in Paris would be warned . . . Randal would have described the jewels. He had only been infatuated with her, and when he knew how vilely she had used him, he would have no mercy on her—be only too eager to get back the jewels, for which he had paid very handsomely.

Her red hair was against her . . . too distinctive. If she wished to disguise herself adequately, she had better dye that flaming hair.

She went straight to a small hairdresser's, and asked to have her hair dyed black.

The man who attended her, exclaimed against this atrocity.

'Madame—wis ze such be-autiful 'air—to 'ave 'im dyed—*quelle horreur!*' he wailed.

Marion smiled grimly at her reflection in the mirror. Her cheeks were ghastly, her eyes dark pools of fear—haunted—glittering.

'Dye it,' she said, almost viciously. 'Black— *noir—comprenex vous?*'

The man shrugged his shoulders and obeyed. Seldom did he see hair of such golden-red—so glorious—so natural. It broke his heart to turn it into a dull, ordinary black. How could he know the grim necessity which she was under . . . the real agony in her heart when at length she saw her beautiful pale face framed in inky, dark, unfamiliar waves of hair. With her great dark eyes she might now have passed for a Spanish woman. But Marion had gone . . . the Marion whom Dion had loved . . . whose hair Dion had kissed.

She left that shop, satisfied that her disguise was more complete. Her next action was to purchase a cheap pair of dark spectacles which disfigured her, but were an added touch of safety. Now, who could recognize the beautiful Lady Courtland in this slim, white-faced, dark-haired woman; the great eyes hidden; the wonderful mouth left pale, untouched by the vermilion pencil with which she usually painted its perfect bow. She might have been a foreigner—pallid, ill, quite poor in her plain dark suit and white shirt-blouse.

Now to find a job. She had only a few hundred francs on which to live, and they would not last long in this great city.

Evening found Marion wandering along the banks of the Seine, homeless, desperately tired, and afraid of every police-officer she met.

She had tried in several places to secure employment, and found it impossible. Nobody in Paris wanted an Englishwoman without a reference, and she was not pretty enough in those disfiguring glasses to attract any attention.

Imagine her thoughts this night, as she dragged her weary steps along the bank of the shining river; looked at the glitter, the gaiety of this city of pleasure, and knew herself an outcast, a criminal, hunted down by the inexorable law. Once she had lived in Paris with Dion . . . lived in luxury . . . beloved . . . madly happy. Now she was alone . . . forever alone . . . without a friend in the world. Not for her the gay music, the brilliant theatres, the luxurious hotels. And the first false step might land her in a French gaol to await deportation . . . later the awful exposure in England . . . her trial . . . all the secret, dreadful things which might come out at that trial . . . the final verdict and punishment.

She moaned a little as she walked along. This was bitter punishment enough but there was more to come. Had not Emm—old Emm, of Moorcoombe—prophesised the 'Dark Death' for her. She shuddered at the memory of the old Devon witch's sinister laugh . . .

Suddenly she stopped dead, pressing her bag to her bosom. She imagined she saw two *gendarmes* pointing at her, on the corner of the road . . . whispering about her. In a panic she turned and began to run blindly across the road.

She heard a voice shout:

'Prenez garde . . . prenez garde, M'mselle . . .'

In her fevered imagination, she thought they were trying to detain her, and she rushed blindly on.

Two brilliant head-lights bore down on her . . . she heard the grinding of brakes . . . the hoarse shouting of men . . . then felt an agonising pain in her side. Her glasses smashed and splintered in her eyes, and she went down with a terrible, long-drawn wail of agony.

*   *   *

In his mother's home at Torquay, Sir Dion Courtland received the following telegram from Inspector Dawson:

'Your wife found in Paris X hospital fatally injured in street accident dying come at once.'

Dion read this, then handed it to his mother and Patricia Westby, who read it together. Lady Courtland shuddered.

'So they have found her—wretched creature! You won't go—surely—Dion?'

He looked at Pat, then out of the window, hands thrust in his pockets, lips set. During the last few days of Marion's absence, he had been through a little hell of his own imagination . . . wondering every hour when his unhappy and erring wife would be found . . . dreading lest she should be dragged back to England and the whole sordid facts of the case be presented all over again to the public. He had felt he could not have borne it, but for Pat's wonderful, unfailing help, and his mother's tenderness.

And now the suspense was over. Marion had been found. She had been injured in a street accident . . . and she was dying . . .

'I shall go, of course,' he said quietly. 'I must.'

Pat said:

'Would you like me to come with you, Dion?'

He gave her a swift look of gratitude.

'Bless you, my dear. But no—you stay with mother. I'll—face it alone. I must. I'll wire that

I'm coming and go straight up to town now, and cross by the night boat. Poor Marion . . . poor, poor Marion!'

But Dion Courtland was not destined to see his wife alive again in this world. The worst part of her punishment was that her husband did not reach her in time to say 'I forgive . . .' She died alone, without one friendly hand to give her courage—without the word of absolution. She died in terrible agony, both eyes blinded, the once-beautiful face hideously cut and disfigured; the once graceful, beautiful body crushed and mangled by the wheels of the great omnibus that had passed over her.

She did not die quickly . . . it was a cruel and lingering death, in a poor French hospital where the doctors were not lavish with morphia, and death from such causes was an everyday event.

Inspector Dawson and his colleague had traced Lady Courtland from Monte Carlo to that hairdresser's shop and had then lost her. But upon reading of the accident to the Englishwoman in whose bag had been discovered the wedding-certificate of 'Mrs. Grey' to Randal Harper, they had hastened that next morning to the hospital, found Marion still alive, and telegraphed, on her behalf, to her husband.

When the unhappy girl realized that she was close to death, and that Dion would not reach her in time, she made a full confession to the

Inspector, hoping thus to win some mercy in the Unknown World into which she was so shortly to be precipitated. The Inspector, hardened though he was to crime, felt cold horror at the things this young and lovely woman had done . . . wrote down the details of her fiendish crimes, shuddering. So now, at last, the world had the truth. Marion Courtland was responsible for two murders . . . Hope Marshall's . . . Jet Saddleman's . . . Marion had induced young Pollock to murder Hope's mother in order to silence her. He was appalled—just as the world would soon be appalled.

Marion's face grew livid and bathed in sweat as she gasped out her confession. She had just sufficient strength to sign it. Then she lay back on her hard pillow and moaned aloud. Her body was tortured . . . the agony in her blinded eyes was unendurable.

She began to shriek, and a nurse came to her side, examined her, then called a doctor. The latter felt her pulse.

'She is dying,' he said, briefly.

Marion could not see. Her lacerated eyes were bandaged. But she imagined that she saw the faces of her victims . . . that Hope and Jet and Hope's mother were crowding around her bedside to watch her horrible death . . . to laugh and jeer and point at her.

Her shrieks rose to a crescendo.

'God . . . God have mercy . . . I can't bear it

. . . oh, my God, forgive me . . . forgive me my sins . . . Dion . . . Dion!'

It was with this on her lips that Marion Grayle expired. She had escaped earthly trial and justice, but she had gone before a Higher Tribunal to answer for her crimes. And thus perished one of the most beautiful and fascinating women criminals ever recorded in the annals of crime.

When Dion reached Paris and was forced to stand by the bedside of the dead girl, and identify her as Lady Courtland—his wife—he saw only a rigid, piteous form—a mutilated face. With the unfamiliar black hair, it was difficult for him to recognize her, but he could not fail to recognize that white and lovely throat; the slender hands; the unforgettable shape of her mouth.

Dawson led him away from the bed; he was shaking and sick at heart.

But there was worse yet to follow for Dion. He was forced to read Marion's confession. It appalled him—filled him with the most indescribable horror.

His wife . . . twice a murderess . . . murderess of poor little innocent Hope . . . of Jet Saddleman . . . and virtual murderess of Mrs. Marshall . . . of Sarah, who had been driven insane by the trouble and punishment she had never deserved.

He gave the paper back to the detective, and hid his ghastly face in his hands.

'God, how awful!' he said. 'How awful!'

'It's pretty bad, sir,' said Dawson, sombrely.

'I feel as though I don't want to live,' said Dion, brokenly. 'Thank heaven you did not find her alive, that none of us will have to go through a trial and see her hang . . .'

'She asked, before she died, that you should forgive her, sir,' said Dawson, awkwardly.

Dion, his face still covered, shook his head. He could not speak—could not bring himself to forgive—just now.

But of course there came a day, many months later, when he could hold up his head again and feel that life was worth living . . . even that he could forgive Marion. But he, and everybody else concerned, did their utmost to forget her and the frightful crimes for which she was responsible.

No matter how black, how hard the winter . . . there is always the Spring. And Spring came back into Dion's broken life . . . and Love came back into his broken and bleeding heart.

That was on the day, about a year after Marion's death, when he led Patricia Westby to the altar and placed his ring on a hand more worthy to receive it; placed his love and faith in a true, loyal woman whom he knew would never fail him as Marion had failed.

Many changes took place amongst the people Marion had known, and who never now mentioned her name. Old Tom Grayle died at the Travellers' Rest shortly after the thrill of his daughter's horrible case had been forgotten. But it had broken his heart and seriously affected his health, and he did not survive the winter.

Sidney Pollock was tried and condemned to death for the murder of Mrs. Marshall, but his sentence was commuted to incarceration in a criminal asylum for life. Sarah Pollock was released, but—poor soul—it was too late for her to begin life again. She was quite stupid, and until the day of her death, remained insane—a dreadful legacy of Marion Courtland's sins.

Old Lady Courtland knew real peace and happiness when she saw her beloved son married to the girl of her heart. With tears of relief in her eyes, she said goodbye to them on their wedding day, just before they left Torquay for London and Italy, where they were to spend their honeymoon.

'God bless you, my dears,' she said. 'I know you will be happy.'

'I shall,' said Pat, her face alight with rapture as she turned to her husband. 'And I shall do my utmost to make my darling equally so.'

Dion—a little grey about the temples—a little older and graver—yet with peace in his eyes—put an arm around Pat, and drew her close to his side. He leaned his head against her boyish one.

313

'I shall be happy, my Pat,' he said. 'Happier than I deserve—with such a wife.'

And there let us leave them with their happiness—and the soul of Marion Grayle to the mercy of her Maker.